Stimmy

An Alternative History Novel

Dedicated to Ben, who provided encouragement and counsel.

Acknowledgements

Thanks to Scott Rakonick for a thorough analysis. Your constructive criticism improved many aspects of this book, especially parts about family relationships.

Jim Spellmeyer, your perspective in the early days of this project was invaluable. Without Linda Mueller's insights into the pandemic-era restaurant industry, sections of this book would have been less authentic.

Bob Shuman provided development ideas without which this book would not have taken its present form. Additional thanks to Christopher and Dee.

About the Author

Joe Kinnison continues a thirty-year career as a portfolio manager and investment analyst. He has seen a few financial stimulus programs. He holds a charter from the CFA Institute.

Joe writes a Substack blog entitled "Financial Fictions," in which he explores both real and literary financial market situations. He is the author of the novel *Illiquid Assets – The Next Market Crash*, a fable about a high-frequency trading.

ISBN 979-8-218-43330-7

Stimmy

An Alternative History Novel

Imprint: Gohomefish LLC

Cover by: Jason Arias

1

Michigan billionaire Benjamin Dosh was a guest in the Senate Dining Room. To host such a visitor, a group of dispossessed senators must have needed a lunchtime distraction. The auto parts mogul was lanky enough to be amusing. As an added attraction, Dosh was good at names and faces, almost to the point of it being a party trick.

For Dosh, knowing the details of each of the assembled senators was a necessity. By attire, it would have been hard to tell them apart. The gathering resembled a prep school lunchroom. School dress code must have required suit coats, ties, and American flag lapel pins at risk of a demerit.

Dosh was not stranger to uniforms. Nearly every person at his company wore a red shirt of some sort. Around the table, the clothes were not the only things in common. The senators shared mischievous smiles and turned-up chins.

Dosh thought that the looks revealed a shared sense of disobedience. "Is it safe for me to sit here?" he asked, as his long legs searched for room under the round table. To the delight of the group, he kicked the table supports more than once while settling. Dosh did not mind their chuckles. He was long past lamenting being all elbows and knees. Besides, he had his own reasons for attending the lunch. "This looks like a group of dangerous men," he said, "especially you, Senator Sasson."

Sitting next to Dosh, the Junior Senator from Indiana must have enjoyed being called out for treachery. He smiled broadly. His teeth gleamed as if they had been whitened that morning. "This fivesome is the brave group that stood up and voted 'present' in the face of the largest spending bill ever to appear before the U.S. Congress."

"Present," Dosh repeated. It was his turn to be entertained. "You will go down in history," he teased. "A thousand pages deep within, the Congressional Record has recorded your achievement. The five votes not in favor of the BOOST Act. Here. Here," he toasted with a goblet of ice water.

Moments after the toast, a server brought frisée salads to the table. As the guest, Dosh was served first. The citric smell of vegetable wash made the visitor yearn for the venue's traditional bean soup. While he picked at the leaves, Dosh noticed that legislators who were not part of this lunch table caucus appeared in door openings and backed away. Men he knew as Tommy, Richie, and Henry, all withdrew.

The barrier was not the room. Tables were set with silverware for dozens. No other seats were occupied. Dosh tried to welcome later arrivals. He unfurled his fingers to wave at a few familiar faces.

His greetings produced a series of pained responses. To rejection, he was not accustomed. Turning back to his tablemates, he said, "I see that the party has ostracized you. I had not realized that sentiment was this bad."

"Nine days have passed since we were excommunicated," indicated Senator Sasson.

Dosh realized that his own status would have been threatened for aligning with this group. He would have been worried had he not known the timing of some news. He possessed some of the inside knowledge to which moneyed lobbyists were sometimes privy.

Speaking like the insider that he was, he shared, "You will not be in the political wilderness much longer." He edged forward and put his elbows on the table. He crossed his arms over his half-eaten salad and in front of his chest. They looked like poles in a circus tent. "My sources tell me to be on alert. We may hear something from the president as early as today."

The information enlivened the group. "If the president's decision is to veto," observed Senator Sasson, "by the legislative calendar, it has to be today." He scanned the other senators. "What are the odds of a veto?"

"There is a chance," Dosh opined. "Lobbying efforts have been effective. Like you senators, a small but vocal group of constituents is opposed."

Five heads dropped.

"For the sake of optimism, what happens if the president does veto the bill?" asked Senator Sasson.

From his seat at Dosh's left, the Republican Whip joined the conversation. "That $2 trillion spending monstrosity gets sent back to the Congress," he said. "It would be held at the desk for several days until reconsideration. Reconsideration enables us to refer the action to committee, introduce new motions, or impose a time delay. With any of those tools, we might be able to kill a congressional override."

Whenever Dosh heard about the procedural elements of politics, he had an adverse reaction. This time his whole body tensed. He grabbed the edge of the table with both hands while his mind wrestled with a few of the arcane details of the rules of order. Each time he engaged in the nuts and bolts of the political mechanism, he blanched. He enjoyed rush week, but he was never convinced that he wanted to pledge the fraternity.

Wearing a forced smile, he fought the unease. If a political second career were in his future, he would have to master the tools of the trade. It had been a long time since he had to function under someone else's protocol.

Like it or not, his next career step was coming soon. The corporate charter for the company that he founded imposed a mandatory retirement age. Nearing sixty-four, he had little thought of slowing down. However, the Board of Directors had announced their intention to enforce the mandate.

Only a year and a few months remained in his business life. He sat, considering whether he could stomach a second career full of cloture votes and points of order. With his mind on his transition, he could not consume any more of the wetted salad.

A waiter in a white jacket appeared. He was carrying a tray of cloches. He rested them on a folding stand an arm's reach from the table. As the server cleared salad plates, a buzzing sound erupted from multiple points in the room. The senators each reached for their cell phones.

"What?" Senator Sasson exclaimed into his microphone. "He did? Veto?" His words sounded as if he had just won $500 on a lottery scratch-off card. "Thank you. Thank you," he repeated to the caller. "Send me the proclamation as soon as you can."

In the next seat, the Senator from Utah raised his arms over his head in a stretch. The phone screen cast a blue light over his hand. He seemed to be channeling its energy, basking in it. "And so our hibernation period has come to an end," he said. "Dosh called it."

Dosh looked around the rest of the table. The senators appeared to be nodding like drinking bird toys. He took that as a good sign. His lobbying seemed to have proven successful.

Ending the economic shutdown had been his highest priority. Blocking the bill might just accomplish that feat. For a man who worked six days a week and ten hours per day, further idleness was unacceptable. Long lunches were barely tolerable.

Dosh craved enterprise. To satisfy that compunction, he required the rest of the country to go along. A veto of the stimulus plan was a big step. Now the rebellious senators needed to do their part.

2

Halfway across the country and a week earlier, darkness was setting in. As the sun disappeared, the Benton Harbor spring season yielded back to winter. Maurice Bakker shivered, standing on an aggregate sidewalk, which fronted his restaurant. The bistro had taken over the raised concrete pad from the storefront all of the way out to the curb. Below the peeling red paint of the curb, a fire lane had become a drive- thru. The dinnertime queue was a long one. Maurice counted a line of cars nine deep.

From the front of the line, a blue Honda SUV advanced. The exiting driver did not likely see Maurice's grateful smile. The concealing mask that he wore, sewn from a patterned cloth napkin, dragged against his two-day stubble. The chef realized his mistake and motioned to wave good-bye to the driver. The driver returned the gesture.

Maurice had few opportunities to interact with his patrons, and he had nearly blown this one. Unsatisfied, he turned back to see a black Hyundai sedan idling in place of the Honda. He tried to make eye contact with the driver. However, even the sapphire that glowed from his eyes failed to connect. If his singular distinctive feature could not breech the space, the windshield, and the patron's glasses, there was no hope.

In the bulk of his 2XL bubble coat, Maurice made a slow turn. His hair, which was gradually turning from blonde to white, blew away from its part. A gust exposed his snub nose out from under a loose-fitting mask. Worse than the blustery cold was the lack of purpose. With nowhere else to go, he backed under the striped awning that was a permanent fixture shading the front of the restaurant.

He stood in the deepening shadow and watched as floodlights illuminated the storefront and the curb. A white canvas pop-up tent, erected over the promenade, glowed. Two members of the restaurant team worked inside. The staff wore stocking caps, face masks, and latex gloves. Packages were arrayed on a folding table. He watched as the workers matched an order to the black car.

When the car drove away, two more vehicles joined the back of the queue.

Maurice and his staff were some of the few people working. At the onset of the lock-down, the government had deemed food service workers to be essential. He struggled to reimagine the role of concierge. Presently, the founder and chief creative was not feeling very essential. He wore his discomfort like a wetsuit, squeezing against every part of his torso.

Although he had been reduced to the minimalistic role of essential food purveyor, Maurice was a James Beard Award winning gourmet. The point of view of the celebrated chef was handcrafted sausages and cheeses. That focus paired well with his family's old country recipes for Danish tarts and poffertjes.

The food marriage occurred on charcuterie boards, and he named the restaurant Full Board in reference to the plating. In the spirit of creativity, the culinary artist could not stop himself from designing food presentations in the form of sculptural elements. Patrons went crazy over the concept. They taped images of their own creations to the restaurant wall and broadcast some to the ether.

A food influencer saw the Internet postings. A year before the pandemic, "Foodielicious" filmed her trip to the restaurant. The heavily made-up, size zero woman strutted her dancewear around the building. In the resulting social media post, the influencer played on the trend of mispronounced foods. To the likes of gnocchi and quinoa, the influencer added metworst. She herself pronounced it "metaworst," evoking cyberspace. The slip went viral, as it was intended.

"The Dutch Masters board is an experience in itself," Foodielicious proclaimed. "Turkey rookworst and pork metaworst frame the board. If you have not tried metaworst before, it is kind of like salami. These treats are elegantly paired with edam cheese wedges arranged in a design. To the left of center is a small stack of Dorothea cuttings. You cannot get Dorothea just anywhere. Dorothea is a goat milk gouda made with spices and potato skins. Both the cheeses and the meats are made on site." She posed for the camera. "Don't forget to order a wine pairing," she vamped. The video closed with Foodielicious holding to the camera a seahorse designed with toothpicks and cheese.

Full Board became the place to go for sausage you could not pronounce. Maurice was gifted a sign that read "Home of the Metaworst." The words were set in a star field. Formerly in a prominent location behind the restaurant counter, the sign now stretched between poles of the pop-up tent. No customers would have seen it inside.

Maurice walked back inside to the front of the house. A single pathway of overhead lights connected the entryway to the closed kitchen door. Black spindle chairs, once occupied by foodies and friends, were stacked atop matching black wooden tables. As it did every time he saw it, the sight made his heart ache. Black wooden blinds, tilted to discourage inside views, rested fully extended to the windowsills. Had he not come from the backed-up drive through, he would have thought that his life's work had ended.

One of the lights shone on his daughter Nova. While Maurice's role had decreased during the pandemic, hers had broadened. He had given her some room to adapt the business to the new reality.

Nova had proven herself to have excellent technical skills. However, her advancement had come with an unexpected and unwelcome element. In the weeks as her involvement grew, so did her entitlement. She had not voiced the words, but her intention was clear. She expected to take over the business. She had come of age, she had dedicated herself for the full extent of one month, and she wanted her inheritance.

Maurice watched as his presumptuous successor unstacked, inspected, and restacked the inventory of charcuterie boards. Three styles of boards moved between stacks atop the former checkout counter. In recent weeks, the former checkout counter had become Nova's de facto office. She recreated order taking and food delivery processes. She installed formal business systems like accounting and payroll. Little survived of her father's legacy methods.

Nova did not look up as he pushed through a swinging door into the kitchen. While the counter had been taken over, the back of the house remained his domain. The food prep workers would be using his recipes and following his guidance.

Masked, gloved, and hair netted employees manned several stations. Maurice could barely tell one person from another with the only visible feature being their eyes. Even those were hard to see through safety glasses. He had new hires working in the kitchen.

One worker had started only a week ago, and newbies were given the job of operating the cheese cutter. The device was simple in design. A grooved plastic platform provided a base. A wire stretched across two posts. The wire was sharper than the string of a kite that was built for slashing midair duelers. While dangerous, it made consistent cuttings. She was doing a decent job of reducing blocks to bite-sized pieces. Maurice watched for a minute and moved on.

He walked past two workers feeding a meat grinder, and he examined the output. The mixture of meat and fat looked right. Even through a mask, he could smell garlic and coriander. The workers had followed his method with precision. He nodded in approval.

Further back in the kitchen, he inspected the stove. Milk was coming to temperature in a three-gallon double broiler. He glanced at the thermometer hanging on the interior side of a pot. The gauge read eighty-five degrees, one degree away from ideal temperature. His apprentices were preparing to add rennet just as the milk peaked.

Completing the walk around, he headed over to his least favorite appliance, the printer. It bulged over the only surface in the kitchen that was not made of stainless steel. The printer fed a steady stream of orders on what looked like a grocery store cash register tape.

Maurice ripped off the tape. Before he could even look at it, the tape was removed from his hands and torn into a stack of orders. "Nova told us to take care of this," a woman from the plating team said to Maurice.

She turned to three other workers stationed around a metal table. "We have additional orders for five Dutch Masters, three Sour Krauts, three more Edam & Eve." They assembled charcuterie boards.

On the table, he spied a run-away "metaworst" slice. He captured it and guided it around the mask to his mouth. The ladies of the plating team expressed their disapproval, chasing Maurice from the kitchen.

Back in the front of the house, he slipped past Nova's workstation. He removed a piece of register tape and several bills from the pocket of his coat. One of the waiting drivers had paid him in cash.

Staring into his hand, he announced, "This check was for $44.26. The customer gave me $90." While he knew that excessive tips came with most orders these days, he struggled to fully understand why. His staff was not waiting tables or busing dishes or filling glasses. How was this earned? How could this last?

He steadied and reminded himself to be grateful. His community wanted this business to survive. Although the restaurant prospered, it came at great cost to the life he once enjoyed. "This cannot continue," he said under his breath. He did not want it to. His family could not survive it.

3

A day later, Nova was stalking Maurice through the opaque plastic window of the restaurant's kitchen door. In the kitchen, she sidled to the doorframe to remain unseen. Long, straight strands of hair were held out of her line of sight by a topknot. With her hair pulled severely back, a few black roots gave away the curated blonde color. Blonde dye on her eyebrows was equally unconvincing.

While she waited for the front door to open, Nova sniffed kitchen aromas. They affected her as if the convections were smelling salts. The early morning baking crew cooled fruit tarts. Pulp and butter singed her nose.

Before the pandemic, she seldom missed a class at CenterRing, her boxing club. She possessed a physical attribute, a seventy-five-inch reach, which made her nearly invulnerable in sparring. Making the most of her length, she trained so that her deltoids and triceps were well-defined.

Concealed and aroma stimulated, Nova was ready for a quick strike. She knew the pattern of her opponent. He was vulnerable early in the round. When she saw Maurice enter the restaurant, she punched open the door and sprang from her corner.

With her momentum going fully forward, she nearly lost her balance when Maurice failed to engage. Following her training, she stayed on the balls of her feet. Stepping briskly, she moved out to avoid losing her range.

While she was ready to spar, the squint of his deep blue eyes indicated a surprisingly intense resolution on his part. He revealed himself to be committed to a course, perhaps more committed than she. Maurice closed the distance to the counter where he retrieved the television remote from an under-counter pocket. He turned on the monitor.

Nova was well aware of his need for noise. Maurice could not handle even a few minutes of quiet. She considered it a weakness in his character. It was one that she would someday use to her advantage. Today, it worked to his. She regrouped and decided that she would come out even harder in the next round.

While Nova could not see the screen, she could hear the program. The Working Group briefed the public. Since the sessions started sixteen days ago, Maurice had been transfixed. He had not missed a daily episode. After each installment, the man would spend the evening dinner service repeating the things that he had heard. "Lost manhours" and "contact traces" were among the new phrases that he was testing.

Hardened by her first experience, Nova approached her opponent. However, footwork was her weakness. Her style favored toe-to-toe instead of dancing. Although her heels were off the ground, her shoes squeaked as they scuffed the tile floor. In or out of the restaurant, Nova wore tennis shoes most days. In anything with heels, she might as well have been wearing foam clogs.

If Maurice heard the squeak, he did not react. While his ears worked selectively, hers heard everything. She listened to the rate of his breathing and the creak in his hip. She kept her stance, ready to counter any move.

On the television, the president appeared. His brown hair was plastered across his head from the part, and his face was a color that had not experienced sunlight in weeks. The president continued, "The hospitals tell me that they want 40,000 doses of monoclonal antibodies. A week ago, they said 30,000. Now they say forty. Who knows? Next week, it could be fifty. The sky is the limit when Uncle Sam is paying the bill." The president gestured to Dr. Felicia Kellum at his side.

"Mr. President, we prefer to keep monoclonal antibodies from being a standard of care," the doctor contributed. Doctor Kellum wore a hunter green, A-line dress with a Gucci buckle holding a sash at the waist. Under a short bob of blown-out red hair, her face swelled from recent fillers. Her skin tone was chemical. Kellum spoke with the authority of the girlfriend of a middle-school class bully. "We think they are appropriate only in extreme cases. If people cooperate with our guidelines and keep six feet of social distance, we may need fewer doses. Social distancing and hand washing are the best ways to slow the spread of this virus."

"How about that Doctor Kellum?" Nova said, trying to stir up what had become a national debate about the woman. She announced her position to prompt Maurice to engage. "She seems like the closest thing that the country has to an expert. And everyone is copying her hairstyle," she added.

Maurice reacted to the feint. However, the dodge was not what she had anticipated. His words had a double message. "Kellum continually stands on the president's left," Maurice deflected. "That means something."

Nova understood the reference. She served at her father's right hand. The posture would make her the front- runner to lead the restaurant's second generation. Her brother had self-selected out of the picture. He was virus scared. He neither wanted to handle food made by someone else, nor did he want contact with customers.

Nova had started looking something like a business leader and restaurant manager. She had ditched most of her usual wardrobe. Black pants and a loose-fitting, buttoned-up black shirt indicated her commitment to her new craft. She had not shown her midriff or displayed her tattoos in a month. Over the black sheath, she had added an additional layer.

Nova had come to wear a kitchen apron. To the best of her ability to recreate it, the apron matched the one her grandmother used to wear. The apron had a white base and a floral pattern. Powder blue cords stretched over her neck and behind her narrow waist.

Nova reengaged Maurice with a clench. It was a soft one, delivered across the shoulder blades. Nova released her perfunctory embrace, and she turned her eyes toward the screen. She wore thick eyeliner and lengthened her lashes with mascara. The makeup created a stark black rim around her whites. She had mastered a happy medium between high fashion and goth. The black outlines were a compensation. She had not received the family heritage of azure irises. Hers were a dismal brown.

"Maurice, can we talk business?" If she proved unable to steer the man's attention, Nova's tactics would get more severe.

"Hold on a moment," he interrupted. "I want to see this."

Nova bristled.

The camera zoomed out. The new shot included the seated White House Press Corps. An optic orange sign was taped with what looked like masking tape to every other seatback. From home, all a viewer could make out was the top line of the sign, which said ATTENTION! in all caps and underlined. The sign must have gone on to say something like, "Sit here at your own risk." Reporters dutifully avoided every seat with a warning label.

Without yielding to the screen, she continued. "Profits have been up." *No thanks to you*, she thought. "I'm using the surplus to bring in additional supplies."

"We could use more of nearly every ingredient," he mindlessly agreed. His stare never moved from the television screen.

Experiencing his avoidance and misdirection, she realized that she and Maurice would not be going head-on. She expelled a lung full of air through her teeth. It sounded as if she had needed an extra push for her last barbell rep. She grabbed him high on the back of his arm and squeezed hard. The grip was an illegal one, but only if a referee saw it. "With the programs that I put in place, the restaurant has never made more money. In the last two weeks, revenues have nearly doubled."

The president resumed command of the podium. "We are invoking the Defense Production Act, which enables the government to compel certain companies to increase their production of products necessary for the well-being of our citizens. If the hospitals need 40,000 therapies, we will call on the resources of the country to get them 40,000, so help me God."

When the president finished his flurry, Maurice disengaged. "I just want this pandemic to end," he said.

"Maurice, you're showing your age," Nova sparred. This argument was one of her planned escalations. "The world has changed. People like this experience. Instead of getting dressed, they can drive up wearing their pajamas. Annoyances like reservations, indifferent waitstaff, and loud diners can be avoided."

"No one likes this," he retorted. "Humans are social beings. Distance does damage."

"Your thinking is archaic, Maurice. People love working from home. The extra time that they have is the origin of our long lines at lunchtime. While I realize that people with the disease are suffering, for the sake of Full Board, I hope the end of the pandemic does not come soon." She waited for him to realize her inevitability and abdicate. It was she who knew the new customers.

4

An hour's drive northward up the Lake Michigan shoreline, a conference call was underway. "Attendance is falling," intoned a voice on the speakerphone. "The retreat is more likely pandemic than product, but no one knows for certain."

Benjamin Dosh, a minority investor in the second or third iteration of the spring football league, had his suspicions. However, he sat quietly in his office and listened to the owner briefing. Listening was largely the role of a minority investor, he knew. Although he understood, he struggled with restraint. Finding a suitable pastime to offset his upcoming forced retirement was proving trying.

Dosh had built a Fortune 400 business. Day-to-day, he commanded more than 20,000 employees. His business was larger and apparently more sophisticated than his sports venture.

He had a financial stake, but not a determinative voice. He must accept indignities, he told himself, like not being invited to the owner's box for a game. He vowed to tolerate uncertainties, though he deemed them poor preparation.

Dosh sat with his back to his slate desk, facing the silvery windows that made up the outer wall of the top floor executive suite. In Grand Rapids, Michigan, like few other places, the skyscraper penthouse was only five floors above the street.

One direction from his desk, he could see a y-shaped splice of pavement. The intersection was the most prominent in the Heartside district. Despite the morning rush hour, the city, on whose industry he thrived, was barely moving below. He saw three cars and even fewer walkers. Be it fear or compliance, most people were honoring the shutdown.

While he fought the mandatory confinement, he made accommodations for his people. Inside, his floor was half occupied with staff who seemed to come to work to access supplies of toilet paper. He supplied it gladly. Hand sanitizer stations were at seemingly every entrance and exit. As a result, the whole building smelled of rubbing alcohol. The recently installed air cleaners did nothing to remove the smell, but they did create noise in the otherwise solemn space.

His recently disinfected speakerphone was set at reverberation volume. The sound was a personal protest against the quieting. "We are going to post a press release," the director of the Portland team blared. "It will say that a player tested positive for COVID-19. Lucky us," he said ironically. "I think this is the second sports figure to have contracted the disease. The NBA had one about a week ago. We have been getting educated on the subject. We do not have a plan for this happening."

Dosh wondered how he had involved himself in a business that lacked a contingency plan. He knew the answer. If not starting a political second career, Dosh wanted to be a sports team owner. In truth, sponsoring a team to promote community pride was his preferred version of civics.

While Dosh envisioned himself as a full-fledged member of a premier league, the existing owners did not. His mere billion in net worth was wholly inadequate. Having been unceremoniously rejected by the reputable owner's groups, Dosh took the well-traveled route of barely billionaires. He pursued franchises in fledgling sports… leagues without contingency plans.

"This player is the only one in the league who is known to be sick," offered the executive PR director.

Good. Only one case. Dosh did not have time for setbacks. His firm's board of directors had spoken. The mandatory retirement age was in fact mandatory. The forced end to a regionally meaningful career was coming. If serious pursuits were taken from him, he would try frivolous ones, like sports.

A different league staffer continued, "Portland's exposure may pose a risk to their opposing team. We asked team doctors about the players wearing masks. We have been informed that masks would pose other problems for athletes. Working with mouthpieces, face shields, and cages adds to the complication."

Dosh was hearing reactions, not visions. Visioning had driven his career to its heights. He could create a mental picture of himself triumphant in a future time and place. He had the willpower to make that image come to fruition. In his current projection of the future, he did not see protocols and precautions. He saw a billionaire sportsman.

Few people outside of his own head would see Dosh as a sportsman. He was paint-layer thin, and only athletic in an NBA center, Manute Bol sort of way. Office chair calisthenics only went so far. However, he believed that competitors came in all shapes and sizes. He had a will to win.

"We are thinking about canceling the Portland game for this weekend," continued the team director. "If we cancel, we may have to rethink the playoff qualifications. The schedule does not allow for make-up games."

No playoff meant no winner. No champion meant no sports owner for whom a statue was to be erected. He imagined his spindly body as a Donatello bronze. The bronze would look good outside of a stadium. It could be a meeting point before or after a game. His forehead extended up past the mid-scalp. He had a natural spot for patrons of the casting to rub. The buffered baldness would shine in the sun.

"You have probably seen that basketball is suspending their season indefinitely," offered the PR manager. "We might follow their example."

New voices joined the broadcast. "If we think we're headed for skipping games, we'll conserve capital by canceling the season. Our broadcast deal requires us to provide the production. We are on the hook for equipment, lighting, commentators, and graphics. In short, we provide everything, and it's expensive. We lose money on broadcasting, about $50,000 per game."

Growing frustrated by the events spiraling out of his control, Dosh furrowed his extended forehead. Coupled with an expensive broadcast, the league was looking at having no gate, no concessions, and no parking revenues. How would they ever attract an audience? He was starting to wonder if this venture would even survive.

Dosh would lose money. He accepted that fact. More devastatingly, the mogul might be losing his sporting future. If he had sufficient cache, he would have exercised it to save the season. Although he had a public profile, he was not a celebrity of the magnitude needed to sway opinion. To the degree that he was any sort of household name, he was the "Billionaire Next Door."

He converted that phrase himself from the once popular investment book *The Millionaire Next Door* and the name of his firm. Dosh thought that team ownership might be his route to that somewhat desired A-list.

The audio medium prevented the group from seeing Dosh's facial contortions. He puffed his pink cheeks and blew out his breath. When he inhaled, he sucked his lips back into his mouth, covering his teeth like a child pretending that he wore dentures. For the first time on the call, he spoke. "The season may not be salvageable. However, we must keep this venture alive. Protect the athletes. We would like to have them back in the future."

5

A gitated by his suspended sports venture, Dosh was feeling time pressure. Forced retirement was a cannonball coming right for him. He could see the black mass of lead. He could feel the rush of air. The business leader's best idea was to marshal support among his peers. A few days after the dissolution of the football league, Dosh convened an in-person meeting at a venue that he thought would be irresistible.

In the 1980s and 1990s, New York's 21 Club hosted business leaders engaging with Wall Street dealmakers. Dosh had been one of the former. No matter what your net worth, the 21 Club gave one the feeling that its rooms were reserved for a society to which you did not belong. Dosh had heard that regulars even felt a certain estrangement. He stared at it from the street, feeling that very sense.

The building featured a wrought-iron entryway that separated itself from 52nd Street. The ornamental jockeys adorning the building's slightly above street-level balcony were once a source of pride. Vanderbilts and Mellons had donated versions. As Dosh observed them decades after their placement, the statues seemed vaguely racist. The gaze of hundreds of concrete cast eyes made him feel as if he were the one on display.

The billionaire steeled himself and descended the historic stairs. It would be one last look at the historic venue. For the benefit of patrons, the Club resisted pandemic protocols for an additional week. Closing looked likely to be permanent.

Once past the front door threshold, a familiar aura presented itself. Not only was the mood the same as a year ago, but also the layout was part of the time capsule. Dosh's eyes took a moment to adjust from the afternoon sun to the semi-darkness that counted as ambiance. Despite the momentary blindness, he knew exactly how to proceed. As it was, as it had always been, the lounge was forward down a hallway. He paced himself between museum-quality Remington paintings and Disney sketches. Dosh did not stop to appreciate the artworks. He suspected few ever did. No one came to the 21 Club to be an aesthetician.

The alcoves around the lounge were original. Walls enclosed three sides with the open side facing the bar. Like everything else in the club, they were decorated with paintings and glass-encased collectibles. He selected a large alcove, big enough to hold a sofa and four chairs. Even the furniture appeared the same as it was a decade ago. During his previous visit, he had secured the financing package for his firm's acquisition of Smart Parts.

For this trip, he planned to mix finance, operations, and hospitality mavens. He knew these titans in the way that you knew of people. He had heard stories about their public offenses. He had greeted them at various charity affairs.

To his knowledge, the men had not assembled in a group before. He felt a hint of danger of a kinship that he planned to assume. His common ground would be their social class. These people, like him, were just outside of the Forbes list. These people were the kind that business magazines would malign as "one recession away from falling out of the billionaire class," as they had written of him. Tech mega billionaires, like Edward Tandy, would be curse words to compatriots in this group.

Dosh eased down to the cushion on the left side of the sofa. When he could control his circumstances, and he often could, he would protect his left arm. An accident had left it weakened, and the best doctors in the world had not redeemed it. With his healthy right, he signaled for the bartender.

An African American gentleman in a white shirt, black vest, and bow tie, responded to his signal. The man's straight black hair seemed wet with gel. He wore glasses low over the mask covering his nose. A tastevin hung from his neck. "How many are you expecting this afternoon, sir?"

"Four," responded Dosh. "Please bring a bottle of Buffalo Trace bourbon, a bucket of ice, and glasses." Dosh reached into the breast pocket of his tweed jacket and presented his credit card.

If the order disappointed him, the bartender did not show it. Bourbon was likely a letdown for someone in command of bottles of wine worth thousands of dollars each. The bartender examined the back of the card, American Express black. "Thank you, Mr. Dosh," he said before disappearing across the room and behind the bar. Swiftly, he returned with the order.

As Dosh sat in preparation, Neal Grigio, the founder of a multinational snack bar manufacturer, slipped into a chair. His demeanor struck Dosh as that of a rich uncle, kind but distant. Grigio wore a pinpoint oxford and pressed woolen slacks. Hinting at wealth and sophistication, the uncle came a little too well dressed to a family holiday gathering. Grigio had a silver head of hair, a hawkish curved nose, and an easy smile.

Grigio selected a glass filled with amber liquid, and he raised it until it sounded against Dosh's drink. With song from the crystal lingering in the air, Neal took a sip.

Having memorized a profile on each of his guests, Dosh engaged immediately. "Neal, I've been looking forward to speaking with you. I enjoyed reading your new book. I thought that you made some good points about business principles."

"Thank you. My team did a nice job on it. You spend your career building up these concepts," his voice trailed off as if closed with emotion. "When you retire, you want to leave something lasting."

"*Top Down, Bottom Up* got a lot of good press," Dosh observed. "The book release must have raised your public profile."

"I'm not looking for recognition," Grigio continued. "Since world events canceled my book tour, what I really want is to unload a basement full of unsigned copies. Look Dosh, I'm retired. I play golf. Why am I here today?"

Before Dosh could answer, Paul Kimball walked in. He wore a charcoal gray suit with the jacket riding high on his collar as if his shoulders were shrugged. A red necktie tugged the shirt and jacket together. Above the tie clinch, Kimball had an inch of growth in his beard. The billionaire was one of the few people that may have looked native to the 21 Club setting.

Dosh and Grigio rose from their seats. Since handshakes were discouraged in the new virus era, Kimball offered the men an elbow bump. "Lucky timing, Dosh. A few days later, and you wouldn't have gotten me here," informed Kimball. "I'm preparing to leave the city. The lunatics running this town are going to lock it down tight."

"So it seems," agreed Grigio.

"I'm going to a state where business is welcome and commonsense prevails." Kimball said it as if his peers would know the place. "My key staff has already been relocated to West Palm Beach. Next week, I'm moving to Florida. I'm headed south… just like this city… just like the stock market."

The men enjoyed the witticism, and they settled into the arrayed sofa and chairs.

Dosh scooted himself forward to the front edge of the couch. He realized the extent of his task. One of his lounge mates was checked out, and the other was about to flee. He leaned toward the men, and he rested his elbows on his lap. "Thank you for consenting to meet. From what I have learned about each of you individually, and from what Paul just said, we hold common views on the lock-down."

Howard Denizen walked into the lounge and directly up to the bar. His black T-shirt and dark sportscoat blended into the gloom of the room such that he appeared as something akin to a shadow. Dosh recognized the spectral form and motioned to Denizen to join the group. "Gents, let me introduce you to Howard," he said.

Denizen ripped a black mask from his face. "Sorry to be late." He reclined into an empty chair. "My hotels had to lay off nearly 1,000 people this morning. These people were good workers and loyal employees. But if I'm prevented from having guests, I cannot justify housekeepers. The direction things are going, this economy is going to get much worse. I am cutting costs as fast as I can. We are preparing for the worst." Denizen selected an unclaimed glass, downed its contents, and reached for the bottle to pour another finger.

"Howard," Dosh began, "I think you will find that we all share your dark mood. Before you arrived, I was saying that I think that the people around this table have some common cause. We are all reacting to it differently, but we think the lockdown is a bad idea. If we save lives and kill livelihoods, what has been accomplished?"

"Amen, brother," toasted Denizen.

"In addition, and I am being a little presumptuous here, we think the stimulus plan, the BOOST Act, is a bad idea."

"It is the size of the thing that bothers me," interjected Kimball. "It's big enough to be a tenth of the whole economy."

Grigio chimed in. "Forcing people out of work, then paying them not to work, is what worries me. Work ethic is the basis of long-term success. This bill takes away the incentive to get out of bed in the morning."

"If you are like me, you have already expressed that view to your legislators," Dosh said.

The men responded ruefully.

"One would think that a billionaire with a Political Action Committee would have some pull. However, we have all learned, one way or another, that the traditional route has not been effective." Dosh sensed general agreement. "What Id like to propose is that we work in concert. The political leadership seems to be able to ignore any one of us, but they may not be able to ignore all of us."

Heads nodded in agreement.

"I am suggesting a joint statement, perhaps along with a financial incentive."

"I have a way to deliver a message directly to the president," offered Kimball.

"Go right to the top," encouraged Dosh. "Fantastic. For my part, I have an idea that might generate some national attention and force an end to this lockdown. We need to get people back to work."

6

A day after the billionaires met in New York, the Junior Senator from Indiana was moved to action in Washington, D. C. He would have preferred to avoid meeting with the president. His benefactors gave him little choice. The threat against campaign funding was plain.

In most situations, the senator and the president had little common ground. The Midwesterner's hopes were particularly low for agreement on the outlandish idea that he was compelled to present. It would take moments of temporary insanity for him to present it and for the president to accept it. His best hope was that this president seemed to make extensive use of his veto power. He was on pace to set records.

Senator Rob Sasson exited the rear seat of a Cadillac Escalade and promptly cleared through the White House gate. He pushed through the olive-painted bars of the perimeter security turnstile. A mocking north wind rushed him inside the gate. It rustled his reliably cooperative hair. Thick, brown, and normally perfect, his strands would have looked fake on an elder statesman.

On Senator Sasson, however, it seemed the fitting cap for someone with the demeanor of a Broadway leading man. He turned up the nubby collar of his full-length wool overcoat. He stood for a minute more of the wintry blast while he gathered his wits. He tried to manage his own low expectations.

Up a short walk, he crossed the reinforced transom of the security door, with who knows how many cameras, lasers, and sensors trained upon him. He came eye to eye with the Director of Oval Office Operations. Really, the connection was eye to lens. Melissa Crawford was wearing black-framed glasses. Senator Sasson had the impression that a stylist for an ad campaign had selected the lenses.

Melissa had been a successful model before joining the staff. She had sharp and beautiful facial features, but she was the kind of thin that came from subsisting on cigarettes and coffee. With the glasses presenting as a prop, she tried to appear analytical. The senator, in return, was trying not to look skeptical.

In a moment of standoff, two starring players from stage and catwalk determined whether the White House version of a red carpet was big enough for both. Melissa broke the staring contest. "You came up about a dozen votes short," she began. "Your amendment did not achieve the necessary sixty-vote majority."

The senator tempered his normally expressive facial cues. His return look was so flat that the wrinkles around his eyes and mouth looked fixed.

"Too bad," Melissa continued. "Apparently, your colleagues believe in welfare. Our struggling citizens will make more money on government assistance than if they were working. As you know, senator, we do not like creating dependency. The White House was rooting for you."

"I could have used a little less rooting, and a little more arm-twisting."

Acting as if the complaint was beneath her, Melissa stretched her frame. She made a turn, stiff in the shoulders with arms slightly extended. It reminded Senator Sasson of a ballroom dancing twirl. He remembered that Crawford had appeared on a season of *Dancing with the Stars*. Melissa proceeded toward the interior of the building. "Put your mask on," she ordered.

The senator reached into his coat pocket and retrieved an N-95 mask. He looped elastic over both ears and raised the formed paper barrier. Out of what was becoming habit weeks into the pandemic, he squeezed the metal clip to tighten the fit over the bridge of his nose. Melissa had distanced herself in the seconds Senator Sasson had consumed himself with masking.

Rob rushed to catch up. The clicks of wingtip footfalls echoed from the tile. He could already feel himself breathing heavier, dampening the mask.

When the senator arrived at her side, Melissa started talking. "I have scheduled you for fifteen minutes with the president at five past the hour." Melissa raised her watch and pointed to the minute hand on its cobalt face. "If I think you're wasting his time, I will cut you short at the ten-minute mark."

Melissa opened a door and ushered the senator into a conference room. Motion sensor lights clicked on. The LEDs illuminated an empty conference table surrounded by brown leather chairs. If not for the heavy drapes over a single window, a standing American flag, and an oil painting of Harry Truman, it could have been a meeting room in any corporate office. "Take a seat," she said, exiting the room and closing the door behind him.

Senator Sasson removed his overcoat, folded it in half lengthwise, and laid it over the back of one of the chairs. His sense of time constraint prevented anything more than an improvised coat rack. He straightened his paisley blue tie and fiddled with his mask. If it was only ten minutes, he would take it.

The president burst through an interior door with an entourage in pursuit. The first Generation X president had vigor. To the senator's eye, the man had a strong resemblance to one of the former occupants of the White House. The president had a bushy moustache that bended with his beard. The beard was well trimmed, just below the chin. The facial hair was brown, and it matched his unruly eyebrows. If he had worn vintage attire, this president could have passed for a Grover Cleveland doppelganger. He sat in the chair opposite the senator.

"Why you are here, senator?" he asked. "I can answer that question. You are here because you got routed yesterday. Got your ass kicked. Congressional leadership threw you under the bus. After toying with your little amendment, they rammed through the BOOST Act. It passed 95-0. Ninety-five 'yes' votes and five abstentions. You were one of the five. That is a blowout."

"Yes, Mr. President." He could do nothing but agree.

The president slid forward in his chair, folded his hands, and put both elbows on the conference table. "You got beat, and I do not like losers. However, I do like fighters. Melissa says that you are here to fight. Lost the battle, not the war. The junior senator is planning a comeback. What's your plan?"

The freshman senator had his moment. He might not get another. He had a message to deliver, and he decided to do away with style points. "Mr. President, for the sake of the country, I think you should veto the BOOST Act."

Through the empty looks of the staff, Senator Sasson thought he could detect dispassion, or was it pity? The president glanced at the gaping faces of his team. "Veto!" he shouted. "You know that I like a good veto," the president said to his roomful of sycophants. "Melissa, remind the senator the veto proof majority in the Senate?"

"Sixty-six votes, sir," Melissa reported. She checked her watch.

"The vote was ninety-five to nothing. Do you have a plan to somehow turn thirty votes? Thirty votes is a lot of votes. I am not sure you have that kind of juice. So I veto, and in a week or two, Congress overrides the veto, and that's it."

He had a second chance to speak. The moment did not seem like it would be a long one. He formed the words as fast as he could. "This bill represents a case of the cure being worse than the disease. The best thing for the country is to have a recession and recover. Let the markets work. That would be preferable to artificially inflating the economy. Stimulus creates distortions. Inflation will be the result. It would make a bigger problem long-term." He had no indication from the president that his argument made an impression. "My constituents are suggesting a veto... for the good of the markets and the good of the country."

"Thank you for your perspective, Senator," voiced Melissa, "your ten minutes are up." She opened the door leading back to the inner sanctum. "Mr. President, you have another commitment."

"You are still new here in D.C. Do you have thirty friends in the Senate?" The president bolted up from his chair and he was immediately provided with hand sanitizer by one of his assistants. The president rubbed in the salve and made a quick exit. His entourage followed, save one.

7

Tunnel vision had prevented the senator from noticing the character sitting across the table to his flank. Appreciating the man for the first time, he could not help having a cartoonish first impression. He sat across the table from an African American version of Clark Kent.

The man's otherwise nubby black hair was combed to a frontal curl. The Superman-inspired forehead swoosh had to be intentional. After a costume change, the man could be heading to a Comicon.

Sasson looked him over. The Man of Steel had aged. This version had the frame of a middle-aged gym rat.

Sasson's mind raced. Was he supposed to know this man? Was this person someone whom he had confirmed to a cabinet post?

Clark Kent spoke. "Senator Sasson." The accent sounded vaguely French. The senator heard his name pronounced "Sah-sohn." The man's voice choked, and he coughed. "I would register an informal request that you exercise some haste in considering the following analysis." He cleared his throat.

Sasson reacted with confusion. The man's precision with words was reminiscent of a scientist or mathematician. After a few attempted phrases, the man tugged on his tie and collar. The senator was even more off put. The man seemed like the type, when not in costume, who preferred wearing turtlenecks.

The man ripped off his face mask. "The limited evidence that the Surgeon General has assembled suggests that masks are not effective against the spread of the coronavirus. You may remove yours, if you so wish."

Senator Sasson unstrapped his mask and drew a breath of air that had circulated through the ventilation system of a 200-year-old building. It tasted of dust and metallic dental fillings. "Thank you. It is hard enough to convey meaning with a full collection of facial expressions, and it is nearly impossible without. Forgive me for my ignorance, but with whom am I speaking?"

"I did not expect you to remember, Senator. However, we have met on a previous occasion. I spoke to you during a break at an academic conference a few years ago."

"I am sorry; my memory fails me."

"No matter. My role has changed. Philip Anaclet is my name," his voice scratched again. "I am the Chairman of the Council of Economic Advisors. You may know my recent work to discredit the concept of modern monetary theory."

The senator's bewildered look betrayed that he had never heard of something called "modern monetary theory."

"Doctorate from Yale," Anaclet tried. "You may see my regular op-eds in the Washington papers?"

When the senator failed to respond, Dr. Anaclet reached downward and struggled with something at his feet. He produced a canvas portfolio about the size of a legal pad and three times as thick. He unzipped the portfolio and removed several documents. He passed the papers over to the senator. "The president is in favor of smaller government. I have been authorized to talk to you on an exploratory basis about your proposal to veto the BOOST Act."

"The president did not seem to embrace my suggestion," the senator pushed back.

"Perhaps not. He wishes to be seen as neutral in what he perceives to be a battle between the 'me' generation and the 'meme' generation. Boomers want things as they are. Millennials want welfare now. They realize that the safety net will not survive another twenty years. The BOOST Act is welfare now."

The senator struggled to respond. He had not considered the pandemic bailout as a generational issue.

"However," continued Anaclet, "the president's financial benefactors come from the former group. Some donors are the same as yours. Prior to your arrival today, he asked my office to run some numbers. If you will consult Table 1, I'd like to discuss our projections with you."

The senator was dumbfounded. This longshot of a meeting had resulted in an actual study by actual government economists. "By all means." He shuffled two papers, quickly finding the spreadsheet marked Table 1.

"These are economic projections focusing on gross domestic product, GDP, the total output of goods and services of the United States."

The member of the Senate Finance Committee was facile with numbers. "If I am reading this correctly, under the BOOST Act scenario, you are calling for the economy to shrink slightly this year. Next year, your office projects 4 percent growth."

"That is correct, Senator," said Anaclet. "You are a quick study. Now please consider Table 2 on the next page."

Senator Sasson slid the second paper close.

Following a quick knock on the exterior door, the lock turned. It was reminiscent of a doctor's exam room visit, that the senator almost expected to see a lab coat at the door. Instead, Melissa Crawford barged into the room. "Oh, I apologize, Dr. Anaclet. I did not know that you were in here. I came to escort the senator to the exit. I have called for a car." Crawford's further look registered the presence of new documents on the table.

"Ms. Crawford, may we have a few minutes?" Anaclet requested.

Melissa made a show of checking her watch, and she let out a sigh that seemed to flare the edges of her mask. "I can give you five minutes in this room. If you need longer, you will have to move somewhere else. I need this space for something more useful." Crawford let "useful" hang in the air.

"I will accept your five minutes," the chairman responded, "and I will see the senator out."

Melissa turned and departed, shutting the door behind her with more force than necessary.

Senator Sasson returned his attention to the second table. "If the BOOST Act is rejected, the Council of Economic Advisors projects GDP to shrink by 11 percent this year."

"Consider, senator, that if our estimates are correct, this outcome would be the third largest economic decline this century. Conditions were worse only during the Great Depression and post-war 1946." Anaclet pointed to the Truman portrait on the wall. "Even the man who ended World War II could not get reelected under those conditions."

"Wait a minute," the senator exclaimed. "These numbers show that the recovery would be greater without a stimulus. The economy would produce double-digit growth next year, more than offsetting the year one decline."

"That is the key point, senator. The recovery is projected to be stronger without the BOOST Act than with it. The BOOST Act creates a substantial debt burden. Interest on the debt will reduce future growth. Moreover, the growth in government reduces more productive private investment. The issue is not the size of the recovery. It is the timing of the recovery that presents a problem."

"These figures are comprehensive." Senator Sasson continued to examine the data. "I am so appreciative."

"The financial analysis speaks for itself," Anaclet concluded. "Now you know the numbers, and we know them. Yet certainly you understand, senator, that the veto that we are discussing is a political decision and not an economic one." Anaclet packed his papers and stood. "We're out of time. I need to get you to your car."

"The president has seen the models?"

"He reviewed them this morning," Anaclet confirmed.

"I believe in markets. Failure is part of the model. If the president acts, I will not vote to override a veto."

"From you, senator, the country will need much more than that."

8

A few days later, Nova pulled off a vacant six-lane thoroughfare. While the street was empty, her strip mall had come back to life. Down at the end of the oblong lot, two cars parked near Nextdoor Auto Parts. Nextdoor Auto Parts was the largest tenant in the strip mall. The anchor store had been closed for two weeks.

Both vehicles rested in front of the auto parts store and as far away from the building as they could go. Back in the pre-pandemic days, employees would park in those spots. She recognized one of the cars.

"Oh no," she said to her windshield. "No." Her takeout system used much of the drive lane. The queue was working flawlessly. As her model succeeded, her father was further compromised. "Do not screw this up," she yelled toward the auto parts store.

Nova braked between the lines of her usual parking sliver. The sight of neighboring activity and the squeak of brake wear reminded her that she had done nothing to maintain her own car. As she had for the last two months, she quickly dismissed the thought. Six miles per day round trip did not add up to much. Nova knew little about the Kia Soul that her father had purchased for her. She knew its color, Latte Brown.

Nova sat in the idling vehicle. She lowered the visor, which had a small tin-like mirror on the back. From her purse on the passenger seat, she removed mascara. Looking back into the visor mirror, she applied it with practiced ease. Lengthening her lashes was like a male executive putting on a power tie and a pocket square. To her, the look said style and confidence. As she finished, both the lighted sign and the interior lights from the auto parts store turned on.

"Oh no," she vocalized again. "Stop." The restaurant suffered in comparative curb appeal.

Although the light was half a parking lot away, beams hit her like glass shards. Especially compared to the building's darkness of the last few weeks, the illumination was painfully bright. It was like someone had slipped into the closed store and replaced every bulb with one twice the wattage. She used a hand to shield her eyes.

"Ugh," she exclaimed. "No good can come of this."

Purse in hand, she turned off her car. When her tennis shoes hit the pavement, the inky asphalt sealer gave way in spots to pencil-lead-shaded bitumen. The surface had grit that remained from salt or cinders or whatever they put on parking lots during the winter. Nova scuffed her feet and kicked some of the grit in the direction of Nextdoor Auto Parts. She noticed two people in red jackets carrying folding tables out to the front of the auto parts store.

"What now?" she lamented. "Do my patrons have to drive around a yard sale?"

Inside, Nova awakened her dark restaurant. She proceeded behind the counter to a computer, which with a touch, booted up. When Maurice arrived, she intended to show him inventory levels and order patterns. Nova fumbled through her first attempts to arrange the numbers.

Creating financial ratios was one thing, but making them understandable to Maurice was a whole additional layer. Maurice had his strengths—she tried not to underestimate her opponent—but financial management was not among them. Until she'd stepped in, the family heritage was at risk. Her grandmother's memory could be sullied.

Nova was not quite ready when Maurice bounded through the front door. She reacted with frustration, slamming her fingers into the keyboard. On the contrary, Maurice could not have looked happier. His squared chin provided a base to project an impish grin. "Have you seen what is going on down the mall?" he asked.

"Bright lights and a yard sale," Nova denigrated. It involved people and trinkets. She knew it would give Maurice some opening to jeopardize her system.

"You should see it," Maurice extolled. "The red shirts have placed tables all along the curb." Maurice called the workers at Nextdoor Auto Parts "red shirts," as did most people. "The tables are filled with windshield wipers, bottles of motor oil, tire pressure gauges, and all kinds of stuff. The wind is giving them fits, but they seem to be figuring it out. One of the red shirts asked me if it was okay to offer coupons to cars waiting in line for our food."

"What did you say?" Nova cautiously sounded. "Tell me you said 'no.'"

"I said yes, of course," replied Maurice. "They have been good to us over the years. When we were the first two businesses in this strip mall, we helped each other. We catered for them. They provided for our auto needs. Those jumper cables in your hatchback are a gift from them."

"I remember," she said. "All of that was a long time ago."

"We have had separate successes. It got harder to find time to take a walk down the mall," he seemed to be regretful. "That may have changed today. We may have rekindled an old friendship. Nothing would make me happier," he pronounced. "They even gave me a coupon." He handed her a red paper coupon.

"Thirty percent off," she observed. "That represents a big discount." Drawing a contrast took her seconds. "You know, Maurice, we are selling at full price. Most people are tipping extra. How can having this comparison be good for us?"

Maurice seemed to ignore the question. To all visual cues, he was brimming with excitement. "I like their idea of going car to car," continued Maurice. He plucked thin winter gloves from his pockets. "I am going to do the same thing."

"Wait. No. Maurice. No. Maurice, that is a terrible idea," Nova cautioned. "Our customers are looking for contact-free meals. They are paying us a premium so that we keep our distance."

Nova watched as his facial expression changed. Maurice's blue eyes blazed. The first look was anger, or what passed for anger in Maurice. A ladyfinger firecracker fizzled to a dud.

His capacity for rage had changed little since she was date raped as a freshman in college. His brief eruption toward her attacker dissipated quickly. He seemed to move nearly immediately to achieving justice and reform. While he may have accomplished both, she wanted to be compensated in blood.

His version of a stern rebuke having vanished into nothingness, Maurice leaned his shoulder firmly into the front door. His weight opened the door halfway on its hinge. He held it open and looked through the pop-up tent, which was active with preparations. Nova could see him assess the line of cars. The wireless exterior camera she had installed had already shown her that the backup had now reached four. On her computer screen, she could see down to the third car in line. The tan Lexus had red jackets on either side of the front windshield. The red jackets were changing wiper blades.

"I am tired of handing packages through windows," Maurice said. "While I respect your point of view, Nova, that's not my idea of service. I am going to start talking to our customers while they wait." He exited the restaurant.

As the afternoon progressed, Nova snatched glimpses of the restaurant host on video. Maurice greeted each car with a friendly wave. Flapping his hands, he urged cars forward until they were a few feet from the bumper ahead. At that point, he held up a two-hand stop. Nearly the photo opposite of a dog on a car ride, he stuck his head into windows. She could not believe that he was so reckless.

Some riders were resistant. In those cases, he took the cue and backed away. However, many would talk to him. She could not believe that, either. Some of the conversations lasted so long that the driver had to decide whether to continue the visit or give up her place in line.

Nova bristled each time he delayed the queue. Every minute he socialized cost the business money. The pandemic was shaping up as a once-in-a-lifetime opportunity to make the business financially prosperous. For her future and the future of the family heritage, she wanted that, even if the chef's priorities were elsewhere.

After the last car of the lunch hours drove away, a weathered Maurice returned inside. His ears looked chapped by wind and cold. His protective mask was below his nose and damp at the mouth. When he removed the cloth, he revealed a toothy smile. "That's the most fun that I have had in a month," he said. "By the way, your grade school friends, Rex and Matt Woods, say hello. You know, you really should reach out to them. They lost their jobs. They lost their mother. They are struggling."

Nova scolded him back. "You're going to get more people sick. You are a super spreader."

Maurice seemed to dismiss the warning. "What would you think about serving some snacks to the guests waiting in line? Some of them are out there for twenty minutes."

"Are you insane?"

"We could individually wrap a cracker and cheese or something. We could do a giveaway like the red jackets are doing."

The swimming eyes and wrinkled brow seemed to indicate brainstorming. His head moved slightly side to side with what must have been each new idea. "How about a sachet? That would be fancy. It could be good marketing. We could put our name and phone number on the bag."

"Our business is digital now. We do not do phone numbers."

"You know what I mean," he said.

"What you are suggesting sounds expensive," answered Nova. She seized the opportunity to try out some new financial terms that she had been trying to incorporate into the business. She hoped the outside help she was receiving did not show. "That would hurt our contribution margin."

Maurice turned stolid. The look reminded her of times when she was a younger child when she delivered some offensive word. He would wait as long as it took for her to reveal whether she knew what it meant.

Knowing what was required of her, with exasperation Nova produced a definition, "We would make slightly less money on every meal that we deliver," she said. "What would we be getting by adding to our costs?"

"Goodwill," Maurice said.

"I prefer tangible assets." She tried to distract him with another financial term. Her retort did not seem to register in his understanding, but it gave her a surge of energy as if she had just swallowed a split atom.

"We should make the customers as comfortable as we can. Our cultural tradition is hospitality. We open our home. We make people feel at ease. That's how your grandmother would've wanted it."

Her father was not allowed to invoke Nova's muse. After a brief fit of anger, she tried to return the conversation to business conditions. "We did not have a shut-down then."

"People are trapped in their homes all day long. They drive here for an experience. Even if the experience is in a car, let's make it a good one."

Nova typed on her computer. A dutiful business partner, she would order sachets. However, as a matter of financial sense, it would be on her terms. Her way was to raise prices to more than offset any costs. A few keystrokes later, the prices of the most popular entrees at Full Board rose by five percent. Service and samples were expensive, and good business was good business.

9

A day after raising prices, Nova noticed activity on the feed from her exterior camera. Cars were filling the far end of the parking lot. For the middle of the afternoon, it was an unusual sight. Lunch service had ended, and dinner service was hours away.

As the cars gathered, a few trunks started popping open. The assembly reminded her of Saturday morning at her alma mater, an NCAA Division II football tailgate. Searching for an explanation for the growing group, she decided on the pandemic. Nova had heard reports of socially distant meet ups happening in public spaces.

Given how much he said that he enjoyed being out in the parking lot, Nova thought to alert Maurice to the crowd. However, he sat across the counter from her, looking like a man who had been on his feet for too long. His polar fleece was upholstered to the back of the wooden chair, and his back pressed hard against the improvised cushion. One leg bent to the floor, and another was propped on an opposite chair.

The television blasted sound. When she realized what was showing, she knew that directing him outside would be a futile exercise. Some people never missed *Jeopardy!* Some never missed *Ellen.* Maurice never missed the Pandemic Working Group. She could imagine an announcer ending the press conference as if it were a serial: "Tune in tomorrow for the next episode."

Nova heard Felicia Kellum speaking, "Today, we are reporting 1,000,000 active cases worldwide. This is the first time that case counts have reached the 1,000,000 level. Here in the United States, the CDC is reporting 503,400 confirmed cases. We believe this figure to be understated as testing supplies remain inadequate."

Maurice voiced, "When is this going to end?"

Nova checked the camera view. Since her last look, a group of people had organized between the rows of cars. One man stood on the bed of a pickup truck. With gloved hands cupped around his mouth, he appeared to be shouting instructions. He pointed toward the thoroughfare.

The open trunks produced signs that looked like foam boards attached to one-by-twos. The signs were distributed amongst the gathered. Nova could read a few of the posters: "Liberty Or Death," read one. "Tyranny Has a Face," read another. It was the face of Felecia Kellum. "Let Us Work," proclaimed a third.

As Nova watched, the band of people numbering nearly 100, walked up the grassy berm bordering the parking lot. They moved over a sidewalk and out into the middle of what would have been a busy road before the shut-down. As it was, three lanes of sparse traffic stopped in both directions. Drivers blocked every lane. Vehicles were abandoned with high beams left aglow.

The assembly quickly swelled to a size well above the number Nova had first counted. The sudden mass of the mob felt overwhelming. It was like she stepped into the boxing ring to fight one opponent and found an opposing fighter in every corner. Those fighters had trunks and robes of many types. She saw military attire, clergy garb, and lots of people wearing versions of red, white, and blue. Nova realized that she could not see faces. She saw stocking caps and sunglasses, winter masks, hoods, and high collars.

Nova rounded the counter, removed her coat from the rack, and headed to guard the door. Possibly sensing something wrong, Maurice turned off the television. He arose and followed.

They arrived outside at the curb, and both stopped fast. Up on the roadway, protestors filled at least a quarter mile of the street. They were circling and chanting, "Disobey! Disobey!" Each repetition came with a little more force. Signs were moving up and down and swaying back and forth. "Fire Kellum," was the next shout they heard.

As the ruckus grew, a central group formed. A mostly single-file line had people moving like the bunny hop at a 1950s wedding. The line snaked around idle demonstrators and circled within the blocked street.

Eventually, splinter groups spun off. Nova could hear a variety of different chants, some taunting and some angry. A few people seemed to be probing for more to do than walk in a circle. They tested the poles holding streetlights and stoplights.

All at once, protesters started setting off emergency road flares. Multiple flares were dropped in front of the parked cars. Further down the road, she could see more tiny flames. Smoke from the flares billowed on the horizon. On the road in front of the restaurant, plumes rose and then lingered. The flares made a cottony fog. The fog seemed to reflect the light from the high beams. At both ends of the protest, Nova saw walls of white.

Maurice seemed to celebrate what he saw. "You cannot keep people shut in their homes forever. They want their jobs back. They want their lives back. Meals together. Families together. Power to the people," he cheered. "Nova, this is what citizenship looks like. Rights must be protected from government abuse."

Sirens sounded in the distance. A few minutes later, a helicopter appeared overhead. The blue and white airship descended, and it hovered above the power lines alongside the road. It was close enough to the ground that the rotors blew the smoke. The white wisps curled away from the blades. Nova saw some protesters holding on to their headwear.

A voice was broadcast through what looked like a megaphone on the front of the helicopter. "This is the police. Your assembly is unauthorized. Leave this area immediately." When few responded to the order, the message was repeated and repeated. As if the volume was the problem, the helicopter moved slowly over the crowd.

The chants had not stopped. They had changed. "Open Michigan," they cried, as rhythmically as the words permitted. "O-Pen Mich-igan," they screamed again. Groups aimed chants to the helicopter, shouting to the sky. Other protesters assembled in front of news cameras where they performed their slogans.

"These are my people," yelled Maurice. "These are my neighbors. I am not the only one that wants this lock-down to end."

Flashing red and blue lights appeared on the periphery of the protest area. After a few minutes, Nova saw policemen gathering. Slowly, the force grew to about twenty officers. The police carried large shields. The shields looked to be transparent plastic and large enough to cover the officers from head to knee. The force also appeared to have helmets, and something strapped to the back of the helmets. The strap seemed to be connected to a black device with a circular offshoot that looked like a walrus tusk. Gas masks, Nova realized.

Someone among the protest group must have distributed American flags, because several hundred flags were hoisted high and waved until they unfurled their full length. A few people ran down the median, flags waving behind them. The passing flags looked like midfield after the home team had won a big game. Nova had never seen Maurice enjoy a Fourth of July parade as much as he seemed to be reveling in this display. A few times she saw him salute.

As the protesters waved Old Glory, the police marched forward to the edge of the flares, some of which had started to reach the end of their twenty-minute lives. The officers deployed themselves shoulder to shoulder until they filled every traffic lane. With shields raised, the blue line walked slowly forward.

Protestors put up light resistance. Some moved slowly ahead of the police. A few taunted them with signs. The more aggressive tried some leftover high school marching band vintage flag twirling maneuvers. Drivers returned to their cars and laid on their horns. The police slowly advanced as the honking grew louder and longer.

As quickly as they had assembled, the bulk of the protestors abandoned the road. They ambled back to the lots from which they started. The parking lot adjacent to Full Board slowly refilled with revelers. The protesters stowed their signs and flags, and they navigated between the parked cars. Members of the group hugged each other.

The police at first seemed startled by the rapid disbursement. All resistance to their wall of shields disappeared. Law enforcement looked as if they were prepared for a fight. No fight ensued.

When the authorities regrouped, Nova saw two officers direct themselves toward the Nextdoor lot. *Go ahead officers, clear them out,* she thought. *Unless they are planning to buy dinners, get them off of my lot.*

One of the red shirts must have seen the police descend the berm. He ran past the protesters, and he intercepted the officers. Whatever message he delivered must have satisfied law enforcement. The officers backed off to the edge of the road. They stood at that distance, taking pictures.

10

The protest ended before dinner service started. Except for two or three cars in front of the auto parts store, the parking lot was clear when the line formed. If anything, the restaurant takeaway business was better than recent highs.

At the end of the dinner service, Nova headed home. She could have gone a few more rounds, but there was no one left with whom to scrap. The staff, including her father, had clocked out. She made haste, knowing that she had another opponent waiting for her at home, and this opponent was her favorite.

Nova's two-bedroom ranch was a cookie-cutter clapboard. The 1970s-era tract house filled half of a private quarter acre in the middle of an originally suburban block. The front entryway divided the house. Both bedrooms were down a short L-shaped hallway on the left-hand side. For Nova's purpose, the bedrooms were where she lived. The front bedroom contained a silver elliptical machine, an exercise bench with weights, and a heavy boxing bag.

The four-panel doors to both her bedroom and the home gym were kept closed without exception. To her mind, the bedroom and fitness room were utilitarian. Utility was not allowed to compete with the aspirational design of the rest of her home environment.

While Nova did not inherit Scandinavian eye color or hair color, she had experienced some of the culture. Her grandmother's home was hygge, a Danish decorating concept that emphasized quiet coziness. "Oma," which Nova knew to mean "grandmother" in Danish, had filled her house with comforts. Living spaces had soft lighting and soft blankets.

Although unsuited to her own adult lifestyle, which took place on the left side of the house, Nova designed a living space inspired by her childhood experience. On the right side, an overstuffed sofa and an upholstered chair and a half filled the seldom occupied living room. The overstuffed sofa was draped with two plush blankets. The chair and a half was so overcome with pillows that if she ever did actually sit there, the pillows would need to be lowered to the floor.

Along with the house providing enough space for her opposing home modalities, she had selected this house specifically for the fireplace in its living room. Along with soft comfort, warmth was central to the hygge concept. The hearth was built of a reddish midwestern brick. The mantle was a solid piece of fruitwood—light, grainy, and simple.

One of the first things that Nova did after closing was to buy candles to fill the firebox. She selected and arranged a dozen pillar candles of varying heights. Unlike everything else in the room, the luminaires had evidence of their use. The wax looked like a root beer barrel candy lozenge, with flecks of lemon and peach within. When they burned, the candles emitted a bright sweet scent. A layer of grenache melted down the sides and dripped nearly to the floor.

The candles were burning when she opened the front door. Before she saw the flames, she had inhaled the scent. The person who had fired the candles sat at the Henning Kjaernulf teak dinette willed to her by her grandmother. The table said hygge through and through.

The visitor wore a long-sleeved T-shirt and jeans. His oxfords were removed, and his stocking feet were on the opposite chair. When she closed the door, he stopped typing on a computer, which had taken over the table with a dock and two monitors. Greater disrespect for the décor may not have been possible. She made a mental note to hold that against him.

The young man's hair was a little longer than she remembered, pompadour style in need of a fade. He looked like he had not seen a barber in the six weeks since their last encounter. She was ready to be offended by that as well. However, she remembered that for at least some of that time, barbers had been halted by the pandemic. While a few weeks overdue for a haircut, he was clean-shaven. He had made some effort, she decided.

"Hello," he said in a sweet and longing voice. "I lit the candles. I remembered that you like them."

In a brief search of her memories, she could not recall how he would know that. He must have remembered the candles that they used for lighting at the Arenal Volcano base camp. She had mentioned her fondness at the time.

Arch Crockett pushed back the chair and rose to his feet. He was tall and trim, with broad shoulders. He had the body of a swimmer, angular from the shoulders. The suitor approached Nova and threw both arms around her waist. He held her like a young lover who had been separated by a tour of duty. Minutes passed until Nova broke the embrace. She was momentarily disarmed.

Nova gazed into his green eyes and caught him gazing at her chest. Disarmament was over. Since puberty, she had possessed the kind of chest that inspired men. Her 36Ds were round and erect, with a deep cleave between them. Arch realized his transgression, but he did not repent. Her body was a thrill ride. He returned his attention to her now scolding pupils.

She glanced over his shoulder. Along the sidewall of the dinette, she saw a duffel bag and two large suitcases. Nova knew Arch to be a minimalist traveler. He prided himself on it to the point of caricature. He had taken only a carry-on bag for their trip to dive the Blue Hole in the Bahamas. Somehow, he managed heli-skiing in Utah with merely a garment bag. Three pieces of luggage could contain every article that he possessed.

"I packed heavy," he admitted with a sincere look and a conciliatory shrug.

"We planned a restauranter's version three-day weekend," she reminded him, "Sunday through Tuesday."

"I know. I know. I realize we had that plan," he said.

"Have you changed it? Without consulting me?"

"Here's the thing." His voice grew both assured and excited. "On Friday, my company decided to close its New York office. The shut-down will last for as long as the pandemic. As of right now, I'm not expected back for at least a month."

A month was far different than a long weekend. So far, the basis of their relationship had been a yearlong series of weekend thrill seeking. Nova went along with the trips because they made her feel special. Arch was a powerful man who would show-off for her entertainment. In addition, he would lavish her with five-star accoutrements.

"I have the equipment that I need to work from home," he continued.

"Home?" she questioned. Nova was not certain she wanted a roommate. She liked things her way. The front of the house and the back of the house should never cross.

"Home can be wherever I want it to be," he explained. "Some people are going to Florida. Most people are going to Florida," he corrected. "I picked your house—your crazy house with a gym in the back and a meditation studio in the front. What I like about it is that it has you in it."

"Crazy?" That seemed like the word to rebut. Was he being endearing or insulting? She suspected the former, but prepared to contest the latter.

Arch must have perceived that his long-term visit was not given the warm reception of his hopes. "If it helps, I have an expense account and a per diem. I can pay rent."

"Keep talking," she prompted.

"Shut-down permitting, we can travel every weekend, if you want."

Daring was one of the things she liked about the man. Arriving with a plan to stay was daring. The presumptuous young man challenged her, and she liked to be challenged. A month-long adventure, she thought, could be little more than a series of consecutive weekend jaunts.

He launched into detail about his work. "The reason that I can stay here is that our hedge fund is killing it. Do you know what a put option is?"

"No, I've never heard of a put option."

"It's a derivative financial instrument in which you make money when a stock or bond goes down beyond a certain price level. We have sizable put options on the hotel companies. Few people are traveling. The stocks are down something like 40 percent so far. My company is making tens of millions on this trade."

She was not terribly interested in put options, but Nova realized something. Arch was facile with finance in a way that she struggled. This knowledge base might be important to her primary objective. His savvy could help her prevail over her father. With live-in help, she would certainly take over the business.

As she had once said to her father, she said to Arch, "I hope this pandemic lasts a while longer."

11

The next morning, Nova tried to sleep in. Blackout shades kept her room dark well into the morning hours. Although undisturbed, she was awake at nine o'clock, her usual hour. The body clock would not relent.

Nova kicked off a flat sheet and the corner of a down comforter that remained atop the mattress. Her bare feet touched the floor. Without hesitation, she started some stretching exercises at the side of her bed. Once warm and limber, she traded a satin nightshirt for a sports bra and yoga shorts. She bunched her bedheaded hair into a scrunchie.

Opening the door, she noticed lights in the center of the house. Arch had been at work, she sensed for hours. She realized that the stock market was already open, and he was probably trading. Although Arch had not disturbed her, she cared little about returning that favor. After all, it was her house. She announced her presence. Nova crashed through the gym door and slammed it behind her.

As she had intended, Arch must have heard. If the door had not prompted him, a few thwacks with her boxing gloves on the punching bag had gotten his attention. Minutes later, he appeared at the gym door.

Although he responded as summoned, Nova was unhappy with the pace. She scowled when he opened the door. To her mind, a live-in boyfriend should anticipate her every want. She wanted attention. Nova kept punching the heavy bag, adding a little more vigor. The grey cylinder rebounded from each blow with the weight of its stand pulling it straight.

He watched for a few seconds. With his full engagement, she showed off with some speed jabs. To her great surprise, he raised his phone and started filming. "Keep going," he encouraged.

She raised pink training gloves to her cheek level. She kept punching.

"What is that move called?" he asked.

"I am doing a routine called jab, jab, cross, cross," she said. "You get in a boxing stance." She shuffled her feet and breathed hard. "Launch two straight lefts, and follow with two rights." She executed the drill with speed and agility. "Then I reverse my stance to Southpaw," she said and did. "Right, right, left cross, left cross."

"Why do you do it that way?" he prompted.

"Works both arms the same. I don't want to get uneven," she said flirtatiously and touched her chest. Nova started a new set of motions. She brought her hands in to her cheeks and launched punches upward from the elbows at her waist. "This is called nonstop uppercuts," she reported. She was ducking between punches.

"What does that do?"

"This works the legs, the back, and the shoulders," she indicated. "Fifteen minutes each of jab, jab, cross, cross, and nonstop uppercuts is a full-body workout."

Arch stopped recording. "I am so in love with you," he blurted. "I mean it."

Nova had been well acquainted with lascivious comments in the gym. She rarely worked out at her regular gym without them. "Whatever," she deflected.

He returned to his computer and watched the video. He edited it, added some comments, and posted it to social media.

Fifty minutes later, Nova had forgotten about the video. Stocking footed and moving as if each leg muscle had been splayed, Nova shuffled into the dinette. She walked slow half laps around the table, occasionally testing each leg with a series of double hops. She moved over near the wall, planted her heel, and bent to stretch her calf.

"What was with that recording?" she asked. It had flattered her, which was a good move on his part. "Just having some fun?"

"I'm trying to show you your true calling."

"I don't believe in true callings. I have food to serve and receipts to process. I need you to be totally committed to helping me with my father. Don't distract me."

"I posted in on the Internet," Arch revealed. "I bet you get a lot of views. You'll see. You'll be a fitness influencer before you know it."

Nova's flushed face reddened further. "Some food influencer came to the restaurant once. My dad loved it. What did that get us? A stupid flag." As she cooled, Nova evaluated Arch's work-at-home attire, which she had failed to notice before. He wore a blue button-down shirt, salmon-colored shorts, and fisherman's sandals. Arch wore a headset, with grey foam circles covering both ears.

After a moment, he hit something on his touchscreen and removed the telecommunications device from his head. He raised his eyes from the screen and engaged Nova. "Hey, your town is in the national spotlight," he said. "The cable news channels have been showing protest footage all morning. I recognize some of the places on the video."

"That should help tourism," she deadpanned.

"I thought you said it was nonviolent," he retorted. "The press is calling it the Michigan riot." Pointing to the headset, he said, "I asked my team to give me a list of every public company headquartered in Michigan. I need to be ready to make some money if the riots expand."

"It was hardly a riot," Nova replied. "It was a bunch of people walking around with signs and flags. I hate that everything gets sensationalized."

"Supposedly a police officer got hurt," he reported.

"Flags and signs," she said. "The protestors fled when the police moved in."

"If that is the case, why is the governor threatening further lock-downs?"

"Further lock-downs? You're kidding me. What else could she lock-down?" Nova asked. "Certainly not essential services." Nova pointed both hands at herself, identifying the shapely features of the essential service worker. *Lock it tight*, she thought. The existing shut-in was one of the best things that ever happened to her.

"I don't know. I read something about curfews."

She walked into the kitchen, steadier now. She squirted water from a refrigerator water dispenser into an aluminum cup. She kept the filled cup close to her mouth and took small, repeated sips.

Returning to the dinette, she was careful to avoid his camera. From a side angle, she looked at his monitors. The portfolio management software he had shown her was running on screen. She saw blinking red and green numbers and text.

Arch must have understood her interest as license. "Let me show you a few things from my true calling." He started spewing financial information. His voice seemed to deepen. "The Dow continues to slip lower. It is down about 200 points. The market is getting skittish about the BOOST Act. Congress ratified it more than a week ago, and the president has not yet signed the bill."

Arch drew a quick breath. His stream of business news continued as if he were a podcaster on stimulants. "Theme parks are in trouble. No attendance. Vacation rentals have no cash flow."

Nova hit pause and lowered the playback speed. Too much information was disseminated too quickly. She grabbed on to a topic she had earlier learned from her personal financial pundit. On an earlier trip, she had been schooled in how to borrow stock and sell it. "Were you short any of those companies?"

"No, but we should have been," he admitted.

"I thought you were good at this," she scoffed. "True calling?"

"We missed those. It happens." Arch smiled. "Nova," he gave her a satisfied nod, "if you understand the markets this well, you should be investing."

"I am trying to pay my mortgage," she said. "I do not exactly have money to invest." She wiped her face.

"Financial Independence, Retire Early," he stated, "FIRE—if you put a little money away now and invest it in the markets. Before you turn forty years old, you accumulate enough money that you may not have to work. Isn't that the goal of working, so you don't have to work? If not that, you could buy out your father. Pay him outright instead of trying to wrestle away control of the restaurant."

"I am not sure," she said. "You tell me every day that the markets are terrible." She had been listening intently to his financial advice.

"How about this?" he suggested. "I will set up a brokerage account for you. Yeah, that's a good idea," he seemed to convince himself. "I will fund it with my rent check. Here's a plan… we add to your FIRE account every month that I stay."

"Okay," she said excitedly. She liked everything about this idea. If he could stay focused on helping her with financial things, she would let him stay. "Give me a good password."

"You could buy stock in one of those food distributors that you like. Or how about that auto parts company near the restaurant, Nextdoor?"

"Something is weird about that store," she protested. "They are defying the lock-down order. They are harassing my customers. I do not know for certain, but I think they were involved with the protest. Mostly everyone wearing those red shirts and jackets is sort of cultlike. How do I short it?"

Arch had a strange look on his face. His facial muscles flexed, holding his mouth from saying something his brain must have wanted to say. "Let me look into that for you," he offered instead. "I will do some research."

12

The next morning, Dosh was back in his office. Dosh's suite overlooked the iconic Blue Bridge spanning the Grand River. The Grand River had a tinge of mud in it, the winter blue tainted by runoff from the first spring rain. It was something of a relief to see clouds do their business instead of providing the endless lake effect drab. Lake Michigan was sixty miles to the west. The cloud cover it generated lasted all winter and followed the river inland once dodging the coastal sand dunes.

"Go ahead and rain," he said to himself. "Get it out of your system. I do not want the weather to dampen the turnout I expect this afternoon."

Staring out the window, he focused on his reflection in the glass. At times, an orderly visage gave him an orderly mind. Like the rest of the red shirts, he wore a uniform. His adaptation today was a long-sleeved polo version and tan slacks. Dosh looked like a maypole trimmed in red and khaki. Fabric hung from a central spike. He looked downward to confirm that the socks he had selected two hours earlier at his bedside matched his pants. Someone other than the wearer had recently polished the brown loafers on his feet.

Four days into the store reopenings, the red shirts were selling enough merchandise to both cover their own salaries and contribute to the utility bills. He considered that a win. Working outside had proven to be a good accommodation to pandemic conditions. The extra pay that Dosh had included with it was well received. He was providing a model of how people could work.

Ready for the next phase of his plan, Dosh returned to his desk. He lowered his coffee mug to the surface. His second cup had lost its warmth. He rolled back an executive chair, one of the neighboring office furniture company's great inventions. The carbon frame with a web seat was invented a few miles away. It felt regal, technical, and airy all at the same time. Dosh admired enterprising people that had produced it. He eased into the chair and inched his stilt-like legs forward under his desk.

Nextdoor Auto Parts had its own inventions. Its logistics systems were revolutionary. One hundred fifty well-provisioned stores dotted Michigan, and 400 more were elsewhere in North America.

Since Dosh had compelled a reopening, violating state stay-at-home laws in some of the more aggressive enforcement states, his business mix had changed. Windshield wipers had become the franchises' top seller. Car batteries moved well. His pit crews installed those too, along with battery terminal kits when they could. Air filters, air fresheners, wiper fluid, and compressed air cartridges to fill tires completed his roster of in demand auto parts. The logistics systems responded to the change in business mix with accelerated shipments.

With more trucks moving, not every truck left the distribution center completely full. In those cases, Dosh filled any empty space with materials to support his other mission. Truck trailers were capped off with bottles of water, road flares, foam boards, and every sort of American flag he could distribute.

With items in motion, he needed to inform his store managers. Dosh's second call of the day was a Grid call, an online video conversation. Nearly everyone in the business world had adopted one of the video conferencing platforms in the past month. His technology team, for some reason, preferred Grid to more popular platforms. His IT was topnotch, and their communication choice matched that of millions of others. Although Dosh had accepted the decision, he was reluctant to use any technology in which mega billionaire Edward Tandy owned a stake. Tandy's only loyalty seemed to be to his pocketbook.

The video chat started with the perfunctory good mornings. Those greetings were followed by well wishes for health. Completing the seemingly mandatory preliminaries were acknowledgements that these are extraordinary times. When the preamble finally ended, Dosh guided his store management team. "I would like your first priority today to be unloading trucks," he said.

"Mr. Dosh," interjected a red shirt with long brown sideburns, "I only have four people scheduled to work today. If two of them unload the truck, I will not be able to provide a full pit crew. You see the same numbers that I do. Larger sales tickets are powering the business. You know that customers are coming to us for the entertainment value of seeing the crews work."

Dosh knew the man with sideburns as Tim. Tim was a hard worker who was money motivated. Any other day, Tim would have been one of his favorites. "Are any other resources available? Could you call someone in? If not, I am willing to accept a partial pit crew for a few hours."

Tim replied in a drawl that was either Canadian or Minnesotan. Whenever he used the letter "O," it took a while. "I will try to call someone in, but you knoooow how hard it is to get people to shoooow up even as scheduled. Everyone is either sick, or exposed to someone, or uninterested in going ooout. What is so critical about last night's delivery?"

"My crew emptied our truck this morning," interjected a red shirt with matching red hair, trimmed beard, and moustache. "We unloaded something like 100 road flares and twice that many American flags."

"This merchandise is not what is selling. Hell, we are selling more air filters than we are road flares. If you don't mind me asking, what's going on, Mr. Dosh?" Tim rejoined. "Is there something we should know?"

Dosh said. "You will all be receiving flares, flags, water, and sign materials." He took a moment to consider what he was comfortable saying on an open call. He checked the roster of attendees, and he found no surprises. "Everyone turn your camera on," he demanded.

A few seconds later, Dosh could see his in-state management team. Every one of the on-screen boxes had a red shirt. The checkerboard of people with red shirts was sufficient evidence to him that it was his people on the feed, and his people alone. It helped that he recognized most of the faces.

He tapped his mouse to bring up the pop-up menu, and he made sure that the recording function was reset to "off." He watched reactions as his staff noticed. Several seemed to lean in to indicate listening more intently.

Dosh took a disclosure risk. He knew that he was making the case for those employees and board members who thought he treated the company like his own personal fiefdom. They had already planned his exit, so playing to their suspicions did not matter to Dosh. "I decided to devote a few resources of this company to do something for the good of our home state."

The response to the Benton Harbor rally had met his expectations. The press and the politicians were stewing. It was time to escalate. "The trucks are filled with supplies for an upcoming protest. A group will be demonstrating in opposition to the lock-down."

"Whoa," said Tim. "What? I am not sure that I want to get involved in something like that."

"I am not asking you to participate in the protest, although you may if you wish. I am asking you to distribute the materials that I have provided."

"You provided?"

"The materials are a personal contribution to several charitable groups."

"What kind of charities do protest marches?" Tim asked.

"Daughters of the American Experiment, Sons of the American Experiment, AMERIVETS, The Fife and Drum Council, and the Freedom Party, to name a few," said Dosh.

"We are supposed to unload the trucks and pass this stuff out?" confirmed the redhead.

"Each of you should expect a small crowd to start arriving at your parking lots this afternoon. The visitors are expecting to be provided with provisions. Please hand out those items using whatever method you feel is most efficient."

"Anything else?" prompted a burdened Tim.

"Yes, please allow the visitors to use our facilities to stay warm and make bathrooms available to them if asked."

Tim persisted. "How many stores are involved?"

"Every Nextdoor Auto Parts store in the state," Dosh replied. "We are providing materials free of charge to registered charitable organizations. If you encounter problems with local officials or local law enforcement, please refer them to me. I'll make myself available to receive calls."

"We are totally going to get busted," said Tim. "Aiding and abetting a riot."

"As far as we are concerned, this is a sanctioned gathering on our private property."

"What if this gathering moves offsite?" The border of Tim's Grid box turned yellow again to indicate audio. "We're located next to what used to be a busy street."

"That activity is not something we'd officially endorse," said Dosh.

"How is this good for business?"

"Tim, we need people to drive their cars. That means we need them to leave their homes. We also need people to work so that they can afford the products in our stores. If these protestors are successful in changing government policy and opening the economy, that outcome would be a positive for our business."

Dosh had provided a forum, but his word was the last word. He had good people, and his chain of command was reliable. "Fellow red shirts, get those trucks unloaded and get those products in the hands of your afternoon visitors. Consider this a priority of the chairman." He reached for his computer screen and ended the video call.

13

Late afternoon, the rain began to clear over Western Michigan. As the sky brightened, Michigan Governor Jovita Bliss could not believe her eyes. A crowd gathered outside of the white picket fences of the governor's summer residence on Mackinac Island. Although the off-season population of the island had grown from its pre-shut-down level, a crowd of any size was an unusual sight.

Dosh had done his homework. The official schedule detailing the governor's whereabouts was a matter of public record. When he discovered that the executive had vacated the capital city, he pounced at the chance to draw attention. He could highlight her flight to the vacation home. In addition, the governor had long demonstrated a penchant to produce word salads when surprised.

"Look outside," Bliss said to her team. "Those people are a lawless assembly." She stared out the window. "This group of extremists is here to cause chaos. It's a violent mob. They're ready to attack us. Force and fear are the currencies of these insurgent factions."

Dosh arranged for a small convoy to leave Grand Rapids in time for the four o'clock ferry from Mackinaw City. Timing was critical. Dosh's pick-up truck and ten other cars roared up I-75 at full throttle. They parked at the ferry terminal and boarded with minutes to spare. Dosh enlisted his group to help him empty his truck bed of armfuls of gear. On the lower deck of the ferry, fifty protesters filled rows of white plastic seats. They drew their signs and unpackaged their flags.

As the ferry cleared the no wake zone, the pump-jet engaged. The watercraft rose on plane, and within seconds, its speed topped thirty knots. A plume of water gushed like an angled geyser from the back of the boat. The translucent surface of Lake Huron skidded past in a rush of turquoise.

Only a few minutes out of port, the lighthouse on Round Island Point was fast approaching. A red base had a white structure built atop it. The lighthouse looked like a sunburnt hand curled around an ice cube. Passing Round Point, Mackinac Island became visible. The shoreline of the most famous of Lake Huron's 30,000 islands shimmered.

As conspirators concocted plans, the ferry docked at the end of a long concrete pier. Dosh and his group of fifty were first on land. Making their way rapidly to the shoreline, they passed two large buildings with green roofs. On land, every church, inn, and Victorian on the wharf looked as if a fresh coat of white paint had been applied but not yet dried.

The travelers, like most Michiganders, likely knew the island well. They would have been here on honeymoons or family trips. Motorized vehicles were prohibited past the pier. Bicycle shops, with racks full of weathered frames of every color, intercepted their route. Otherwise, the group moved briskly through the shoreline shops.

Up from the waterfront, the island's natural features first announced themselves with a substantial hill. The group reassembled at a trailhead for one of the island's many paths. A steep rise of a hill up Fort Street forced a pause to slow breaths and pulses.

Dosh and company arrived at the governor's summer mansion like a flash mob. A man with a tricorn, revolutionary war hat, led amplified protest chants, "Throw Her Out! Throw Her Out!" Signs, banners, and flags unfurled.

On the grounds of the mansion, the tall lanky man poorly disguised himself in sunglasses and a baseball cap. He carried a sign low in his bad arm that said, "I Will Not Stay Home." The message was a direct affront to the governor's order from a month previously. He walked around the mansion, gathering additional demonstrators. He recruited a dozen.

As Dosh circulated and rabble-roused, the governor appeared in one of the windows for a second time. He and Ms. Bliss made momentary eye contact. She did not recognize him. Had she done so, it could have been a blow to his business fortunes in the state. The short timer did not seem to mind.

The governor wore a muumuu with reddish-brown tones and a vine-like print. The color complimented her dark skin. The dress draped loosely, concealing her corpulent frame. African jewelry hung from her neck and ears. Bliss turned and left the window in a sudden move.

A few minutes later while he was circling, Dosh's phone buzzed. He received an email from the governor's office. Most of the citizens of the state likely received the same correspondence. It said, "Under Executive Order 2020-21, all public and private gatherings of any number of people occurring among persons outside a single household are temporarily prohibited."

Dosh's experience in being an organizer was progressing well. If a reminder email were the full response to a protest, the governor would find her efforts insufficient. She had no idea what else to expect.

Upstairs in the summer residence, two aides rushed into the executive office. "Governor," began a young woman in a winter white, knee-length dress, white gold jewelry, and low heels, "you should turn on the television." The woman selected a remote control from the governor's desk and activated the information appliance. WNLS News, Channel 6, broadcasted from the front lawn below.

"Why do I need to see footage? What will I see that I haven't already seen? Do we know something that we don't currently know? It's happening here. Is something else happening everywhere? Something nefarious is going on," screeched the governor.

"Watch," requested the aide. She keyed in other channels. Broadcasting from the state capital in Lansing, Channel 10 aired a protest march. Channel 47 showed a "Live, Breaking News" banner. Their reporters covered a demonstration in opposition to the shut-down. The smoke in the air identified this feed as coming from a third site. WLAJ 53 reporters were on site at the Towne Center shopping mall. They filmeds what appeared to be a fourth separate uprising.

Down on the lawn, the group seemed to be dividing. A band of people waving signs and flags aligned themselves along the sidewalk. Another group faced the windows of the mansion, directing their slogans to the governor and her staff. In the center, some bound their signs to the stair railings. Dosh moved from group to group.

A few minutes later, four police officers appeared at the scene, two men and two women. The officers were dressed head to toe in black. Bulletproof vests made them look bulky, and weapons dangled from their utility belts. After what appeared to be a brief surveillance of the scene, the officers walked past some of the protesters. The small force entered the mansion without incident. The governor and her staff met them.

"This uprising is interfering with the business of the state," began the governor. She was not sure she believed her own statement, but it was the most officious thing that she could think of saying. She was trying hard to communicate her executive capacity.

"You are looking at the entirety of the island police force," responded the woman identifiable as the police captain by her insignia. "We have two officers off-duty and off-island, and one sick. We count seventy-five people out there, and others were joining as we entered.

"This is an invasion. Start making arrests," instructed the governor. "Start with that tall guy in the ballcap. He stands above the crowd. The man is openly defiant. Thinks he's above the law. We already sent out a broadcast to remind the citizens of the regulation."

"The protesters appear to be nonviolent, ma'am. With our limited manpower and limited resources, the safety of our officers would be at risk."

"This is an attack on democracy," continued the governor. She could not help herself. She continued, "it is an affront to the rule of law." Irrelevant political phrases gushed from her lips.

"Yes, ma'am," the captain responded. "We are here to protect, but we are not equipped for what's going on outside the mansion."

The aide took a call on her smartphone, pinning dangling hoop earrings to her ear. She announced, "We are getting reports of protests in Detroit, Ann Arbor, Grand Rapids, and Dearborn. You already know about Lansing, governor. These illegal actions appear to be statewide."

"Call out the National Guard," the governor erupted. "Martial law. Set a curfew." She had lost the room long ago, but she could not stop herself.

The room fell silent, and officers and aides looked around. Finally, one of the aides spoke. "Ma'am, the State Guard has already been activated. About 5,000 guardsmen and guardswomen are engaged in sourcing and distributing personal protective gear."

"How do I get a force on the ground? Military gear, nonlethal weapons?" she asked. "We need to control this situation. I am in charge here," she insisted against disbelief.

"You would need to invoke Title 10," offered an aide. "That would activate remaining National Guard forces of the state, and give us access to Federal members of the force."

"Title 10 means Federal control," recalled the governor. "This is my state. I am in control. I mean business. The buck stops here."

"Yes, ma'am," placated her aide. "You'll need to call the president."

"Who is the head of the National Guard?" Bliss asked. "Can I call that person? I'd rather not call the president. He's a denier. He aligns with the teabaggers. He's probably responsible for this riot."

Silence suggested that the room had heard enough. "We can go that route, Governor, working backchannels, but activation may take several days. Even after that delay, the decision still must go through the president's office. It is a simple matter of how quickly you want troops."

"I want them now. Make the call," she instructed.

Moments later, Melissa Crawford knocked hard on the door of the president's study. She opened the door and stuck her head into the room. Melissa was without her fashionable glasses, and her hair was pulled back into a bun. "Mr. President, the Governor of Michigan is on the phone for you."

The president looked up from the television monitor. "I was under the impression she hated me. By the looks of things on the news, her situation must be desperate."

"She is asking for additional National Guard troops," Melissa said. "It might be wise, Mr. President. The people now on the streets have been idle for weeks. They have been stuck in their homes… doing nothing. Letting off steam could escalate."

From a nearby chair, Philip Anaclet said, "If we give them more help in the form of stimulus money, and the period of idleness and unrest could last for years." Anaclet tugged on his turtleneck.

"Time for action," concluded the president.

14

Early Friday night, Nova's computer was open on the restaurant counter. She stood at the keyboard. Two floodlights beamed down upon her, making it look like she was performing a synthesizer solo for a rock show. If bills and receipts were her music, she was not enjoying the genre. Her arms tensed, and her head bowed. Her apron hung loose from her neck, untied from the back. She had also unbundled her hair, batting it away as it fell in front of her face. She looked something like a shoe halfway untied.

Her dark mood matched the dark restaurant. The restaurant had closed thirty minutes early. To Nova, it was an unimaginable result: a failure of her system. Demand had started a doom loop. First, they ran out of tarteletter. Then, the rod polse dwindled. After scrambling to remove several items from the menu, Nova ultimately had to stop accepting orders altogether.

She had lost a fight, her first since being a freshman in college. In the darkness, she attempted to process what happened. While sorting out the present day, she flashed back to her past trauma. Then she had been naïve and unprepared. This time, that was not the case. Her buying had boosted supplies.

She had prevailed upon her father to increase production. A streamlined delivery process had enabled the restaurant staff to serve more cars than it had a week ago. She had raised prices. However, her preparation and training had proven insufficient. Like the last time she had failed, she was bruised and seething.

Partly out of spite and partly out of business sense, Nova took another digital price increase. On the bright side, customers had continued to favor the restaurant with outlandish tips. Gratuity sums were averaging 50 percent on each check. Half of that went directly to the restaurant. With high cash flows, the business was only a week away from being debt free.

As she closed a spreadsheet tab, a metallic crash sounded from the kitchen. Curious, she responded by walking to the swinging door to look through its cloudy window. Seemingly energized by the early close, Maurice had made a beeline to the back room.

An hour later, Nova realized that he must still be excited. He was seldom so clumsy with the tools of his trade. He retrieved an empty pan from the floor. After recovering the fallen member, ten bread pans were arranged side to side at the far end of the stainless-steel counter.

Maurice had changed into his full chef regalia. His trousers were black and white houndstooth. His double-breasted jacket covered the swell above his waist. The jacket fastened a few inches left of center with black snaps. A rimless hat, a toque blanche, covered most of his sandy hair. Nine o'clock shadow seemed to complete the black and white contrast.

Nova had seen this attire many times before. She considered it somewhat of an embarrassment, akin to her father dressing up to take her out to trick-or-treat as a child. The outfit often indicated a creative phase. The collection of pans led her to think that Maurice was inventing a new bakery item. A new product meant new ingredient needs.

It was the last thing that a restaurant that was unable to finish its dinner service needed. Yet there it was. On the counter nearest to the chef, a chunky mass of dough sat atop a layer of flour. Maurice divided the dough into his line of pans, filling each about half full. He sprinkled some sandy substance on top of each loaf.

After applying a thorough covering, he selected a deep brown rootlike item from the table. Dragging a zester over the root, he cut shavings to fall into each pan. After finishing his toppings, Maurice gently rubbed each dough ball and then carried pans two by two to a convection oven.

Beyond Maurice, what looked like the full kitchen staff was at work. If that were not the case, Nova would have lashed out. She needed food product for the next day's service, and for the days following that. With everyone attired in white hair nets, white masks, white disposable aprons, and white latex gloves, it looked like ghosts dancing in the ballroom of a haunted mansion.

When Maurice turned from the ovens, he must have caught sight of Nova at the door. He headed straight for her. As he crossed over into the front of the house, she saw blue eyes illuminated with purpose. To look at the man, one would think that he had just discovered electricity or invented the Internet. For Nova, seeing him with such purpose felt like body blows on top of unhealed contusions. It was as if her painkillers had suddenly worn off.

"We'll know in about thirty minutes," he said, "but I think that I have perfected your grandmother's recipe for suikerbrood!" Maurice spoke reverently. "I give all credit to her. I don't know if you remember, Nova, but my mom had what she considered to be a special method. She would push brown sugar cubes right into the dough. The cubes would partially melt in the cooking. They would drip and caramelize. The finished bread would have crunchy medallions that were extremely sweet. While those bits were wonderful, the rest of the bread was a bit chewy, and the dough was often moist. Do you remember?"

Nova's memories were vivid. The sweet Dutch bread appeared at the holidays. Grandmother Oma would be dressed in her white apron with its imprints of tulips and clogs. She would bend to the lower oven. Using the apron to cover her hands, she would remove the loaves from the heat. As the bake cooled, Oma would playfully slap young Nova's hands away from the melted sugar cubes.

However, Nova would always succeed in pulling off a few of the warm sweet melts. When the bread was later sliced, she was allowed to take a piece along with dinner. On those occasions, Nova thought she had pulled one over on Maurice. She had dessert for dinner.

Few things troubled Nova more than reinvention of old recipes. This assault was her father rewriting heritage. Suikerbrood was family legacy. The sweet bread reminded her of goodness, sweetness, and love—all things that she felt that she had lost.

"You were putting on some sort of topping?" she queried. "When I think of suikerbrood, I don't think it had a topping."

"Your grandmother taught me everything that I know about baking, and I love her to death, may she rest in peace. However, I have an idea to improve upon the sugar cubes."

Nova hoped that the heavy eye makeup concealed the squint that accused him of treachery. "What's that?"

"Sanding sugar, lemon zest, and roasted ginger. It will give the bread some great aromatics. To provide the crunchy element that we both remember so fondly, I am going to brûlée the top of the dish."

Not only was he ruining her holiday memories, but he was also creating problems in the present. Nova reluctantly added brûlée torches to her mental list of equipment to buy. Was it too much to ask the man to keep from complicating everything?

"Suikerbrood could be a little something special for our customers," he continued. "We have not had a new menu item for a few months." He elbowed her playfully. "We can sell more dessert and expand the amount of our average check."

This point, average check, her calculation for the restaurant's average sale per diner, was not the one ratio that she wanted him to take from the financial discussion. Higher average check did not mean for him to go invent something new.

Flummoxed, she removed her apron and tucked it behind the counter. She felt she was on the brink of losing a second round.

She extracted her coat and her purse. "Good-night, Maurice," she announced. "I'm going home."

15

Later that night, when Nova slumped through the front door of her home, she ran right into Arch. The man must have stationed himself on the small, upholstered bench just out of reach of the in-sweeping door. Arch rose to his feet and blocked her way. Nova could not imagine why, and she was in no mood to find out.

Nova put up a halfhearted forearm block. She tried moving in the direction of the coat closet. Again, Arch slid into her path. "What's your dysfunction?" she asked. It was like having to do a post-fight interview when what she really needed was a trainer.

Forced to her corner, Nova took him in. Arch had a strange look on his face. His eyes and chin slanted upward, and his mouth was pulled into a tight smile. It looked as if he had to unburden himself of a juicy secret. It was either that or the puppy-like houseguest needed to relieve himself on the lawn.

As if interacting with a pet, she reached up to muss his hair. As she did, she noticed that it had been trimmed. She also noticed that he was still wearing work clothes. Any collared shirt qualified as work attire these days. His was a navy golf shirt with a European bank logo on one sleeve. She wondered what project kept him working six hours after the market closed.

He did not seem able to stand any further delay. "I submitted those papers you signed. I set up an account. This account is the one that you will want, you know, for the rent checks."

Nova knew Arch was a brilliant guy, a University of Chicago MBA, but he was having trouble telling her whatever he was trying to tell her. She sort of understood that she was in possession of a cool brokerage account.

"You know that auto parts store?" he continued.

"Yeah, obviously. I work within 100 yards of that store." She wondered where this ambush conversation was going, and why it was taking so long to get there.

Breathy and conspiratorial, he said, "I learned something from one of our word recognition algorithms…"

"One of your algorithms?" she challenged. "I have an account and an algorithm? What are you talking about?"

"You do not have an algorithm," he corrected. "An algorithm is a computer program, a very sophisticated one. It can take a room full of IT guys to come up with one of these algorithms. One of the programs operated by my team searches for information from company conference calls and press events. The algorithms can even analyze things like language from police scanners. The algorithms search for key words. Often repeated words can be predictive."

"Okay, big shot, you have a fancy computer program. So what?"

"My firm's algorithm picked up a disclosure. I think the information means that the FBI is going to raid the headquarters of Nextdoor Auto Parts."

"Raid them? That sounds bad."

"Federal officers crashing through your front door. Yes, that's bad."

"What did they do?"

"You said it yourself," he replied. "Something struck you as wrong about the company."

"I know that the store next to us violated the stay-at-home order. Do the Feds arrest people for that?"

"No, a bunch of companies have been fighting for the right to stay open. What the algorithm found is more concerning. The word search produced multiple hits on 'aiding and abetting.' Those words are often used for something criminal."

"Something criminal," she repeated. "That sounds salacious." Nova removed her coat to give herself time and space. Arch finally allowed passage to the closet. "So what does this have to do with my new brokerage account?"

"I shorted the stock on your behalf," he replied. If he were honest with himself, he would admit to shorting for his own purposes as well. The trade was a small one, but the gesture meant something. "The news must be leaking out. The stock is indicated down three bucks in the after-market."

"The stock is down. I am short, so that is good."

"Right."

"I borrowed the stock, right?"

"Yes."

"I sold it?

"At $28 per share," he agreed.

"I can buy it back tomorrow at $25. I pocket the $3 difference."

"Exactly," he coached. "A 12 percent two-day return is the kind of stuff we Wall Streeters dream about."

Nova had no such dreams, but she was learning quickly.

16

The next morning started early. At times, Dosh woke so early that some might consider him starting the day during the night before. Dosh's overwhelming enthusiasm for morning was one of the reasons that his wife had given up. Single parenting while sleep deprived had threatened her health. Over time, it became clear that his passion for work exceeded his concern for her condition. With room for his gangly arms and legs, he slept comfortably in the center of the bed.

Since the third grade, Dosh began every daybreak with a recitation. "Early to bed, early to rise, makes a man healthy, wealthy, and wise." His namesake, Ben Franklin, was credited with the phrase. Dosh had so incorporated the idea into his life that he conducted further research. He discovered that Franklin adapted a sentiment that had been in use since the 1400s. That history made him like it even more. As long as there had been a place named America, there had been a spirit of enterprise. He saw himself as a worthy inheritor. In Dosh's experience, the country was exactly the land of opportunity that its slogans promised.

Rising to his full height was like running a flag up a flagpole. Dosh rounded the room, opening the blinds to see the barely perceptible twilight. A tabby cat at the foot of his bed lay in a curl and failed to move. The aged cat had been Dosh's only home companion since his wife had left fifteen years prior. The cat's stillness seemed to be a form of coping with the hour. After straightening the blanket, Dosh stroked his pet. Its eyes opened halfway, and it produced a sound more like a yelp than a purr. It was the only contact with a living thing he required.

Marriage had not been the motivation and delegation job share around which the rest of Dosh's life was organized. Amicable and quick, the divorce gave Dosh the house. What he really coveted was the garage. A concrete coating made the floor of the four-car enclosure shimmer. The garage had a lift. The tool bench would have been the envy of most body shops.

The garage and the house sat on an acre-sized lot, typical for the neighborhood. What was not typical was the surrounding green space. As Dosh's fortune grew, he bought the neighboring houses on each side of his home. Once secured, he tore the houses down and planted groves in their places. Other than their linearity, the groves blended with a mixed stand of mature deciduous trees on the slope behind the house and grounds.

He took a glance out a window. In the hints of light, he could see green buds forming on tips of the branches. He looked down the hillside where the sprouting stand ultimately gave way to riverbank. Dosh had a degree of privacy and a view. He never thought he needed more.

After a shower, he dressed in a red shirt and khakis. He headed straight for the garage, where a year-old Ford F-150 SuperCrew Platinum Edition pickup filled slightly more than its allotted single stall. Not only did he drive an American car, but he also supported the local industry. Dosh bought a new car or truck every single year.

The drive from the township of Ada to his office was a moderate one. His commute lasted about twenty minutes. He drove in silence to keep his brain filling the void with new thoughts. He had the beginnings of a concept for a new promotion. It was something that would drive traffic to his recently reopened stores.

When he turned into the parking lot, he coasted in between the lines of the space designated for the president of the company. His spot had red stripes, differentiated from the yellow lines everywhere else parked. He parked, locked his truck, and sauntered into the lobby.

The lobby of the Nextdoor Auto Parts World Headquarters was a glass atrium. A center console desk had seating for three. A small conversation area flanked the crescent-shaped console. Modern chairs with clean lines and black upholstery provided a waiting area. The chairs faced inward centered on a somewhat gaudy, red-patterned area rug. The rug was partially hidden by a concrete-textured occasional table. The seating area was bordered by glass cases.

The cases contained relics from the brief history of the company. The evolution of the company logo could be followed from its presence on patches, hats, and signs. Pictures of Dosh shaking hands and cutting ribbons were interspersed with the swag.

Dosh's legal counsel, Jack Trainor, met him inside the door. Jack was a short, round man. His belly spilled well over his belt, a product of many long dinners at Washington, D.C., hotspots. He had bushy salt-and-pepper eyebrows, which distracted from his mole-marred bald head. Standing next to Dosh, the two men produced a respectable showing of forming the lower-case letter "b." Trainor was wearing a dark suit and tie, and he was carrying an attaché case. After elbow bumping Dosh, Trainor raised his index finger and put it in front of his mask covered lips.

Three seats in the reception area were in use. Two seats facing the console desk and open to the front door were occupied by men who may have just aged out of one of the Seal teams. Having watched more than his fair share of John Wick movies, Dosh's impression of the men was that their white shirts and black suites were tactical. A woman with the build of a softball player sat with her back to the door. Above the seat cushions, Dosh could see a badge on her belt.

Dosh walked into the lobby and gave a silent bow to his visitors. He swiped his wallet containing a security card against the access control system's wall unit, and he motioned for the group to follow him into a conference room, which was walled-off behind the console desk. The group quickly divided with Dosh and counsel going to one side of the conference table and the visitors occupying the other. They proved rigorous in keeping separated by six feet of distance.

"Benjamin," began Jack Trainor, "let me introduce you to Special Agent Carol Weisman. She and her team are from the Detroit office of the FBI. I have arranged this meeting at her request." Trainor made a long, sweeping motion with his arm, which seemed to convey that he was handing the meeting over to the agent.

The agent turned from the lawyer. Her eyes augered into Dosh's. "Mr. Dosh, are you aware of the slew of unlawful gatherings that have occurred throughout the state over the past few days?"

"Is anyone with a television or a web connection not aware of the protests?" asked Dosh's lawyer. "Certainly Ms. Weisman, that is not your question."

The agent bristled, and she sat up higher in her chair. Her considerable shoulders rolled forward, her posture communicating gravity. She extended two fingers toward the commando in business camouflage to her right. She flexed her fingers repeatedly, until they became hooks.

The man pulled a laptop from a black leather bag and presented it to her. She opened the laptop. It immediately booted to a video screen. With the press of a button, a video played. She turned the laptop so that Dosh could see. The video was a splice of short clips showing protesters with road flares and flags. "Mr. Dosh, do you notice anything about these video clips?" she asked.

"This video appears to be highly edited," the lawyer objected. "Who did the editing, and what was its purpose? Special Agent, you could be accused of presenting selective facts to elicit a particular answer from my client."

The agent gave a death stare to the lawyer. "What I notice is that the people in these videos have the same road flares and the same flags. Both are dangerous items. The flares are obviously a burn risk, and the flagpoles are potentially blunt force weapons. Whoever supplied these devices is guilty of several felonies."

"Flags are considered weapons?" challenged the lawyer. "You might want to consult the First Amendment to the Constitution. For the record, my client does not believe that either road flares or flag standards are weapons."

"Mr. Dosh, are road flares and flags such as the ones viewed on the video sold in your stores?"

"Finally, a question my client can answer," said the lawyer. "Go ahead, Ben."

"Yes," indicated Dosh. "My stores to sell road flares and flags."

"Good," the agent replied in exasperated relief. "How have sales of those items been lately?"

"My client operates a public company," said the lawyer. "The Securities Exchange Commission prohibits him from disclosing financial information to the public without submitting a public filing. I'm sorry, but he cannot disclose sales data, as it may be germane to the value of the company's securities."

"Mr. Dosh, have your stores been handing out any road flares or flags free of charge in the past two weeks? That information would not be financial in nature—do we agree, Mr. Trainor?"

"Yes, agreed," said the lawyer. "Ben?"

"Our stores provide items at no charge to charitable organizations from time to time."

"In large quantities?" asked the agent. Before the lawyer could object, she voiced, "Withdrawn."

"Where is this going?" prompted the lawyer. "Say what you came here to say."

The agent settled back into her chair. She closed the laptop and slid it back across the table to her colleague. Establishing direct eye contact with Dosh, she began, "Mr. Dosh, the Bureau has evidence that you, through the auspices of the Nextdoor Auto Parts stores, have been aiding and abetting unlawful demonstrations throughout the state."

Dosh did not react.

The agent took a deep breath. Lacking a confession, it appeared she had been given specific instructions. As if she was reading from a card, she spoke. "From leadership at the highest levels of the government, I have been asked to tell you in the most strenuous terms… to stand down. Stand down. Do I make myself clear?"

Dosh gave a solemn nod.

Trainor rolled upright out of his rolling chair. "I think we are done here."

All three agents made a hasty exit.

Making his own exit, Trainor patted Dosh on the shoulder and smiled. "In the United States, we do not arrest billionaires."

"Good," replied Dosh. "I am going to New York to meet several of them now."

17

The White House

A PROCLAIMATION

The American people continue to struggle with the terrible COVID outbreak. It has disrupted our lives, especially since the shut-down nearly two weeks ago. We are slowing the spread. However, our businesses are hurting, and our people are hurting.

Prior to the pandemic, the United States had the strongest economy in the world. The Administration is committed to recapturing that strength. We are engaging American companies to manufacture the hospital equipment and protective materials that we need to protect our citizens. Our Federal Reserve has already lowered interest rates to zero in support of new investment in our nation.

Rest assured that your government is working night and day toward recovery. However, it is the opinion of our experts that the legislation recently passed by Congress is not the right path for this nation. The BOOST Act, as written, intends to add $2.2 trillion in government spending. Quite simply, this bill represents a government takeover of a sizable portion of our economy. Ronald Reagan said it best, "The scariest phrase in the English language is 'I am from the government, and I am here to help.'"

Trillions in new deficit spending is not the help that our nation needs. Our debts are already too large. Instead the country needs to return to normalcy and get back to work. This Administration will do everything in its power to make that reentry a safe one.

Congress may try to override my veto. We are ready to fight for the American people. Fight for your freedom. Fight for your jobs.

A veto is one of the powers of the President. It is not used regularly, and it is not enacted without deliberation. We believe that the best path through this time of difficulty is to rely on the compassion and ingenuity of the American people and not the checkbook of Congress. Our faith in America, its institutions, its businesses, and its citizens has never been stronger. God Bless these United States.

NOW, THEREFORE, I, KENWORTH J. JOHNSON, President of the United States, by the authority invested in me by the Constitution and the laws of the United States of America, hereby veto H.R. 748, known as the BOOST Act.

IN WITNESS WHEREOF, I have hereunto set my hand on this fifth day of April, in the year of the Lord two thousand twenty, and of the independence of the United States of America two-hundred and forty-fourth.

KENWORTH J. JOHNSON

Seated in the Oval Office, the president spoke to the television cameras in a midday national address. He posed for the lens with a slight turn of his head. His mouth was open with his teeth clasped together. He looked as if he was holding a bitewing at a dental exam. "Many of you are aware that it has been nine days, nine long days since Congress passed the BOOST Act. The Act would have increased costs $2 trillion. Trillion with a capital 'T.'" The president loosened his clench and swayed with confidence. "By law, the President can either sign the bill into law, ignore it, or veto. On the advice of my Cabinet and for the best interests of the American people, I have decided to veto."

18

A few hours later, the Senate Majority Leader emerged from a behind closed doors Republican conference. Two tall, thick cherry wood doors with carvings inset opened out to a tiled hallway. Senator Robert Sasson was right behind the leader, slightly ahead of a duckling-like row of legislators. He looked ashen.

The Majority Leader walked straight ahead to what looked like a prearranged press conference. Sasson saw a glass podium framed by four posted American flags. The display was semicircled by few members of the Capitol Hill press. They were armed with cameras and microphones, and black cables drooped from the instruments to the floor.

Sasson could see that the legislator was going to drop the figurative bomb that he carried. Apparently, the man could not wait even a few minutes. There would be no failsafe. A photo op had been arranged. Whatever time Senator Sasson thought he had evaporated.

Sasson and the president had their differences, but no one deserved the rug pull that was coming. Senator Sasson saw an empty stretch of corridor, and he cut to the left. He accelerated, walking briskly, as if only wingtip shoes prevented a full run. As he raced, he dialed his cell phone. With his first words, he could hear his voice muddled among the echoing caverns of the capitol building. "I need to speak to the president."

The operator must have heard enough to sense the urgency in the senator's voice. Senator Sasson heard a few clicks. "This better be good," said Kenworth Johnson. "I have got Edward Tandy dumping shares of airline stocks. Some patriot that guy turned out to be. He owns a stake in a national asset. When the going gets tough, he gets going. What do I say to this guy? Has he ever heard of civics? I think I'll tell globalist Edward to go buy some more Chinese stocks. Maybe he should move to China. Sunnyvale would not miss him. Everybody thinks this guy is some sort of a Jimmy Stewart citizen figure. It could not be further from the truth."

"Mr. President?" he interrupted. "You need to know something. You need this information right away. The Senate has decided not to override your BOOST Act veto."

"You are my man on the inside, Senator. Got what you wanted. Good. Maybe I underestimated you. Maybe you are a player."

Senator Sasson tried to temper the enthusiasm. "Mr. President, it is not what you think. You are not going to believe this."

"Spit it out. Say whatever it is that you want to say."

"The veto was sustained because the Senate Republicans have decided to withdraw support for your administration. It is a total repudiation. The majority will refuse all new bills. They will reject any cabinet nominees. They will defer any judicial nominees. Given the decision, you would be wise to withdraw your nomination for the Supreme Court," he said. "The conference is angry. They are vindictive. You are on your own until after the election."

"How can they do something like that? Are they going into recess for the next five months?"

Back down the hallway, the press conference was beginning. Senator Sasson watched a ceiling mounted monitor. The Majority Leaders's eyes looked as if he had spent the day reading in semidarkness. Members of the caucus knew that he had not. The squint was likely intended to portray gravity. The senator's somewhat famous barrel chest seemed to distance him from the podium. To close the gap, he patted both sides of the dais, like he was greeting an old friend.

"The president is a disgrace," he stated flatly. "Despite overwhelming support by both the Senate and the House, he has seen fit to veto the BOOST Act. The legislation provided stimulus checks to members of our population at greatest need. In addition, it promised funding to our business community. The Congress believes the BOOST Act to be the catalyst for our nation's recovery from this terrible pandemic."

The Majority Leader suddenly smiled. To a viewer, the change was startling. "The Republicans in the Senate have expressed extreme contempt for the president. In our assessment, he has failed to represent our constituents, and he has failed as the leader of this party."

The nine-term congressman turned the top edge of a paper upward from the podium. As he had intended, it gave the impression that he was selecting every word. "Based upon a roll call vote, which was held a few minutes ago, the Senate lacks substantial votes to overturn the president's veto." He went on to recognize the senators who wished to be named. "Given the president's outrageous act, twenty-nine Republican senators have withdrawn their support for the bill. Ten Democrats will join, making this a bipartisan decision.

"We hereby turn our backs on the president," as he said the words, he performed the action. He stood for a few seconds for the cameras to capture the moment. Several senators shouted, "Shame, shame," off camera.

The Senate Majority Leader left the podium and walked out of camera and microphone range. To watch, the junior senator could swear that the majority leader had a spring in his step. A member of the press overheard the leader say, "This man will be the next Herbert Hoover if I have anything to say about it."

19

The next day, Arch was back at work in Nova's home dinette. He had entered a splashy trade for his firm. He had Nova to thank for it, not that he would tell her that fact. She had a way of claiming other people's legwork, and his mad money exploits were his.

Had he not opened a brokerage account for Nova, Arch would never have experienced fractional share trading. Any number of shares not rounded to 100 were considered fractional shares. Fifteen shares were fractional. Eighty was fractional.

As a professional investor, Arch routinely dealt with thousands of shares at a time. For Nova, he was buying and selling fives and tens. These were minor quantities, personal finance level stuff.

However, once Arch became acquainted with fractional shares, he discovered what he considered to be fractional options. He preferred trading options, or anything else that involved leverage. Acute risk focused his mind.

Zero-day options were often options tied to less than 100 underlying shares of stock. As an added feature, zero-day options expired within the subsequent trading day. The option's lifespan was less than thirty hours. For a trader, timing needed to be perfect. That challenge compelled him.

Previously unknown to Arch, zero-day options had become popular within the last few months. Like fractional shares, zero-day instruments appealed to people with limited funds to invest. The options were cheap. They cost pennies and dollars, instead of hundreds and thousands. Mom-and-pop investors, known as retail investors to people in Arch's trade, dominated the day trading market.

Beyond zero-day options being used by unsophisticated investors, Arch's newfound toy had some other advantages. Different from his usual derivative holdings, zero-day options were extremely liquid. The trading tools had become so popular that some days, zero-day options were half of volume of the entire market.

The odds dramatically favored the sellers of zero-day options. Eighty percent of the derivative contracts expired worthless. Arch wanted in on that action. For each one or two option buy that someone entered on their online brokerage screen, Arch took the other end of the trade. He sold. Speculators paid Arch a quarter to take a dollar's worth of upside exposure. If the market fell, Arch would be pocketing most of the quarters.

He pressed his advantage by using his firm's algorithm. The algorithm had collected a bulk of negative words, like "down," "correction," and "volatility." The words suggested a negative market sentiment. Arch spent the entirety of the previous day guiding execution of option trade after option trade. He only sold call options, those that profited from a higher market. He ended up with a large bet against US stocks.

To Arch's great delight, the president's veto of the BOOST Act destroyed the market. The New York Stock Exchange (NYSE) normally began trading at 9:30 a.m. Eastern Standard Time. However, when the exchange attempted to open, trading halted within the first five minutes.

Automatic circuit breakers, which were put in place after the Y2K crash to calm volatile trading, tripped. Enacted when markets indicated a decline of seven percent, the first circuit breaker required a fifteen-minute trading pause. When trading started, Arch was about to make a great deal of money.

In the few minutes of quiet, Arch had trouble wiping the smile from his face. He had found the information. He had made the right interpretation. He had exploited one of the popular new trading tools in the market. On the one day that mattered, he cornered the zero-day option market.

The brilliant move had broadened his firm into a whole new marketplace. Risk be damned, he did it with stunning success. The firm would make tens of millions. Preparing for opprobrium, he practiced false modesty. "Nothing ventured, nothing gained," he whispered to himself. It was one of those idioms, among many, that Arch's father repeated endlessly when Arch was a child. Heard often enough, some things stuck with you, even those from an absentee father.

When the stock market finally reopened, trading lasted a tumultuous ten minutes. The market cascaded downward in lurches. Collectively, stock prices fell an additional six percent from the first halt. At that point, the second circuit breaker triggered. Stock trading paused for another fifteen minutes.

A victory lap around the dining room did nothing to satisfy the budding Wall Street icon. He tried to pass the time watching CNBC. After a short while, watching the business news became like watching a sitcom rerun in which he knew all the jokes.

Arch was amped up. With the market closed, he had no way to express his feelings. The adrenaline was wearing off. He wanted to keep the high. He wanted more.

He did not want more money. He had grown up with money. With the seven-figure bonus that was coming, he already earned more than he would ever need. What interested him was the danger. He went in search of a bigger bet, a riskier bet, a more exotic wager.

20

Arch kicked off his loafers, flipping them against the wall as if aiming for the receptacle. Rising from the most profitable dinette set in the history of dinette sets, he moved over to Nova's seldom-used sofa. Arch jumped for the corner pillows. Airborne, sideways, and perpendicular, he landed shoulder first.

He removed the smartphone from the pocket of his cargo shorts. Responding to his touch, it seemed to have survived the fall. If the impact created another crack in the screen, it would have been hard to notice. The glass looked like a spider web. The protective casing for the phone looked like an eager pet had chewed it. He extended the pop socket on the back and angled the phone forty-five degrees from the sofa cushion.

Since he was idle, Arch knew that his trader, the man who bought and sold on his behalf, would have little to do. Skyler Ruffin had been Arch's shadow since the day Arch had started at the company. Having Skyler around was like having a needy girlfriend with an awesome sports car. Skyler was diligent and loyal. The trader picked up on the first ring. "Why are you calling me?" Skyler asked. "You know that the market is halted. I cannot trade. My hands are tied."

"What are the odds of Joe Burrow being the number one pick in the NFL Draft this week?" Arch asked his trader. The stock market may have been shuttered, but sports gambling stayed open around the clock. A risk was a risk, and an information edge was an information edge.

Skyler had a large fleshy face, and he used it to fill the video on Arch's screen. Talking to Skyler was like having someone invade your personal space. On a glance, one would have guessed that the trader figured out a way to zoom the self-facing camera. The reality was not that technical. He held his phone inches from his chin. Skyler could not give up on the idea of holding a phone to his ear. He realized the presence of the camera, so he compensated with a half measure, a phone four inches from his cheek.

The quirky trader was not a bookie, but he might as well have been. He knew the lines and the odds. Arch valued this side of Skyler's personality, even more than he appreciated the man performing nearly all of Arch's required office tasks.

"Who is the number one pick?" started Skyler. "You are kidding me, right? Really? The markets are so bad that they had to shut them down, and you want to talk about football? Have some perspective, man."

Resting his head on the cushion, Arch watched with one eye as Skyler caught his breath and turned his own head to the side. Arch saw his left ear in sufficient relief to see hairs sticking out. "Dude, have you ever heard of a personal trimmer?"

"Hey, while you are working on perspective, get some manners too," Skyler said. "I have to make sure that the market is not reopening after the latest halt. It is not. We are done for the day," he confirmed. "Twenty percent down. You will have to wait to collect your winnings until tomorrow."

"I'm so bored," whined Arch.

"We have thousands of zero-day options in the money. Is that not thrilling enough? How much action do you need? What's wrong with you?"

"It's actually hundreds of thousands," he corrected. "I am not calling it a day at ten in the morning. There is money to be made."

"Fine," Skyler said in apparent disgust. "You need stimulation." He filled the screen with his balloon of a forehead. "If you want to know the answer to your original question, the betting line from TheDunesOnline is negative 300 on Burrow going number one."

"I want action, but I am not laying out $300 for the chance of winning $100. C'mon, Skyler, I know that you know about this stuff. What do you have for me? I need a good prop bet."

Skyler's eyebrows shot skyward, and his forehead wrinkled. "You are a freakin' professional gambler in your day job. What's the difference between the stock market and a sports bet, dude?"

"You know this answer, Sky. None. Some of the best gamblers in the world work on Wall Street. What do you think that book *Liar's Poker* is about? The market is closed. You said so yourself. What's a guy to do? Give me a good money line."

"Why can't you just go work out or something? Bleed some energy."

Arch talked like a guy whose seminar you paid to hear. He continued as if he was pointing out highlights on a PowerPoint presentation. "While the Wall Street game has been around forever, this sports betting stuff is brand new. Only a few of the players are sophisticated. Not much competition. Even better, it takes a while for the house to get probabilities exactly right."

"Dude, now I'm totally sure that you're a degenerate gambler. Remind me not to give you any of my money to manage."

Arch did not respond. Skyler would come around. He just had to give him time.

Judging by the changing light reflected on Skyler's face, Skyler was toggling between screens on his computer. Arch couldn't help but think that Skylar's head looked like a candelabra light bulb, the kind with the slight turned tip of glass on top. The bulb flashed blue, then white, then back to blue. Skyler finally spoke. "Here's something interesting. This might be more fitting for a guy selling call options hours before a market crash. How about betting on which college will have the most players selected in the first round? Top choices are Ohio State and Alabama."

"Interesting," said Arch. Skyler seldom disappointed him. "What are the odds on a bet like that?"

"The action is around Ohio State at 0.75 more than Alabama. Basically, if Ohio State has one more first-round pick than Alabama, you make money. Betting the over will cost you $125."

"I like it. I'm in. Dig deeper. What else?"

Skyler continued to scan. "Hey, wait, we could bet on the number of wide receivers picked in the first round. Many people wager on the number of quarterbacks selected. However, other positions are less popular bets. That one could be mispriced. The line on this one is hovering around four—four wide receivers taken.

Hell, I think both Alabama wide receivers will go. The over on the number of receivers pays plus 200. I say we smash that number."

"Brilliant," confirmed Arch. "One of the wideouts that Joe Burrow threw to at LSU will go high. From what I've read, three other wide receivers have first-round draft grades. I'm all over this bet."

"How much are you putting up?" Skyler asked. "After today, you have some money to throw around."

"You'll get a nice bonus, too," he reminded Skyler that the trader rode on his coattails. "For me, I'm going in for 5,000. That's enough to make it interesting."

"Want to do anything else?"

"What else do you have?"

Skyler filled the smartphone screen again. Only his eyes, nose, and mouth were visible. It looked like a spreadsheet help agent. "I love this one. You can bet on the duration of the first round."

"Doesn't it take about four hours?"

"Yeah, but this draft will have a few twists. First, Miami forfeited their pick. People will forget. The first round will only have thirty-one selections this year."

"I like it."

"Second, this will be a virtual draft. That has never happened before. Everything will be online. Faster, I think."

"I could see fewer trades being executed."

"Exactly. Last, the first and second picks are a done deal. Burrow first. Chase Young second. Along with the forfeited Miami pick, this draft will be three deliberations shorter than any other."

"Information edge. This is what we do. I like your style, Sky man. I'm in for $20,000. Entering it on my screen now." Arch picked up his smartphone and toggled it to the black and green screen of his favorite sports betting website.

"As I said, my friend, you are a degenerate gambler. If you don't start practicing some self-control, I'm afraid something bad is going to happen to you."

"Taking big chances is what makes life worth living."

21

Oozing with personal and professional winnings, Arch headed to the airport with Nova in tow. He could see that she did not appreciate being woken and rushed out of the house. She was half conscious, and her features looked fuzzy without her usual makeup. It was like she'd colored outside of the lines.

He tried to compensate for her sluggishness with conversation. "You will like this trip. It is not the longest flight we have taken." He felt he had plenty of goodwill on which to draw. Previous trips had five-star accommodations and exotic experiences. Some of their best moments as a couple had been on adventure trips. He hoped that this one might pave over a few rough patches at home. "Have I ever let you down?"

No response. She looked out the window.

He tried to engage her with compliments. "Nova, you have strength and fortitude. You can endure physically challenging situations. You're fearless." He looked at her across the back seat. These were the features that made her a good companion for his type of travel.

She refused eye contact.

Arch worked to avoid revealing how much he was enjoying the one-sided conversation. He parsed his lips to keep from smiling. Nova was usually volatile. When she wasn't in control, she was even more explosive. Having her on edge enhanced his experience. He started talking about himself, knowing it would agitate her further.

"Have I told you about my mom?" he prompted. "When I was growing up, my mother and I were never able to travel. She was chronically ill for most of my school years. Depressed. We did not leave home much. Because of that, I vowed to myself that if I ever had money, I would use it to see the world. I owe it to my mother to visit the world's best sites and have its most profound experiences."

Nova maximized the distance across the back seat until they arrived at epartures.

At the drop-off, Arch extracted both suitcases from the trunk of the Uber. His baggage was a carry-on and hers at least twice that size. He set her suitcase on its wheels and pulled up the telescoping handle. Appreciating its bulk, he shook his head, knowing that his reaction would set her off.

"It's hard to pack light," she sassed, "when you refuse to tell me where we're going."

"Somewhere exiting," he said. He had voiced the same phrase at the house. "We'll be back in three days." Further explanation was not forthcoming. As they entered the terminal, he asked, "Have I ever told you that the only trips that my parents took were to business conferences?"

"Is this a business trip?"

"No." He made his point emphatically and continued with this story. Now that he had started, he was determined to tell her something about his upbringing. "At best, my parents would extend a work trip by a day. They'd give themselves a few hours to see a few sights. My dad was a workaholic. I think the sights my parents saw were in Detroit, Cleveland, and Toledo."

"How short is this flight? Tell me we are not going to Detroit or Cleveland," she protested.

"Longer than that, but we're not leaving the country." He pushed forward with his story. It was his version of meeting the parents. "My mother taught me to have experiences while you can. She never left home after getting sick."

Arch led Nova into a nearly empty airport terminal. Arch observed two other people he thought to be travelers. He scanned the terminal and found the video board listing arrivals and departures. Only two departures were listed. Both went to Chicago, and both were on time.

Nova noticed the same information.

"We are going through Chicago." He emphasized the word "through."

A single attendant stood behind a kiosk at the American Airlines check-in. She wore a mask and gloves. Arch set Nova's bag on the digital scale next to the ticket counter. He glanced at the readout—forty-seven pounds, barely legal. He handed his driver's license to the attendant in one smooth motion.

"Heading to Los Angeles, Mr. Crockett. Premier status." The attendant returned his ID card. "I will need to see hers as well." Nova processed the destination and produced her drivers' license. The rep gave it a cursory look. The blue suited worker reached under the counter and pulled a long, white sticker from the printer. She fastened it around the handle of Nova's bag and hoisted the bag onto a moving conveyor. "Gate One," she informed, handing the tickets to Arch.

Nova and Arch were the only passengers on a twelve-seater to Chicago. They sat together in the second row. With less distance than the car, but with the same lack of eye contact, Arch spent the entirety of the short flight telling Nova more stories about his parents: How his father had taught him to work hard; how the man had taught him to take chances; how his mother was undemanding, which did not seem to work out so well for her.

Compared to the short hop, the Chicago to Los Angeles leg was crowded. Thirty passengers spread out. Each had his or her own row for the three-hour transit. From the row behind, Arch watched as Nova tried to distract herself. She tried to sleep. She tried movies. She spent a half an hour in the bathroom apparently applying her makeup. Mostly, she kept looking back between the seats.

After landing, Arch decided that the time was right to address her lingering questions. "For our adventure," he said excitedly, "we don't even have to leave the airport."

Nova stood, stunned.

Arch could see that he needed to give her more of the picture. "We are not leaving the airport right away," he corrected. "Later, we have a room for two nights at the Fairmont Miramar. The hotel is on the beachfront. That's why I had you pack a swimsuit." He gave her a paper with the itinerary. She folded it and put it in her purse.

"Why aren't we leaving the airport?" she questioned.

"You aren't going to believe this," Arch effused. "I sort of can't believe that they are still doing this during the shut-down." The big reveal came with exuberance of a fifth grader at his first air show. "We are going on a zero-gravity plane ride."

"A what?"

The story that he had quarantined for hours came out in a burst. "They only do this sort of thing at a few sites on the West Coast. That's why we had to come to Los Angeles. Here's how it works." He fused his fingers and straightened his hand, using his hand as a jet. "You go up in a big plane, a passenger jet. It angles up to 32,000 feet, and then the pilots drop it straight down. During that descent, for fifteen or twenty seconds, we'll be weightless. After that, the plane levels off at something like 24,000 feet, and we do it again. The experience is as close as you can get to feeling what it's like in outer space! Zero gravity! You are going to love it," he promised.

"How long is the experience?" she asked.

"It's five hours, and you experience zero-g about ten times." As he answered, Arch was scanning for signs, and found a valet holding one with his name on it.

Nova and Arch took a shuttle to a private terminal where a 727 was waiting. In the terminal, they were given blue jumpsuits. The short sleeve, button-front coveralls had patches on the lapels and sleeves. Once changed, Arch thought they could have passed as astronauts from NASA.

He was stoked. "This is going to be so awesome," he kept saying. "Awesome." For the next hour, he kept asking her if she had the right stuff. Once or twice, he channeled the first *Top Gun* movie and called her Goose.

"Easy does it, Mav," she partially played along. "You don't want to crash and burn."

Along with a family of four, they were ushered up a set of airstairs to the back of the plane. They were asked to stow their footwear and to take a seat in one of two rows. Arch got his first glimpse of the arrangement.

The whole midsection of the aircraft was open. The ceilings, walls, and floors were padded with white foam. That was the floating area, he presumed.

As the plane taxied, an instructor relayed the ins and outs of g-forces. They would be experiencing two or three g's during the rapid climbs. They would be floating weightless during the descent. They could spread eagle, or do the Superman pose, or even hold hands. They would be alerted one or two seconds before the drop ended, so they could either get their feet under them or find a spot to drop on the floor.

The first cycle was over so fast, that Arch felt like he had barely reacted. Nova and Arch rose tentatively from their seats and extended gingerly into the air. They had barely moved when the warning sounded. "That sucked," announced Arch. "We only have nine more of these drops to go. We have to get more out of it than that."

When the second zero-g session arrived, they were ready. Arch timed the gravity well and launched himself into the air. Two seconds later, he was flying up toward the door separating the cockpit from the play area. Nova was not as springy, but she followed along. She caught up and reached barely in time to hold his hand. He held tight when the gravity resumed, and they sank to the floor pads together. "Much better," he said.

"That's more like it," screamed Nova. She gave Arch a kiss on the cheek and sprung back to their seats. The next few cycles were orgasmic. However, the eighth descent made her airsick. Nova went back to the seats and buckled. She prepared to sit out the next cycle.

Arch took her absence as permission. When the gravity subsided, he launched himself to the ceiling. Then he pushed off to the far wall. From there, he gathered himself and shot across to the opposite side. The family seemed to have predicted what was coming, and they floated in place near the back. He pushed from the wall to the ceiling to the floor to another wall, each time with more speed and more abandon.

Trying to get in one more pass as time expired, Arch was twisted in midair when the gravity resumed. His momentum took him hard into the side of the jet, and he dropped like a watermelon to the seam between the wall and the deck. Everyone aboard heard a sickening crack.

22

An hour later, a hooded, face-masked, and face-shielded woman met Nova in front of a white tent. The tent seemed to be plastic-coated fabric, and it bulged gently in the ocean breeze. From a short distance, it looked like it was breathing. The tent blocked the entrance to the Emergency Room of Cedars Sinai hospital. Marina del Rey, with its rows of sailboat masts, was directly behind the tent. From the tent's front flap, it looked like it was filled with people and equipment.

The woman, wearing so much protective gear that she could have come from a clean room or a nuclear site, stopped Nova on her tentative approach to the front opening of the tent. The only thing not white on the woman was a decal with the letters "RN" on her lapel. She greeted Nova in a fashion befitting an unwelcome guest. "What can I do for you, missy?"

Nova was not expecting to have to answer a challenge. It took her a second to regroup. "I, I, I'm here for my friend," she said. "He was brought into the ER in an ambulance maybe a half an hour ago."

"What's his name?" asked the nurse. One of her gloved hands held up a tablet computer. She looked through glasses, mask ends, and face shields to the screen.

Nova tried to look at the screen, but the nurse turned it away. "Arch Crockett," replied Nova. "C-R-O…"

The nurse cut off Nova's spelling. "Yes, I have it," said the well-layered RN. "This is the right hospital. Possible concussion and a compound fracture of the right ulna."

Nova blanched at the words. It was a graphic injury, and first aid could only accomplish so much. To the already airsick Nova, the plane could not land fast enough. "May I see him?" she asked.

"You are not from around here, are you?" asked the RN.

"No. Why?"

"California pandemic protocols don't permit anyone other than the injured or sick patient to enter the hospital." The RN looked her over. "That means no family." The nurse stared at her left hand on which there was no ring. "And certainly no friends, missy." The woman continued to scrutinize Nova. "By the way, pull that mask up further over your nose."

Nova adjusted her mask. "So I cannot come in," she repeated as if for her own understanding. The shock was wearing off slowly. She took a moment to remember how she had functioned well enough to reach the tent.

"Missy, under HIPPA regulations, no one at this hospital is going to be able to communicate much to you about his condition. The law prohibits us from discussing medical information without the patient's permission. In the case of your," she paused, "friend." She checked her device. "He will be going into surgery soon."

Aggression rose inside of Nova. However, something kept her from throwing punches. It may have been the hazmat suits. The attire seemed so foreign as to be inhumane. On second thought, Nova understood that the nurse communicated what she could.

"Once he recovers from the anesthesia, he'll be able to sign a form giving you access to his health information. It will be several hours, three or four before he'll be in recovery. I cannot let you stay here. By the looks of you, you need some rest. Is there somewhere else you can go?"

"I am not sure that I have a place to stay." Nova pulled the paper itinerary from her back pocket. She unfolded it as if she was looking at origami folds. "A room is booked in his name," she said.

Nova showed the paper to the nurse. "Will the hotel let me check in?"

The nurse handed back the document and dismissed Nova's concern. "Hotels are nearly empty. You will not have any trouble getting a room."

Processing the trauma of her day from the sudden exit from home to the violent end of the zero-gravity experience, Nova's last words to the nurse were, "I am something of the victim here."

23

Awake the next morning at seven o'clock, Nova was a product of the time zone difference. She opened the window shade to see the flat rays of the morning sun turn the beach a shade of tangerine. Further out, the waves had a gentle curl. Above the curls, she could see a swimmer in what looked like a wetsuit. The man or woman was beating a steady cadence.

The scene made her think of home. Summers on the western side of Lake Michigan produced scenes like this one. Cold, clear water and a windblown chop. She had to admit that somehow the prospect of sharks and surfboards made this different.

Nova decided to bleed some energy and go for a run. After dressing in a lime tank top and black leggings, Nova pulled a ponytail through the elastic closure on the back of a ball cap. Her suitcase produced socks and running shoes. Equipped, she decided she had not overpacked.

She felt some vindication that Arch's packing turned out to be the problem. He wouldn't be using any of it. She looked at his bag, handle up and zipped. It was resting on the patterned carpet at the foot of the bed. The sight of it burdened her.

She walked past Arch's luggage and headed to the lobby. As it was during her late arrival the previous night, Nova was the only customer in the lobby. She felt a sense of kenophobia. Vast marble floors held an abstract design. Open triangles intersected with closed circles.

The floor looked polished, and it gleamed against natural illumination angling in from skylights. Dark woods provided contrast. In front of the mahogany reception desk stood a round wooden table large enough to seat a wedding party. Atop the table was a bouquet. The bouquet had palm fronds, which among other tropical plants, extended well over her head.

The plants made her feel as if she were somewhere exotic. That feeling was her first on the trip. To this point, Arch had promised wonders, but he had delivered nothing of the kind.

Outside a revolving door, she was surprised by the coolness of the morning. Goosebumps rose on her skin, and she folded her arms to hold heat. She almost turned around for the jacket in her suitcase. However, she resolved that the running would warm her and calm her soon enough.

Alternately raising her knees to chest height, she warmed up along a white metal railing framing the porte cochere. Around a circle drive, she made her way to a sidewalk. The walkway twisted between a fifty-foot drop off and Ocean Avenue. The sidewalk had green grass on each side. The grass was so brilliant of a shade that it looked like it had just sprouted from seed. Being near Hollywood, it crossed her mind that the grass was fake. She bent and brushed her hand through it. It was reedy and damp, the real thing.

Looking up, she saw palm trees lined the path. From where she stood, it looked like palms would provide a corridor. Nova checked her fitness watch and ran. Her mind went faster than her legs. She passed the Santa Monica pier with barely a notice.

Nova had woken to a ringing cell phone. After a few exchanged words, her impression was that Arch was more groggy than she. "My arm is throbbing," he had muttered. The cockiness, the only side of him she had really seen, was gone. Instead, he was pitiful. She was not much for pity.

Shaking off the memory, her eye caught a landmark, Fourth Street. Nova turned and jogged inland from the coastal path. She crossed the empty two-lane road. The opposite curb had a row of patio sets fronting restaurants. She dodged the obstacles. A few blocks later, Nova found the fitness attraction she'd found on her search engine, a set of stairs.

For a set of public concrete steps, the rise had some immediate appeal. Rounded wood handrails jutted from the troweled walls. The outside edges of the walls were planted with jasmine. Sprays from the bushes shaded the path like Chinese folding fans. Nova smelled the jasmine on the wind, and she saw a few star-shaped blooms. The four-wide expanse of the 180 stairs was just expansive enough for passing. She leaped past a few walkers on the way up. She nodded at masked runners on their descent. After one cycle, she had already doubled the number of people she had seen on the trip.

By her third cycle, she had established a routine. That permitted her mind to recapture more segments of the night before. "How did I get here?" he had asked. Nova was not sure whether the anesthesia or the concussion was talking. The emergency landing and the stretcher were more than she wanted to recollect. "They're releasing me in the morning," Arch claimed. Nova was not sure whether to take him seriously; bones did not heal in a day. She had no idea what she would do with him if he were released. A nursemaid she was not.

With her thighs burning and sweat tingling in the cool, Nova headed down to complete her fifth set. Keeping her momentum, she ran hard back to the coastal path. She continued to run away from the hotel. A few minutes later, she reached an intersection of sorts. The Marvin Braude Path started from a Y. One side of its pavement led down the cliff, and it continued over the top of beach sand. She raced downward to the path over the sand. Venice Beach came into sight.

Finished with the stairs and miles down the path, she had pushed her limits of exertion. The only noise in her head became that of her heart pounding. She stopped on the path. She felt she needed her faculties back.

As she stood, partially bent over and panting hard, a man approached on a bicycle. He was dressed in a blue and white cycling jersey. As he passed uncomfortably near, she heard the rumble from his knobby tires. Hands on her hips, she straightened. She came up ready to attack, until she saw his law enforcement insignia.

The policeman turned and slowed. He made another pass at a speed just enough to keep the bike upright with a wobble. He had a Hispanic complexion and a moustache. Black hair rimmed his helmet and mirrored sunglasses hid his eyes. He looked something like a cross between a highway patrolman and a leader of a peloton. "You cannot stop here, miss," he voiced in a deep bass.

"Huh?" she panted. Relaxing her defense, she waited for either a punch line or a pick-up line.

The officer produced neither. "The beach is closed by order of the governor," he said. As if he were reading a legal document, he said, "Public spaces might serve as venues to spread the virus." Not seeing a reaction, he continued, "You are allowed to transit the beach. Transit," he repeated. "Loitering of any kind is not permitted."

"I'm just catching my breath," she protested.

"You'll have to catch it while in motion," he said. "I cannot let you stay here. I had to arrest a swimmer when he came ashore earlier this morning. Move along, please."

Nova started walking, then she resumed her run. The biker followed for a minute, then he turned and sprinted off in the opposite direction. By the time she arrived at the famous Venice Beach outdoor gym, she already knew what she would find.

Muscle Beach was empty. Black glossy exercise mats covered a platform one step up from sand level. A blue-rimmed fence enclosed the entire platform. Someone from the parks department thought enough of their patrons to leave bars, racks, and benches outside, as encouragement for fence hoppers.

However, the usual free weights and dumbbells seemed to be locked away. She would have rather shown her stuff, but the cop was around somewhere. It would have to be enough to be at the place where bodybuilding began. She looked up at the stadium seating, imagining it full of onlookers. She would have given them a show.

It was hard not to feel dismayed by a gym she could not use, a beach she could not experience, and a hotel with no guests. This trip wasn't what she deserved. She noticed restrictive fencing and "Closed" signs everywhere. With each one, she grew more dismayed with Arch.

Nova turned toward the hotel and resumed her run. Just when running started to feel like trying to escape, the phone that had been pressed into an outside pocket of her leggings buzzed. She brought it to her ear, and she slowed to a walk.

Messing up her own tantrum, Arch was fuming. "You're not going to believe this shit," he ranted.

Nova was shocked by the difference a few hours had made. Damaged had turned to infuriated. "What's going on?" she prodded.

"I am going through checkout procedures," he said. "I am dressed and ready to go. The discharge papers are signed. One of the last things they had me do is take a COVID test." He seethed. "I tested positive. COVID positive. Can you believe it?"

"How could you be positive? You were fine yesterday. Not even a cold symptom."

"No idea," he said. "I must have gotten exposed in the hospital." Arch took another big sigh. "Now get this. They asked me where I would be going. So I told them to the hotel and then a flight. As soon as I said that, the nurses freaked. They said that the hospital cannot let me leave. A hotel room is not considered to be a quarantine space. With a positive test, I will be refused travel. The hospital will not discharge me. A nurse tore up the release order. I am not allowed to leave forget this—two weeks. I've been moved into isolation."

She was quick to process the added information. Arch was trapped. She could not help him. She could not even see him. On top of that, she had already discovered that her own movements were restricted. This trip was no great experience. It was more like a hellscape. It was all his fault.

Her reaction was a swift one. "I'm getting out of here," she resolved. "My best chance of getting home is to hop on a plane before they start contract tracing. I am going straight to the airport."

24

A week after the veto and the crash, Dosh was back at his desk for another Grid call. His facial expressions did not keep his feelings hidden. It would be plain to all participants that he was bothered. Try as he might, he could not make personal connections with video images and avatars. Without seeing skin shades change and fingers curl and uncurl, he was missing the data he needed to relate to people.

As he fidgeted, Dosh's mood darkened further. He was wrong to okay standardizing on Grid. Every time he looked at his screen, he felt the presence of Edward Tandy. Tandy the traitor was at least partially responsible for bringing technology from a hostile state actor into his place of work. Dosh groaned aloud when he thought of paying for the privilege of communicating through this matrix of dizzying squares.

The members of his senior team began to join the call. Dosh knew that conducting a meeting in his current state of mind would not go well. He turned off his camera and rose from his desk. Bumping twice into the furniture, the desktop and the corner, somehow made him feel the physical connection that he was missing, a gangly body banging off of hard surfaces.

A minute later, he returned to his chair with a throbbing knee and a bruised thigh. During his circle of the office, he had passed a folded and framed American flag given to him by a veteran's group. The idea that it generated so possessed him, it changed his entire orientation. With the slanted smile of a man about to pull one over on his video guests, he activated his camera.

The idea was perfect, he decided. What he was about to do would be meaningful to him and unassailable by others. It had layers. Oh, did it have layers. It was a tribute to his patriot namesake. It was a protest against both Tandy and his foreign friends. It sent a signal about the FBI encounter for which he was about to be chastised. Dosh started the Grid meeting by using his phone to play a recording of Whitney Houston's version of the "Star-Spangled Banner."

When the song finished with "the home of the brave," Dosh's chest swelled with pride. When he saw that some of his team had risen to attention, and most had hands over hearts, his pulse pounded. The response was the most nationalistic thing he had seen in weeks.

Encouraged, Dosh decided to strike another blow against invasive and impersonal Grid calls. "Before we begin today," he started, "I would like everyone to change their Grid Backgrounds."

He could see his staff leaning forward and tightening their stares onto their home screens. Many stroke keys.

"Before you get too far," he stopped them, "I have a specific idea in mind." He felt his inspiration to be on brand for the firm.

"Please change your Grid Background to be that of your favorite automobile. It can be a car or a light truck. Your choice can be modern or vintage. It would be even better if it could be a vehicle that you own now or once owned. I have one stipulation. The car must be American badged."

Screens began to populate with Corvettes, Shelbys, and Hemis. Dosh posted a 1982 Pontiac Firebird. He had kept it running with a steady diet of parts. At home, auto repairs were his extracurricular activity in high school.

"I never named my cars," continued Dosh, "but I know that naming them has become a popular thing to do. Many of you have told me the names of your vehicles. I have heard some good ones. If the car that you posted has a name, go ahead and upload it in the text thread."

Dosh watched as the text thread populated with names: Rusty, Bandit, Beatrice, Earnest, and Roger.

"Well done," Dosh said. "We have to discuss some bad news about the auto industry today. As we do, never forget that our passion is to keep everything on four wheels rolling." He paused. "The ride-sharing service Hitchhike went bankrupt last night. We have a relationship with Hitchhike. We offer their drivers a 25 percent discount on parts."

He called on his Chief Financial Officer, Ryan Nicholson. Nicholson was Dosh's age and pudgy. He had an unusually dark tan, and he wore a red-accented Hawaiian shirt. Mandatory retirement was deliciously close for the man who had been Dosh's go-to man for two decades. "Ryan, what are our financial exposures?"

Nicholson replied. "Thankfully, not big. We only do a couple of million dollars in business to all of the Hitchhike drivers combined. Our relationships are with the drivers, not corporate. At this point, bad debts look quite manageable. We have reserves for situations like this one."

"Excellent," Dosh said. "Let's focus on the revenue side of things. I assume that we have information on the Hitchhike drivers in our Customer Relationship Management system?" Dosh asked.

"Should we do something to try to retain business from the good ones?"

A different red shirt unmuted herself. Chief Marketing Officer Katrina Marx was a middle-aged woman with black hair and beauty marks. She wore bright red lipstick, which matched both her blouse and the red accents on the crown comb in her hair. "We have the customer records. Perhaps we can retain them if they move to another ride-sharing service or if they maintain cars for their personal use. We could send a coupon. How about spend fifty dollars and get twenty dollars off of your next visit?"

"That will work." Dosh said with finality.

Nicolson spoke up. "Should we talk about car rental companies next? One of the big ones went out of business this morning. Fewer travelers seem to translate into lesser demand for rental cars. When I was traveling last week, I had a whole parking lot full of cars from which to choose."

"I saw that news too," said Dosh. "My first reaction was relief. They weren't our client. Given our other relationships, we may not be pain-free. However, your finance team made a good decision to avoid the weakest of the competitors."

"Part of their fleet will be liquidated," Nicholson replied. "That's my concern. A high volume of cars going to junkyards creates new competition for us from pull-a-part lots. It could also drive parts prices down."

Everyone on the call heard Dosh's cell phone ring. The boss muted himself from the Grid conversation and put the phone to his ear. The executive team could see the silenced chat become animated. They all watched the CEO touch the screen of his cell phone and place the phone on his desk.

Dosh slid both elbows up to his desk and both forefingers went to his temples. He rubbed his temples in circles and squinted his eyes shut. An instant later, as if he realized he was being watched, his hands shot downward to his sides. He raised one hand back to his mouse and selected the unmute button.

"As if ride-sharing and car rental bankruptcies were not bad enough," he began, "I am sorry to have to deliver this news." Dosh was having a tough time grasping it himself. He had realized something in that instant. The economic problems were profound. "However, I have just been informed that one of the big US auto manufacturers has filed for Chapter 11 bankruptcy. This day is one of the darkest in Michigan history. One of the great companies in the United States is in the possession of its debtors."

"Each of the big US producers represents about 20 percent of our parts business," interjected Nicholson clinically. "Our inventory levels are okay, but they will not last forever if the automaker's plants shut down."

A few seconds later, Dosh recaptured himself. "My information is that some of the plants will be idle for a month." He straightened in his chair and leaned into the camera. "Here's what I want," Dosh continued. He had seldom felt so certain. Helping distressed American companies, preserving American brands, and supporting customer choices of American products was civics. "Ryan, contact the bankrupt car rental firm. Offer to buy every US badged fleet vehicle that they are willing to sell us. Fill our parking lots. We will do our own pick-and-pull and have a reservoir of cheap parts. We will keep America on the road. Get busy!"

Dosh understood that he had to stop being the resistance and start leading to recovery. First, he had to negotiate the right to turn several strip malls into something resembling used car lots.

25

A few days later, Dosh was looking forward to a Nextdoor Auto Parts Board meeting. He wanted to see one of the board members in particular. The man was one of the few people in Dosh's life with whom he could talk both business theory and football rosters with equal vigor. Dosh called him "the professor."

The professor of Supply Chain Management at the Tayler School of Business gave the board some intellectual firepower. Just as important, the professor was a lifelong Indianapolis season ticket holder. He also had a notorious lead foot. The professor could make the drive from campus to the stadium in three and a half hours on game day.

The twelve-mile trip from campus to headquarters would certainly have taken him less than ten minutes. Perhaps due to driving speed, the professor was usually the first to arrive for board meetings. Dosh counted on it.

Dosh was a leader, and he relished being in charge. However, being in that position generated many leader-to-subordinate communications and little else. Conversations with people who treated him as an equal were rare. He had not had such a conversation since the 21 Club. Most of the time, he liked the deference and the power. After weeks of being only the boss, he needed perspective, and he needed a friend.

Dosh waited in the lobby for the bespectacled man with a helmet of brown hair to walk through the door. The professor was early as usual. The frames of the academic's glasses were something of a statement, perhaps compensating for some of his other plain features. The wide plastic rims were often a demonstrative color. Today's choice was teal.

The professor spoke as soon as he entered the room. "Please tell me that you have something positive to say at this meeting. I need to hear some good news for a change."

"Teal," Dosh observed. "Miami." Dosh did have some news. Was it good?, he asked himself. It was hard to find good news anywhere. This news might be good for him. It might be a career lifeline for Dosh. "I have an idea that I think you'll like," Dosh assured.

"I just came from a faculty meeting. It was an absolute funeral. We academics have had it so well for so long that no one knows how to deal with adversity. You probably saw that the state cut our funding."

"I saw that. They took eight percent out of your budget."

"Small and community colleges fared worse than most. We're cutting sports programs. Track and Field is gone. Wrestling is gone. Lacrosse was cancelled. A few others."

Dosh shrugged. "If those are the only things, it is not that bad. That cannot impact more than a hundred students. Did they save the football program?"

"Of course. We live in Michigan."

"Something else must have happened. Why was the meeting so morose?"

"We were counting on relief from the BOOST Act."

"Sorry. I may have had something to do with that veto," Dosh said.

"Aw, you are killing me, Dosh, why?" the professor led Dosh into the boardroom. "This hurt us on so many levels. First, we lost stipends and research funds. Then we lost salary for faculty. Most of our professors do not want to teach in person. No educator wants to risk their life for some kid who is on campus to explore his or her alcohol tolerance."

"What about the students?"

"The kids won't be getting the student loan relief in the bill. These students were already leveraged to the hilt, and now the bulk of classes are virtual. Worse yet, all on-campus activities have been eliminated, including communal meals."

"All of the cost of college, but none of the experience," Dosh observed.

"The students must have had the same realization," the professor affirmed. "Earlier today, the administration informed us that enrollment for the fall semester is down by more than a third. Housing is closing two dorms. Most of the adjunct professors have not been retained, and some of the tenure-track faculty were released. If all of that was not enough, the university has started discussions about cutting more than a dozen degree programs."

"Not business, I hope," Dosh relied on Upper Peninsula State University as a feeder program.

The professor shook his head. "My department is safe. Business programs are safe. I might need you to guest lecture a few times."

Dosh did not mind. He could identify the best kids for his future staff that way.

"What are we going to talk about at this meeting today? Something uplifting, you said."

"I thought I would start with how many games Indianapolis is going to win with Wendall Case at quarterback."

"That implies we're going to have a football season. I guess that qualifies as uplifting these days. I'm hearing if they play at all, it may not be in front of fans."

Dosh got serious. "We are talking about the future of the company. I have a big idea. If we proceed, the project will delay the timetable for my exit. I could spend more time on the business and less time on figuring out my next career."

"Are you putting whatever football league you're trying to break into on the back burner?"

"That depends on your support."

26

A half hour later, Chief Executive Officer Dosh stood at the front of the Nextdoor Auto Parts board room. He was the sole occupant of the short end of a wooden trapezoidal table. The room smelled of furniture polish, as if it had been detailed a few hours previously. He sensed that if his career was going to continue past the mandatory retirement date, this was his last stand.

Dressed in a gray suit and red tie, and turned in a chair, Dosh looked like a barber pole. He was clearly uncomfortable outside of his uniform, and he pulled at his collar. He looked at the seven faces in the room. Not all of them were friendly.

A gold-framed portrait of Dosh hung on the wall under platinum lettering, which read "Nextdoor Auto Parts Chairpersons."

The uncentered painting left little doubt that a second portrait was expected soon. The pandemic created some conditions that might prevent the board from acting on their plan. He might be able to stop them. He might.

Dosh stood to start the proceedings. "Good afternoon, esteemed board members. The meeting will now come to order," he began. "The first order of business is to approve the minutes of the last board meeting. Do I have a motion to approve?"

A motion was offered and seconded. The board members voted, "Aye," in unison.

"On to the second item of business," Dosh continued. "Management has prepared a presentation on a disruptive force in our business." Dosh's executive assistant turned on a slide projector. Slides appeared on a pull-down screen behind him.

"Prior to the pandemic, electric vehicles (EVs) captured about three percent of the auto market. You can see the trajectory." The graphic showed a steeply rising line.

"Next slide," he signaled. "The electrification trend, which was started by Tesla, has been joined by the traditional auto makers: BMW, GM... each nameplate is expected to have an EV offering by 2025. Next slide. Wall Street analysts project EVs to capture over 20 percent of the new auto market by 2030. As EVs age and need parts, our business will face a period of change the likes of which few of us have seen before."

If he was forefront in leading the firm through an emerging and existential threat, he could not possibly be forced to retire. He needed to convince them that he was proactive in identifying the challenge, well educated on the subject, and timely in his solution.

"Are you saying that EVs have become a threat to our business?" asked a woman seated to Dosh's right. Nancy Brill was the mom of one of the mom-and-pop competitors Dosh had earlier acquired. The fifty-year-old wore a topaz-colored sheath dress, and she looked as if she had just left a blow-dry salon. Brill was as smart as people came. At times Dosh considered her an ally, and at times, he viewed her as a succession threat.

"Please be patient," Dosh answered. "We have materials to address your questions. Next slide. As the EV transition proceeds, we expect the market for oil changes, spark plugs, and engine additives to get smaller." He presented another chart, showing lines descending toward the x-axis. "Those categories represent about 15 percent of our sales. Next slide. Batteries are another 15 percent of our sales. These batteries are the type used to provide starting power. This power source is not expected to have an application on EV platforms."

"Well, that's pretty glum," said the woman. "Our old school CEO is driving this business right off the edge of a cliff," she said to the room. "Move away from the peripheral business lines, talk to us about parts."

"Skip ahead two slides," he instructed his aide. "Behind me, you will see a parts list for the drivetrain of a typical electric vehicle. The diagram shows the engine, transmission, and drive shaft. Each label is a part, and the part count is nearly 200. Next slide. Here, you will see the part count of the power plant of a typical internal combustion engine driven vehicle. While you cannot see the details on this slide, I hope that you get a sense of magnitude. Light vehicles of the type that we now service have about 2,000 drivetrain parts."

He liked how he sounded. The situation sounded ominous. He had learned long ago never to present challenges without having a solution in your back pocket. His back pocket was full.

"Dosh," said the professor. "To the credit of you and your management team, you're identifying a technological change in the marketplace. The change will no doubt affect our business prospects. Per your numbers, we need to adapt now, or the business will flounder. It might not recover from this pandemic period."

"I would challenge your timetable," Brill interjected. "This EV threat is no cause for alarm. Even if Dosh's numbers are correct, which I doubt, it will take ten years for EVs to have material market share. It could take five years after that before the aftermarket auto parts business is pressured. This supposed EV threat is a lifetime away."

"The pandemic has moved several trends forward," rebutted the professor. "You have seen that phenomenon in several businesses, like home delivery and streaming. Look, I don't think anyone knows how this will play out. Did anyone else see the GDP report this morning? The economy shrank 16 percent in the second quarter. With the economy falling apart right now, who know what transitions are possible?"

The professor had his back. Dosh pressed forward. "Our projections show margin pressure in the next few years, and revenue declines out a decade." He put up a supporting slide. "Regarding the present situation, yes, the economy is weak. We are doing better than most. The business has low leverage. Cash flow is only slightly negative. Our staff is being creative in finding revenue, and they are doing a good job controlling costs."

"I sit on three boards," voiced the Chairman of the Audit Committee. The retired big three accounting firm partner had thick glasses and hearing aids. He looked like he had been confined to a recording studio for the last four decades. "Your team is to be congratulated. This presentation is excellent."

"I will pass that along," said Dosh. "Thank you." He turned from the board member back to the screen. Dosh waited about five seconds for further discussion. "Today, I would like to present a plan on how the company can thrive in the long term. Next slide. You may have noticed that many EV component companies raised money in the public markets last year. Behind me, you can see a partial list."

"Unfortunately for them," he continued, "several of these stocks started trading in the weeks before the pandemic outbreak." Dosh signaled his aid to flip slowly through the next five slides. "You will see that in most every case, the stock prices of the EV component companies have declined. Many are down by half or more. The substantial decline in their valuations may present an opportunity for us."

Dosh started directly at the professor indicating, he hoped, that he was about to deliver the proposal that would extend his work life. "Fellow board members, I propose to you that Nextdoor Auto Parts could enter the EV parts market. Management suggests buying one of these newly public EV parts businesses. We believe that we have the resources to take advantage of the distressed securities prices."

Nearly before Dosh finished his sentence, Nancy Brill spoke up. "Dosh, we've heard your proposal." She paused until the room fell silent. "Frankly, I would challenge your whole premise. Do you really think that EV is an imminent threat? From what I've read, the vehicles have limited range, less than 300 miles. They are heavy as hell. The weight makes every accident a bad one, so they are expensive to insure. These cars use the same amount of energy as gasoline vehicles. The only difference is that the pollution stays at the power plant. Eventually, even the greenies are going to figure that out. Why would Nextdoor Auto Parts want to divert from a being profitable enterprise to support a limited use product with a climate promise that it cannot fulfill?"

"That sounds like a political statement," said the professor.

Dosh detested the cancel culture. He knew too many people who had been deprived of careers and relationships due to the expression of ideas that the prevailing culture deemed offensive. Although Dosh knew some of Brill's statements to be true, he also realized that some of it would offend. If Dosh did not say something to soften her points, some of the board members would cancel her. Like it or not, it was exactly what he needed.

"Let the man speak," said the Audit Committee Chair.

"Next slide," Dosh voiced. "My executive team believes that the company could spend up to $200 million without restricting our operating flexibility. Behind me, you will see a list of three candidates in which we believe Nextdoor Auto Parts could acquire a meaningful stake."

"The facts presented here suggest that doing nothing is a risk to long-term shareholder value," said the professor. "Along with the opportunity presented by the current markets, I would support development of this idea. Dosh, how do we start?"

"We will need a motion authorizing funds."

27

osh awoke at four o'clock in the morning. He had been resting on his injured arm, and it tingled from shoulder to wrist. Most days this hour would have been slightly early for healthy, wealthy, and wise. Now his heart was pounding, and a cold sweat formed on his brow.

It was a recurring dream. Rather it was a recurring memory. The numbness in his arm may have set his mind racing. More likely, it was possible loss of his role at the company. He had sacrificed everything for the business. Including the full use of his arm. If he lost the business, it would be like losing an appendage.

The accident was a vivid imprint on his brain. He accepted that it might always be. The mere thought of crushed bones gave him a bout of dizziness. Sitting up in bed, he had the urge to empty his stomach, one way or another. He tried to stop his reaction, but he was only so effective in controlling his emotions.

Over the last few minutes, the scene had played in Dosh's head: The distribution center for Nextdoor Auto Parts was getting behind schedule. The company had expanded into ten additional strip malls. An additional set of truck trailers set to serve those stores backed to the cross-dock. With a wider set of codes, the computers were slow to generate picklists.

Dosh had trained himself to drive a forklift. At that time, he considered it a necessity to know each aspect of his business. However, when the need arose, he had not operated one for several months. The usual drivers, the kind who saw themselves as driving for Team Penske if not for the multiple failed drug tests, were happy to see the boss doing what they called an honest day's work.

With the business growing faster than the infrastructure, the facility was an adapted one. The new bays were in a previously abandoned section of the old building. The concrete warehouse floor did not align perfectly with the truck beds. To make it work, the company used metal ramps to account for the slight difference. Despite the added complication of the ramps, the loading was proceeding. Forklifts were running up and down the loading dock.

Clear plastic wrapped pallets of parts were loaded on each truck. Often they were stacked one atop another.

After completing a pallet stack, Dosh backed his forklift out of a truck trailer. Clearing the door with forks descending, he began a turn. His thought was to get the forklift moving in the forward direction as soon as possible. However, in his haste, he drove the back wheel off the side of the ramp. The distance was just enough to tilt the forklift back toward the edge of the truck. Dosh lost his balance, and the machine tumbled behind him. He ended up on the floor with his arm pinned between the fallen forklift and the solid edge of the truck trailer. Extraction required firemen to spread the machines using the Jaws of Life.

Dosh was in the hospital for a month. Doctors were rebuilding bones and blood vessels. Dosh spent his days planning surgeries and therapies around his work schedule. He grew Nextdoor Auto Parts overcoming IVs, pins, and traction bands.

The time in the hospital was additional time away from his failing family. His long incapacity may have given his wife her lifestyle back, but his inattention at home made her more resentful. As his days extended and his arm was saved, she visited less and less. Partially at his request and fully supported by her, the young child was kept from seeing him bedridden.

Dosh came to decide that he did not mind being alone. He felt more self-reliant during the recovery. He was doing the work, real work, and rehab. He rethought his priorities. His priority was the company.

Regaining control over the present, he squeezed his unhealed arm. It reminded him of the pain, the memory of which he still could not face. He rose from the sheets, went into the bathroom, and threw up.

After cleaning himself up, he started his day. The memory of the hospital stay gave him a new motivation. The hospital was a non-profit. The BOOST Act had the potential to be a government takeover of the nonprofit sector. The sector was to be flooded with money. He had stopped it. He had a part in preserving the charity-based system. It reminded him to send them a donation check. Community service was part of his business plan, and it was one that he had recently neglected.

28

Arch sniffled. "I feel like a have a cold." He sat nearly upright in the same hospital bed in which he had resided for the last seven days. The laptop that Nova had sent overnight rested atop the rolling table. The table, normally used for meals, extended both above and below his bed in a sideways horseshoe shape. White wires ran from Arch's computer to earbuds in his ears. The wires crossed his injured arm, which was splinted and resting atop a pillow. He looked into the Grid app on his screen. "I had a day, literally one day, with no energy and a little bit of pressure in my chest."

"Sounds pretty mild," Nova said. "You'll bounce back."

"Damn right. For me, this virus is more of a nuisance than anything. I'm getting tired of being isolated. The only people that I see are nurses. These ladies are buried underneath protective gear. Even with the plastic suits, I only see humans once or twice a day."

"Are you alone? Do you have a private room? I heard the hospitals were crowded."

"I'm in a quarantine stall. It's only big enough for the bed and the nurses to stand around it. Otherwise, I'm surrounded by plastic sheeting on three sides. The plastic is thick and cloudy. I cannot see out. While I cannot see much, I hear activity around me. I think I am in a row of four or five people, all in the same COVID situation."

"Have they given you any update on when you get to leave?"

"I tested positive again this morning," replied Arch. "The positive result means it will be at least two more days until I'm released." Arch raised his splint so that the camera showed the black Velcro. He hoped visuals might help. "If I stay here all week, the nurses might take out the stitches before I leave. I guess getting them out would be one less thing to have to deal with when I get home."

"How many stitches?" The question seemed perfunctory.

Arch realized that Nova was losing interest. "I'm not sure." He tried a more stimulating subject. "I was pretty drugged up when they told me." He smiled at the camera. "That's one good thing about this place," he said. "The drugs keep coming." Arch paused as he contemplated the ache in his arm. He panned the camera to a chart behind him on the wall. It showed emojis intended to represent pain levels. "Whenever I'm asked," he reported, "I point to one of the frowny ones."

While he made light of the pain, it was much worse than he let on. According to the resident orthopedist, the arm had nerve damage that might never heal. That news wasn't information he intended to share.

He knew he would not get far with the drug allusions. Nova had told him many times that she would never take part. He needed a new topic, and he needed one fast. Keeping her on the phone was a necessity. Buzzed Arch almost said, "I miss you." He had enough presence of mind to stop himself. That would never work.

What would work was to get her talking about her restaurant takeover scheme. Even operating below his usual mental capacity, he knew that would keep Nova on the video call. "How is it going with Maurice and the numbers? Have you been able to show him why over 60 percent of restaurants fail?"

He could see her energy rise. She tossed her hair. "He seems to understand a few of the ratios you taught me. However, getting him to apply those numbers to the business is another story. He doesn't seem to want to be metrics based. He still thinks that everything depends on the food."

"So much for the numbers," he said.

She paused for a few seconds and looked up and off screen but seemingly not at anything in particular. She resumed speaking, "Maurice has been on my case all week about personal stuff."

"Personal stuff?" Arch had known her long enough to know that she seldom talked to her father about personal stuff. After what had happened in college, he was surprised they talked at all. He was relatively certain that Maurice didn't even know his name. "Personal stuff, like what?"

"With you away, he wants to have his say on our relationship."

"He doesn't even know me," Arch protested.

"He knows that I'm getting outside help on this finance stuff. After our previous weekend trips, I told him enough about you he's been able to figure out that the numbers are coming from you."

"And that bothers him?" Arch asked.

"Not exactly. No. It's personal stuff," she replied. "Some of it relates to you and some doesn't."

"Like what?"

"I'm not sure that you are in a mental state for this," she rebuffed, "but okay. He thinks that I hate my body. That's why I do all of the training... to fix it. He thinks that's a normal response to rape." Arch could hear her emotions rise. "He is so off base. Hate could not be further from the truth," she affirmed.

"You love the training," Arch confirmed.

"My dad doesn't want me to devalue myself physically, just because of the rape. Girls do that, you know. You lose the thing of most value, so you think everything else is worthless."

"This conversation is a lot more intense than I thought we would have."

"I warned you," she said. "Do you want the rest?"

Arch wanted companionship. Besides, he did not think he could say "no." "Keep going."

"He thinks I need personal space at home. He thinks that I need to think for myself. He doesn't like me bringing your ideas into work."

"Wow."

"Yep. Here's the big one… He says that unless the heart is involved, what we are doing is transactional. Consulting with benefits." She struggled to choose her next words. "It may be an even exchange, but we're using each other." Nova tried to lessen the weight of the words. "What a thing to say. Maurice is full of it sometimes."

This was his chance, thought Arch. As much as he wanted to, he never had an opening to connect with Nova's heart. He had tried to express his feelings. He remained unsure of hers. He took his shot. "Is the heart involved?"

"You're on drugs," she snapped. If someone had asked her at a high school slumber party whether or not she liked boys, she might have said the same. For a moment, it looked like the screen would not contain the tilts of her head. "Don't worry about Maurice. None of his advice has teeth."

Arch waited for more, but that dismissal was the end.

Nova continued, "Back to the business. As much as it pains me to say this, I must hand it to Maurice. His new dessert is selling. Almost every dinner order specifies it. Our average check keeps going up and up."

Arch could only follow along. "I know that you don't take his advice, but did you take mine? Did you pay off the loan?"

"As of yesterday, the restaurant is debt free," Nova said proudly. "After retiring the loan, I had some cash left over. With that money, I decided to prepay some of our expenses."

"Smart," Arch encouraged.

"Can we talk about something else?" she asked.

Anything, he thought. Just keep talking. "Yes."

"I got a job offer today," she reported.

"A job offer? Are you giving up on the great restaurant takeover?"

"More than anything, I want Full Board to be successful. It's my family heritage," she said. "The job offer is your doing."

Her statement sounded accusatory. "Do you remember that boxing video that you posted?"

"Jab, jab, cross, cross," he confirmed. "Thousands of hits on TikTok. Every teenage girl is getting psychotic over their relative lack of perfect arm muscles."

"Somebody from Sprocket must have seen it. You know that hot new indoor cycling brand. They contacted me. Apparently, the company needs trainers, and they would think about expanding fitness options."

Arch got enthused. "That sounds perfect for you. I could totally see you as a fitness influencer. That fits your lifestyle and personality so much better than the restaurant. Did you take it? You should take it. I cannot believe that my video did that."

Something he said must have drawn offense. Nova glowered at the screen. Through gritted teeth, she retorted, "I do not spin."

"I think you should reconsider," he continued. "Think about it. You would get paid for workouts. Did they say how much?"

"A salary and free equipment," she snapped. "My priorities are elsewhere."

"Okay," he said. "I don't really understand that, but okay. Let's talk about it some more when I get home."

"At least two more days?"

He thought that she said it like she relished the time. "It might be longer," he softened. There was a lot of baggage to unpack, and he was not sure he was up for it just yet. Suddenly, he noticed the throbbing in his arm. "Another airline went bankrupt overnight. I might have a tough time finding a flight."

29

A week later, Nova was disinfecting her home gym when she heard the front door open. It squealed on its hinges. Slightly startled by the sound, she raised her defenses.

Arch opened it tentatively, turning the knob with his undamaged arm. When the door had opened wide enough for him to pass, he retreated to the porch. Relying on his good side, he raised his overnight bag from the concrete landing. Arch hoisted it up three-quarters of a foot to clear the threshold. He heaved his bag into the house.

Slow to the entryway, Nova missed dodging the bag. Efforting around the obstacle, she reached the front door in time to see Arch's body relax. His shoulders fell and his lungs expelled what must have been remnant whisps of air from bad hotels and failing airlines.

Smells of mildew and cheap coffee kept her from getting closer. She understood it to be residue from the quarantine halfway house in which he had spent two days waiting for a flight. Still, it knocked her back on her barefoot heels.

"Long few days," he said. "I've had shorter trips overseas." Arch had been on an airplane since dawn. The first jet sat on the runway for an hour before connecting in Phoenix. From Phoenix, he had a plane change in Chicago. Finally, he made the commuter jet jump to Benton Harbor. He looked like he was feeling the full effects of three hard landings.

Arch had called along the route, so often it had become a nuisance. He had been double masked. No one would give him a drink. The stewardesses still working were the ones with seniority. Normally intolerant of passengers, the crews treated him as if his presence constituted attempted murder.

Nova's eyes went immediately to the sling. Seeing it in person struck her much differently than seeing it via video. A black strap that looked like it should have been on a duffle bag looped around his lower arm and up over his neck. The strap had a thin foam cushion at its height. Behind the strap she could see his splint. The black wrapping with Velcro ties covered him from the fingers to halfway up his bicep. Her eyes returned to the fingers. They appeared wrinkled, like hers looked when she arose from a long soak in a therapy tub. They also had a color that she considered to be an unnatural shade of grey.

Nova realized in that moment that Arch had been overselling his recovery. She'd seen injuries at the gym and on some of their adventure trips, but nothing as bad as this appeared. The man was defenseless.

Nova continued to examine the arm and the medical apparatus. "Can I touch it?" Without waiting for an answer, she did. She felt the fasteners and the lashings. Her hands moved all of the way up his arm until she hit the skin. She kept going until she reached his shoulder. At the apex, she gave the shoulder a squeeze. The squeeze was not comforting or affectionate. Instead it was a test of his mettle. He was soft and unsteady.

Arch must have understood that he was being appraised. "Do you want me to remove the splint?" he asked. The absence of an answer was not a "no." "The doctors say I am not supposed to do that, but I will." He started to pull on the Velcro. "Do you want to see the place where they inserted the rods? I can feel that my arm has a bump in it." She probed a finger under the edge of the loosened upper fold of the splint. "At least the stitches are out. One of the nurses removed the stitches before I left."

"No," she stopped. She removed her hand and wiped her finger on her shorts as if she had touched something foul. "No, no, no. I don't want to see any more. I don't want to hear any more."

"It feels as bad as it looks," he said.

Nova realized that Arch was probably smart to withhold information from her. If she was going to have a relationship with a man, she had a need for him to be capable of coming to her defense and bludgeoning anyone who caused her offense. Had she known that he had lost that capability, she would have spent the last two and a half weeks withdrawing.

"How long does this thing take to heal?" She poked his arm again. She noticed him recoil. "It has already been more than two weeks, you big baby."

Arch winced as he tightened the straps. After a few long seconds, he spoke. "Six to eight weeks in total."

"When it heals, you'll be good as new?" she asked hopefully, trying to decide if she could tolerate another month of this condition.

"We'll see," he responded. "That's what they say."

It was not the answer that she wanted, and disappointment showed on her face. Nova did not know what to do next. If he wanted pity, he was not going to get it. If he thought she would be happy to have an invalid in her house for a month, he had misread her.

While he was at the door, she thought about sending him right back out. In a moment before dispatching him, she composed a mental ledger: He treated her well. He knew about money. He was generous with his knowledge. He acted as her advocate. He inspired her to take risks. He said he loved her. Was that enough for her to endure his convalescence?

"How about a welcome home?" Arch raised his good arm, throwing it forward near Nova's shoulder height. He appeared to be soliciting a hug.

Nova moved toward his healthy shoulder. The hug that she delivered was more like an embrace given to a favorite cousin. Arch tried to kiss her cheek. However, she was not offering. He ended up kissing her ear, making the sound of an awkward *thwack*.

"I need some rest," Arch declared. He separated from Nova and retrieved his carry-on. Seeming to expend heroic effort with groans and gasps, he transported it back into the bedroom. Nova watched, trying to determine if his supposed pain and exhaustion was a sympathy play or it was for real. She decided that it did not matter. Her disinterest would be the same.

Back in the bedroom, Nova had arranged Arch's suitcases. The luggage was open, and unzipped tops were leaning up against the wall. The clothes inside were sorted and folded. She had added a pillow to the bed to support his arm, and she poured a cup of water for the nightstand. She thought of it as hospitality in her family tradition.

"Thank you," he told her. He unzipped the travel bag and removed a clear plastic bag full of toiletries. He selected some clothes from the laundry that she had prepared. As she watched him struggle with his splint, he headed for the bathroom. "I really need a shower," he said.

Nova sat on the edge of the bed. She waited and processed. She was stunned at how feeble and awkward he looked. She wasn't prepared for this degree of infirmity. She didn't like how it looked on him. She started thinking of ideas on how she could fix him. The man she had left in L.A. was not tired, tentative, and soupy.

Given the length of the wait, he must have used most of her hot water. When Arch finally opened the door, curls of steam escaped the bathroom. To Nova, it looked like he had been announced as a starter for a sporting event. That was a look she liked—trained, toned, and ready to play.

In the light of the bedroom, however, that vision looked different. Arch's hair was wet and stringy. His chin had two days' worth of growth. He resembled a member of the hacky sack crowd more than the varsity. The man wore a loose T-shirt over boxer shorts. He could have passed for a person twice his age. A huge splint covered his entire chest.

After attempting another hug, which Nova rebuffed, Arch walked to the nightstand. "The hospital prescribed Vicodin, and I saved a few for the trip home." He showed her pills carried in his bad hand. Arch picked up the water glass and downed the pills. "My arm hurts, and it has been a long day," he said. He climbed into bed.

"That's it?" she asked.

"Oh, there's one more thing that I didn't tell you. My company has called me back to the office. I'm supposed to return to New York in a week. We can talk about it tomorrow."

Her first reaction was a strong one. So strong that she chastised herself for being emotional. She was wounded. Seemingly oblivious to Nova's tumult, Arch fell fast asleep.

Nova sat motionless on the side of the bed. She pondered in the dark what she deserved and what he provided. After a long while, she made a decision. He was worth saving. She would make an attempt.

The man in her bed was a wreck. If Arch was going to have a role in her life, he needed his manliness back. To be the anti-Maurice she needed him to be, Arch needed strength and virility.

Given his state, she decided that the reclamation would take her most terrifying weapon. It would either shock him back into being the man she needed, or it would crush him once and for all. She gave him an hour for recovery. She stripped, and then dressed in a satin robe, which she left open and untied at the waist. She put on training gloves, black leather with open fingers and padded knuckles. Nova woke Arch with a stinging strike to the thigh. As he startled, she followed with a blast to the midsection.

30

Maurice trained his eyes on the television. On the Tuesday after the Memorial Day holiday weekend, he was expecting a long episode of his favorite show, the Pandemic Working Group. In his mind, a treatment or cure could have been discovered over the long weekend. Without that miracle, he knew that his relationship with his daughter would be further tested.

President Johnson grasped both sides of a cherrywood podium at the front of the White House briefing room. The furnishing piece angled from the floor like an upside-down triangle. At the apex, the leader's hands framed the presidential seal. The man leaned on his elbows, which were touching the bottom ledge. The posture gave his shoulders a slight hunch. Behind the president's head was an oval image of the executive mansion, white with a light blue background. As he spoke, the president leaned from side to side like he was piloting a motor scooter at low speed. Members of the Pandemic Working Group stood behind the president.

"I am here to recognize the efforts of the Pandemic Working Group," he said. He rose and performed a brief clapping motion. "We commend the twenty professionals that served on the taskforce. Planners from military and logistics were joined by experts from the medical and infectious disease fields. They led efforts to produce and distribute personal protective equipment and ventilators. These heroes directed the research so that we all learned about the mortality rate of the virus and its R0. I think we all added a new word to our vocabularies in the last few weeks, 'rho.' Rho is the rate that a virus passes from person-to-person," he explained. "We have the Working Group to thank for that."

The president's face took a reddish cast as if he had held his breath a bit too long. "The focus of this administration is shifting. Pandemic response is no longer the priority. Going forward, we will be focused on recovery."

The briefing room erupted with questions. "Mr. President? Mr. President?"

Kenworth Johnson continued speaking over the inquiries. "Our new task is reopening the economy. Safely. We care about safety," he insisted. "We will safely return people to their jobs and their lives." He paused and straightened. "Effective today, the Pandemic Working Group will be disbanded. Today will be the final briefing."

Maurice could not remember a childhood Christmas morning that felt as good as it felt to hear the news. "It's over," Maurice gasped. His mind rushed. He could lessen the burden on Nova at work. Better yet, her houseguest would be leaving. "The pandemic is over," he proclaimed.

From across the room, Nova seemed to be sizing up her opponent. Although he was no match for her physically, he had acquired some muscle tone. All of the time on his feet had made improvements to his baker's physique. She seemed to appraise other signs of resilience. His face had the healthy ruddiness of an outdoorsman. It was tanned around facemask lines.

Maurice had noticed her watching him. From the time of her first volleys, he had become more formidable. Now events were going his way. Confidence allowed him self-deprecation. He turned from the television. Hardly suppressing his joy, he spoke. "What am I going to do, Nova? My favorite show is ending." He laughed out loud as if he thought that it was one of the funniest things he had ever said.

"Quiet," she said in a stunning role reversal. "I want to hear this."

The president continued. "For the final time, I would like to introduce Dr. Felicia Kellum, the nation's top immunologist. Dr. Kellum helped lead the country through the early dark days of the pandemic. She will be retiring from government service after today's press conference. I accepted her resignation earlier today." The president turned to the doctor. "Felicia, if my sources are good, I hear that you have already been hired by the World Health Organization. We wish you good luck in your new career."

As Dr. Kellum stepped forward, the members of the press rose, masked from their socially distant seats. The standing ovation lasted more than a minute. The doctor smiled a satisfied smile as she absorbed the adulation. She waited for the last echo of the last clap. "Thank you, Mr. President. The nation has endured over 70,000 deaths due to infection from COVID-19. That number of people is greater than the number of U.S. servicemen killed in action in the Vietnam War. The country continues to average about 3,000 deaths per day. We may have made it through the worst of the pandemic, but it is far from over. Reports from Johns Hopkins University indicate that the health system is managing 1,000,000 active cases. We have no means of prevention. You can continue to protect our vulnerable citizens, and I hope you do so, by masking, testing, and social distancing."

Maurice talked over the television. "When should we reopen the dining room?"

"C'mon Maurice. It's not that easy," replied Nova. "For one thing, Michigan hasn't ended its lock-down."

He expected resistance from her. She had acquired power over him that she would exercise. That was natural, and she had been waiting a long time for a cudgel. "The pandemic is over. The president just said so."

The president had returned to the podium. "Currently, twenty states meet the reopening criteria. So Vermont, Idaho, Washington, New York, New Jersey, Massachusetts, Nevada, Rhode Island, Colorado, Kansas, Missouri, Pennsylvania, and Georgia, it's time to get moving. Get businesses open and put people back to work."

"See," Nova said, "no Michigan. My guess is that we'll be one of the last states to open back up. We don't want to open and invite a visit from the police."

"We should resume table service," he responded. "I could create some new food shapes. Better yet, we could have a contest for the best new design. It would be less stress on you… like it was before the pandemic."

"You really do not get it," she scoffed. "Flow from the kitchen would be tricky. It's much more profitable to be a ghost kitchen and send food out the front door. We'd have to manage table service, carry out, and delivery all at the same time. We've never done that before."

"A few months ago, we ran a restaurant where people came to interact with both the food and each other. Full Board was a place where people made friendships and had experiences."

Nova rose from her seat and circled Maurice like an animal going in for a kill. "That model was not working. We were not turning tables." She silenced him. She had won a round.

Maurice realized how much was irretrievably lost.

31

That same day, Arch was alone in his makeshift office occupying Nova's dinette. "I am a god dammed master of the universe!" Arch screamed at his computer monitor. He saw his face reflecting from the screen. His brows were raised as if he was looking for assurance. The reflection lacked commitment. He tried again. "The market will bend to my will!" That sounded even more disingenuous. He looked sheepishly around the dinette as if he needed to explain his behavior to someone within earshot.

Nova would probably have reacted favorably to the shouting. She seemed relieved when he angered at her bedroom stunt. She wanted a fight. When she got it, she turned strangely affectionate.

Arch had tried his hardest to overcome the impact of his injury. First, he had to untangle his headphone cord from his sling. The cord caught under the strap and tugged at his head. Arch used his healthy hand to rip slack into the wire. The tug jarred his arm and sent pain fizzing throughout his body. He used the pain as further motivation. "I have an advantage," he said, more convincing to himself this time.

Arch engaged his headset and speed dialed his office. "Skyler, let's make some money," he began. "I'm in the mood to wreck something."

"Whoa. Hold on, Arch man. First of all, where are you? Did you go back to Michigan?"

"Yeah."

Skyler must have leaned further toward his camera. Arch could only see an investigatory eye. "Who was happier that you got called back to New York—you or the girl?"

"Wait! What?"

"From what you told me from the hospital, she has been ice cold ever since the accident. Remember? You were not sure she wanted you back."

"Yes, I remember," he said. "She's apparently not the type to take that 'in sickness and in health' vow," Arch continued.

Skyler seemed energized by the reference. "I knew it. You were thinking about marrying this girl. Imagine Arch, the risk-taker,

Arch the wild man, tied down? I guess it makes sense. Plenty of excitement with the girl who fights." In a moment of silence, Skyler seemed to be rationalizing the union. "Whoa, this is an item for the ticker tape. Although you're probably not heading to the jewelry store after that Los Angeles disaster." Skyler must've had another realization. "You're not giving up. That's why you went back to Michigan. Man, you must be really whipped."

Arch sank back into his chair. He regretted the inadvertent reveal. It had provided enough information to get Skyler close to the truth. Arch thought he loved Nova. Nevertheless, coming back had been a setback. Nova trying to humiliate him in bed was not his idea of a step toward a permanent relationship.

Despite the injury and perhaps because of the ignominy, he was finding some of his nerve. He needed to change the subject before he lost it again. "What's the market doing? Give me the whole picture."

Skyler understood that it was time to move on. "We've got minimal bids on most of the market. We aren't seeing much volume from institutional buyers." He continued, "The market is just about to hit the down 55 percent level on the year. You already know that we had another trading halt a few days ago." He paused and seemed to be reviewing notes. "Economic news is bad. Employment data is bad. The only thing really going on is annual index reshuffling—the list of companies to be added or subtracted from the index funds comes out this week."

"Wait," exclaimed Arch. "That's perfect. Absolutely perfect."

"What's perfect? The fact that a bunch of new companies get added to the index funds? It happens every year. For the few lucky companies added to the list of index representatives, we get artificial demand. Massive mandatory buying for no real reason other than that someone added them to an index."

"Absolutely. It's perfect. Some real garbage companies made their initial public offerings before the pandemic crash. I mean real garbage—highly speculative. Limited resources."

"You're saying that now these awful companies have artificial demand for their stocks?"

"Oh, this situation is full of promise," Arch savored. "You remember SPACs?"

"Yeah, sure. Special Purpose Acquisition Companies."

"Pure garbage. These are blank-check companies. Most of them came public with no products and no revenues. Few of them even had systems. These firms had nothing but a cash balance and a management team. Their entire purpose in life was to use investor proceeds to go out and buy other companies. In many ways, these were nonbusinesses. Until they acquired a real enterprise, they'd constantly leak money."

Skyler shuffled a few papers. "Yep, you're right, as usual. A bunch of SPACs are being added to the indices. Dozens of them."

"You know what that means," he stated as fact. "Shorting against forced buyers is easy money." Arch's headphone wire tangled again. He decided he was finished being restricted. He raised his arm by the sling. He pulled the sling over his head and discarded it, gritting his teeth the whole time. "The first rule of investing is that liquidity matters more than fundamentals." The phrase may have been another self-comfort, but he said it convincingly.

"Yo, dude, as I look at these SPAC names, I'm seeing some buy volume, as we expected. The electric vehicle wannabes seem to be getting the most action." Skyler's face filled the screen with his brown, stringy hair falling in front of his eyes.

Arch typed a few keys. "I'm seeing it," he agreed. "I think we can make some trades. Five and 10,000 share blocks are moving."

Skyler disappeared from the screen. When he returned, his tenor changed. "Are you sure that you want to position against EV stocks? That move would be like betting against a biotech company who is developing a cure for cancer. You cannot bet against a cure for cancer. Can you bet against a cure for climate change?"

"If it were not for environmental credits, these businesses would be hemorrhaging money," Arch continued to rant. "How did this turn into a political discussion? When did everything become a political discussion? Can't we just sell short some lousy companies? Go big or go home," said Arch, with growing confidence claiming it as his mantra.

"Go big or go home," Skyler repeated. "I'll prepare the trades."

Arch decided to confide in a friend. "Nova said that she wants one thing. She wants to have the old me back."

"As far as I'm concerned, she can have the old you," cajoled Skyler. "Some chicks dig assholes, I guess."

"I'm going to finish the week," he admitted. "I need to see where this goes."

32

Two nights later, Nova sat alone at one of the restaurant tables. Her apron was across the table carefully folded. She had rolled up the short sleeves of her top, freeing the streamlined arm muscles beneath.

She was working on the business. However, even she would admit what she was doing was busy work. She kept finding valueless tasks that kept her from going home. At home, she had seen Arch trying. That was just it. It took effort.

Against kind, in boxing parlance, she was dancing. Nova was ahead on points after a knockdown. Her opponent was limited. With a minute left in the round, she was running out the clock.

Maurice took a different table for himself. He dropped into a chair and raised his feet to the spindles on the opposite side. He groaned. Seemingly intent on making noise, he dropped a tin index card file box on the table. Opening it with a creak, he paged through his mother's recipes.

"You don't have to stay," Nova told him. Somehow the man always knew when she was dealing with something borderline emotional. He would not be leaving. He would wait her out. Uncomfortable presence and the occasional piece of unsolicited advice was the Maurice version of parenting.

"I have been wanting to look at these old recipes," he said. "You are giving me a good excuse. Your grandma had some winners, and she had some real losers. Tastes have changed since the 1970s."

Derogatory mentions of Oma would often bring Nova to fury. However, this time she fought the reaction. She needed to hide her intent. Someday she would relieve Maurice of that file box.

Paging through index cards, Maurice kept talking. "You know, Nova, the recipe for a good relationship is to cherish your time together."

Typical Maurice, she thought. Nova kept her adverse reaction concealed—a bad segue to some teaching point.

"It is best when two different recipes complement each other. What do you kids call it, a mash-up?"

If Maurice were going to force her to talk, the talk would be about business. She looked up from the ones, fives, tens, and twenties she had counted and grouped. "We might have to stop accepting cash," said Nova. She placed the ordered bills into a silver bag. Had she been a dozen years younger, the bag could have passed as a pencil case. "Cash is dirty. It spreads germs."

Maurice followed her lead. "Cash sales are important to the restaurant," he said. "Nova, we can move on from pandemic ways of thinking. A few weeks from now, touch-free will be a thing of the past."

"Parts of the shut-down may be over," she admitted, "but it's still a mess out there. Do you know why I'm dealing with this cash?"

"Because you do not want to go home."

His accuracy enraged her. "I am doing this because our bank branch closed. You probably did not even know that, did you?" Nova did not wait for the answer she already knew. "I have to make a fifteen-minute drive to make a deposit." She picked up the pencil case and gathered her apron.

"Are you ready? I will walk you out."

"I don't need walking out," she scolded.

"Women at night should be escorted," he said. "You can tell your friend that I said that. Chivalry is not dead."

"Escort? What are you going to do if something bad happens?" Vinegar delivered playfully was still vinegar.

The words seemed to sting Maurice. He lashed back. "I have provided for my family to the best of my ability." No longer self-restrained, he continued, "I have another message for you and your boyfriend. You should not be fighting. There is nothing gallant in a man sparring with a woman." His voice raised an octave. "You go tell him this—tell him nothing matters more than the dignity with which men and women treat each other." He seemed to have no idea that he was talking to the guilty party.

Maurice walked his rebellious daughter to her car. Two cars held fast to their emergency brakes against the gentle incline of the last row of the parking lot. Her Kia and his decade-old Honda Crosstour each kept to their unassigned but permanent spaces. He waited at her front bumper until she closed the door behind her. She activated the headlights and they spotlighted on his trousers. She lowered her window. "You're going to have to move. I can't pull out with you standing there."

Maurice turned and shuffled back into the restaurant.

Exiting the parking lot, Nova experienced traffic for the first time in months. She was going to have to pay attention to things like speed limits and stop signs once again. As she dropped an envelope through the chrome commercial deposit portal, she wondered aloud,

"What good does it do to rescue Full Board if the bank holding the proceeds fails?"

The extra driving time gave her a chance to vent. "Maurice is wrong about everything," she said to herself. "He trashes the memory of Oma. He knows nothing about the business. He is wrong about the pandemic. All of this chivalry stuff is ridiculous." She continued to rant. "Who uses words like 'cherish'? What does that even mean?

"Dammit, Maurice." She knew what it meant. She cursed him again. She knew what she wanted. Now she was not so sure that the things she wanted were the right things.

33

The longshot bid to extend his career put Dosh on the road. The presentation sold the Board of Directors the idea of diversifying into electric vehicle parts. His argument had been effective in positioning himself as the solution. A drastic challenge in the business would require his stewardship longer term.

Now the reality had to meet the vision. He piloted his truck in silence. For the first time in months, he felt he could see his future. Investing in one of the largest auto plants in the world, with its prestige and its problems, would keep him in his executive chair for years to come.

Dosh approached the former Big Three assembly plant at nine in the morning. The plant was so large, it had its own highway interchange. Dosh cornered his truck through the spaghetti turns into the parking lot. The asphalt pad seemed like it could have supported a mega mall. It had space for hundreds of cars. As he drove the lot, paying no attention to lanes and parking stripes, he could see that his truck would be one of a dozen vehicles on the pavement.

Dosh selected a spot and stopped. He downed his second thermal cup of coffee and he reached into the passenger seat for a hat. The baseball cap was embroidered with a UAW logo. He wanted to feel a connection with the place. The plant had been a union shop where "Made in America" meant something.

From the lot, he made his way toward the administration building directly ahead. Two stories of concrete slats and long tinted windows looked like the opposite pattern of a piano keyboard. The black windows were the big keys, and the white slats were the small ones. The structure looked like it was the kind of place an engineer could love.

He stopped at the top of the sidewalk. A deep breath of air gave him olfactory hints of rust and rubber. While he drew in the smells, he took a long look. Past the office building, a water tower rose. The elevated squat sphere was reddening around the seams and the joints. "Fremont" was spelled out in block blue lettering. The plant had its own water works.

To either side of the administration building was what he knew by sight to be the assembly lines. Massive buildings, at least three stories tall, were camouflaged with a dusty beige finish. Seeing them, Dosh pictured the gap in the centers of the concrete floors through which the conveyor system progressed unfinished automobiles. What he actually saw was corrugated metal that extended for what must have been a mile in both directions. Awesome hulks.

A gust of wind caused something unfastened to whistle. In Dosh's mind, it signaled a change of shifts. Hardhats and lunch boxes, visible only to him, filed in and out. The workers wore safety glasses, jeans, and flannel shirts. He imagined what it would be like to manage thousands of people working in choreographed sequences.

As he turned back toward the business office, Dosh continued to appreciate the plant. Industry like this is what made the country great. The previous owner had closed the facility only a few years ago. Lacking preservation efforts, weeds and dust had initiated their take over.

He entered the building by its central doors. The doors opened to a small lobby with a reception desk built into the wall. A small seating area opened to the left. Dosh felt awash in history.

While channeling the memories of famous auto executives past, Dosh found a half full coffee pot and helped himself to a refill. He took a few sips of mildly warm, budget coffee while he surveyed wall hangings. Chevy Chevelles in various stages of assembly dotted the walls. He took a long look at the photos. To see one better, he pulled a pair of reading glasses from his pocket. He wanted a clear view of the Chevelle's famous big block engine.

A door opened, and a man with thinning white hair and black-rimmed glasses appeared. He wore a crosshatch patterned business shirt and a quarter-zip pullover. He looked like he had come from a spa visit at a corporate retreat center.

The man motioned Dosh inside, and he stood with his foot propping the door, pushing hard against an automatic closer, a silver cylinder and a strut. "You must be Ben Dosh," said the man. "Sam Colbert. C'mon in."

The CEO of fledgling Fremont Motors led Dosh down a hallway and into an office. "We're a little short-staffed, as you see. We bought the plant for a song, but it used up a lot of our capital."

Colbert continued toward a paper strewn metal desk. "If you're a potential investor, you did not come here to see pictures of the old Chevelle. These are the pictures that you will really want to see." Colbert handed Dosh glossies of the firm's new EV product. From the front, the SUV had no grill. From the sides, it had a modernistic design with a large singular racing stripe.

"You're looking at the concept version. We put a few units together for the Detroit Auto Show. It looks great, doesn't it?" Colbert didn't wait for an answer. "The Thunderbolt is the modern refresh that the SUV category needs. It's sleek. It's powerful. Better still, it's a zero emissions vehicle."

"It looks great," Dosh admitted. He flipped from photograph to photograph. "Do you have a prototype that works? How does it run?" asked Dosh.

"It does run," insisted Colbert. "I'm not surprised that you asked that question. Many EV prototypes don't operate unaided. This one works. If you are a car guy, and you seem like a car guy, Mr. Dosh, you won't be impressed by the zero to sixty."

"How about the range?"

"You will not be impressed with that, either. Three hundred miles."

Dosh understood that the mechanical parameters were barely satisfactory. The need for money and the indistinctive features were likely why Fremont management had accepted the meeting. "I appreciate you showing me the warts, Sam. I insist on candor with my own people. Instead of dwelling on the bad stuff, tell me what is special about this truck."

"As a parts guy, you'll appreciate this," started Colbert. "We have an innovative design that puts electrical motors in the wheel hubs. The hubs are efficient in transmitting electric energy to create on-road performance. You have heard of all-wheel drive?"

Dosh affirmed.

"We're calling this every-wheel-drive. Every wheel has its own power plant."

"I have done some homework on those wheel hubs," Dosh admitted. "They appear to be wear parts. They will take some abuse from the road, and they will likely be damaged in any accident. Our studies say that your EV SUV design is one of the most likely to produce aftermarket parts demand."

"I like a man who gets right down to business. So Dosh, you're looking for a parts deal. I can tell you that you are the first. However, I need to warn you. You may be getting ahead of things. All the parts that we can make will be going onto the original equipment. The first 500 units of every part is already spoken for. It could be years before we have a regular stream of replacement parts for people like you to sell."

"We both know that you cannot produce a vehicle with no means of repairing it. You will need a parts partner. One who understands the product. One who loves this old plant." Dosh was already convinced. "Why don't you show me around?"

34

Dosh left Fremont with a signed parts deal. With supplemental funding from Dosh, Fremont Motors agreed to manufacture more parts than the company needed for the first production run of its pickup truck. Nextdoor Auto Parts would buy those parts on an exclusive basis. Since Dosh was paying for many of the components a year before they would be produced, he was buying them for cost.

The factory tour had not been a total loss. The floor was filled with racks and bins of component parts. While he saw materials, he wanted to see conveyors, cranes, and air powered tools. The equipment present seemed to be in disrepair.

He wanted to fanboy over the inside of the structure. The facility made an airplane hangar look small by comparison. However, in all of the space, little was moving. The few workers walked around in hardhats.

Dosh could envision the plant in action. If Fremont was going to assemble them, Dosh was going to buy one. He negotiated a deal with the CEO. Once agreed, he walked back through rows of T-shaped steel racks. Each rack held quarter panel stampings. He found the panels that corresponded with his order, number 341, and he signed his name with a Sharpie on the interior surface of the parts.

Signing gave him the sense of being a tourist. He had long heard stories about industrial tourism at European auto plants. Customers would travel to the facilities to see their orders in preproduction state. The owners could sign their parts and try to find the signatures when the vehicle arrived. If an unassembled automobile could be a tourist attraction, Dosh wanted to be counted in.

Dosh spent the drive home in something of a dream state. He realized that financial support was not likely enough. The company needed management talent as well— management talent that excelled at logistics, like he and his team.

On his journey west, he crossed the Maumee River. The Maumee was a working river, and it flowed past a Great Lakes port.

CHAPTER 34

The mental picture that he was composing had him filling the river with barges. Not only could he renew the plant and the river, but also he could redevelop the Port of Toledo. From there, light trucks could ship to the world. When he was finished, he would be remembered by the industry with the same reverence as Lee Iacocca or John DeLorean. All of this would take him five years or maybe ten.

While passing a string of green rectangular mile markers and large blue fast food exit signs, he decided that he could not wait. He started making phone calls. An investment banker was quick to agree to financing. By the time Dosh passed Battle Creek, Michigan lawyers had started to pen an offering document. With the CEO moving north along the coast, his treasurer started accumulating stock.

Back at home, Dosh watched every tick of the stock using an app on his phone. He observed a steady rise. He phoned his treasurer. "Are we moving the stock? How aggressively are you buying?"

"It's not us," the Treasurer reported. "The buying program we're using gets us the average price of the stock during periods when we are in the market. The Wall Streeters call it VWAP, volume weighted average price."

"Wall Street has loose lips." Dosh had consummated two acquisitions during his tenure as CEO. He had never seen an acquisition in which either the law firm, the accountant, the banker, or the political lobbyist did not leak. "Either it is one of our supposed partners, or there is another buyer. What's our next move?"

"How badly do you want the company?" asked the Treasurer.

"I want it." He really wanted it. He would work every hour of every day to get it. Dosh felt like his muscles were pushing through his skin to grab this company. "Nextdoor Auto Parts has already become the first parts retailer to transition to EV. It is a potential game changer for us." He meant for him. "We will be the first in our industry to secure the company's future." He meant the CEO's future.

"Our initial bid was at a 30 percent premium to the stock price. The stock is already up half of that sum. The Fremont Board was initially agreeable. However, if I were them, I would already be thinking about a higher valuation."

Losing the company meant losing his job and his passion. Although his business mind was balking, he knew he would pay whatever sum the deal required. The alternative was too painful. "What is our best course to get ahead of this escalation? How do we get this deal done?"

"Take away time," replied the treasurer. "Make our offer public right now. Announce our intentions to the world."

35

Arch's phone rang a few minutes before the market closed on Wall Street. "We have a problem with one of your stocks." Skyler started. "Fremont Motors, the ticker is ESUV, is gapping upward. We're taking losses."

Arch paced around Nova's house in socks, a T-shirt, and basketball shorts. The armpits of his t-shirt were wet with perspiration from a just completed jog of the neighborhood. His shoes were kicked off tied and lying next to the door. The world-beater's splinted arm swung freely in the absence of a sling. He was forcing himself to regain his power. With some lingering COVID effects and numbness in his arm, it was taking all his strength.

Catching a look at himself in a hallway mirror, he could see darkened eye sockets. Strain gave him the look of a raccoon.

His smartphone was tucked into the space between his triceps and the splint. The white earphone wire extended from the splint to his ears. Skyler had interrupted a podcast on lithium-ion battery technology. "Fremont, one of the electric vehicle shorts?" he confirmed.

"We have a few minutes left to trade. How about covering that short? Take the loss. Dump the pig."

Arch's fragile ego did not respond well to the prospect of being wrong. He was certain that he was right about the specific facts—the company had no finished product and no cash flow. He wondered about the asset class. Arch was breathing heavily. He stalled to catch his breath. "What are the rest of the SPACs doing?"

"Not much of anything. Down with the market." Skyler's phone image moved from nose to ear. "Now that you say that, I'm not sure shorting these stocks was such a good idea. Artificial demand for stocks is hard to measure. We could buy to cover all of them and start over."

"We aren't wrong," Arch insisted. "We might be early, but we aren't wrong!"

"Early is wrong. You know that. We borrow money to put on these positions. Interest is due. Timing is everything." Skyler showed his whole face. "What is wrong with you, brother?" Without an answer, he continued, "I'm asking this as a friend. You're not being disciplined. You're holding on to your losers. This behavior is not what made you successful in the past. Do us both a favor and give me the order to stop our losses."

"The buyers are dumb money, man." He realized that he sounded like every smarmy Wall Street broker he had ever done business with. He tried to save his point. "That company is out of money. Management overspent on parts and real estate. Fremont is months away from first production, and they may not live that long without market intervention in the form of new capital. You see, Skyler? This decision was not a hasty one. We have the information resources. We have the insights. If anything, I would press the short."

"I really would not do that, Arch. Take a look at your screen. Somebody is accumulating this stock."

At the prompting, Arch stroked a few keys on his laptop. "I see what you're saying," he admitted. "It makes me want to give our speech recognition algorithm another pass at this company. I'll see what I can find. I'll do that tonight." He allowed that his mental acuity might not be at its peak. He would check himself later. "In the meanwhile, my gut tells me that upward price pressure in a worthless stock is a reason to double down."

"Don't do it," Skyler cautioned.

"Short more of Fremont Motors into the close. That's my trade order. We might be able to eliminate our losses in a hurry if the stock capitulates on this move. Sell another 10,000 shares."

"I know that you like to take risks, Arch, but this is a crazy one. You're drawing on an inside straight. You're betting on Detroit to win the Super Bowl."

"Exactly. You've said those things to me many times before."

"It's your funeral," Skyler retorted. The next sound was that of a dial tone.

How could the stock price of a seemingly worthless company not go down, he reasoned. The stock market itself was already down more than 50 percent. The rate of decline had slowed, but it continued to go down most days. Interest rates were headed below zero. Corporate earnings were terrible. Holding an underperforming short position didn't seem like much of a risk.

Arch flopped into his chair at the dinette. His splint was suddenly heavy, and his arm drooped. The offending arm reminded him of his conversation with Nova from the night before.

"Business is softening," she said. "We get fewer cars every day. Making things worse, tip amounts are nearly back down to prepandemic levels. We are getting the traditional 15 percent."

In reflection, Arch had a second thought. What if a weaker pandemic response meant that the economy was actually strengthening? If the worst of the lockdown was over, the market would sense it. Perhaps it did.

Arch replayed more of the conversation. Maurice must have felt that business conditions had changed. He'd asked Nova to reduce his salary to one dollar and to use the money to preserve restaurant staff levels. Especially since Nova was not willing to make the same sacrifice, Maurice's actions gave her a newfound respect for the man. Arch even heard Nova call him "Dad" once.

As much as Arch's trade was in peril, so too was what he understood to be the basis for his relationship: a hostile takeover of a family restaurant. He was not sure that he could muster the strength to solve both. On the relationship side, he had an exit path. If a more imminent decision was needed, that choice was not one he would make. Either way, Arch felt certain that his time in Michigan was short.

36

Nextdoor Auto Parts has acquired Fremont Motors for cash consideration of $350,500,000. The Boards of Directors of both companies have voted in favor of the merger. The companies do not expect an antitrust review. Deal closing is expected to occur by the end of next month.

Benjamin Dosh, CEO of Nextdoor Auto Parts, stated that Nextdoor has entered the electric vehicle market in a big way. In conjunction with Fremont Motors, the firm will produce America's next great light truck. The acquisition is expected to be accretive to earnings by 2024.

Dosh had made ready the press release when his phone rang. The area code showed Sunnyvale, California. When he saw the exchange, he did not know the number. Neither did his caller ID.

While intent on releasing his big announcement, something told him to pick up the call. In business deals, there was always one more thing—he answered after the fourth ring. "Hello, this is Ben Dosh."

A gravelly voice on the line identified itself. "Edward Tandy here." Although Dosh had never met The Sultan of Sunnyvale, in three words, he knew he would never forget the voice. It was like hearing the late Vincent Price narrate a vintage horror movie.

As he held the receiver, Dosh pictured the public images of Tandy he knew. The seventy-year-old maintained a swinging septuagenarian image. He had thinning hair, colored and combed over. He kept clean-shaven, and he wore rimless eyeglasses to conceal his vision limitation. Tandy dressed as if the temperature always required a sports coat. However, any business partner knew the retirement home picture to be that of pure fantasy.

As Dosh's blood boiled, he started a thought: To his friends, Dosh had made no secret of his contempt for Tandy. The timing of the call would have been perfect for a prank. He started questioning. Why would Edward Tandy call him? How would Tandy have gotten his number?

"Yes, Ed," he said flippantly. "How are things?"

"Fine," he answered. "Fine." The line was silent for several seconds. "Since we are being friendly, I hear people call you Dosh. Although we have never met," continued Tandy. "I do know something about you from a mutual friend, Paul Kimball.'

Kimball was behind this prank, Dosh thought. Kimball did not love the protest idea. He had expressed his opinion that it was too bold. Flags and flares seemed over the top to the new Floridian. It was Kimball messing with him. "Oh," he said to the otherwise convincing voice of Tandy.

"I hear that you run a good business," Tandy creaked.

Dosh would have to congratulate the perpetrator of the call. The idea was a funny one. The man who held up countless corporate titans was trifling with Ben Dosh. Not only was it humorous, but also like all good practical jokes, it attacked a personal weakness. Tandy had everything Dosh wanted, control of his own destiny and a public image.

"Dosh, I am afraid that I am calling with bad news."

Of course he was, thought Dosh. He wanted to signal that he was in on the joke. He tried to think of some reference to one of Tandy's television commercials. "You will save me money by moving my data center to the cloud?"

The mega billionaire did not seem the least bit amused. He cleared his throat with hostility. "This call is a courtesy. Do not try my patience. You are better than that."

Dosh sobered quickly. He realized he misjudged. It really was Edward Tandy on the line. "My apologies."

"I have a number of business interests," Tandy continued. "I own a company that is a leading electric vehicle producer in Taiwan."

Dosh knew. His silence was an affirmative answer.

"While we make a good sedan, my companies do not have an SUV concept. Sports Utility Vehicles are critical to this market, as you know."

"Yes, I know."

"Second, the firm could use a point of entry into the U.S."

Did Tandy want a partnership? Did he know about Fremont? Dosh tried to sense Tandy's angle.

"I am sorry to have to tell you this. I know your team has worked hard. However, I have a need for the business that you attempted to purchase. I cannot let you have Fremont Motors."

Dosh's business mind went into overdrive. He had a signed deal. He had a closing date. He had accumulated a block of stock. The press release was in his hand. "What do you mean you cannot let me have it?" he responded. "I have it."

"This news must be a shock," Tandy's voice softened to a hiss. "I should not have waited so long to make this call. Lawyers get overzealous," he deflected. "Deeds often do not match intentions."

Tandy seemed to see little reason to explain himself further. "This's the way it is," he stated.

Dosh felt a wet shiver up his back.

Tandy continued, "My holding company has made a tender offer for Fremont stock. We are paying fifteen dollars per share. I believe that your deal was for thirteen. As you might expect, the Fremont Board has reconsidered your offer."

"How can that be?" Dosh dropped the press release, and it floated to the floor. He saw the remainder of his career flash before his eyes.

"I would encourage you to check the business news wires. I have some friends at Bloomberg. News stories will confirm what I have told you. Go ahead. Take a look. I will wait."

Dosh set down the phone and opened a browser on his computer. It was not hard to find the headline. The Tandy offer was the top story. Once he saw it, he felt like he had just been fitted with a lap band. Bile rising, Dosh retrieved the phone. "I see it."

"In that case, you are probably trying to decide if you can make a counteroffer."

Dosh's body gave a further wretch. Could the man read his mind, too?

"To the best of our analysis, Nextdoor spent about as much as it could afford on the first offer. A counteroffer may be beyond your means. Even if you were able to find additional financing, it would raise the risks to your company. If you choose to be foolish, we are prepared to top another bid."

Dosh was aghast. He was short on resources. He could not compete. Both men knew it. Dosh felt he was experiencing the legendary dark side of Edward Tandy. Ruthless. Matter-of- fact. Brazenly stealing his deal. Another American asset might be falling into the hands of someone aligned with a foreign power.

"Our sources tell us that Nextdoor Auto Parts accumulated about six percent of the outstanding shares of Fremont Motors prior to the standstill agreement." Tandy was showing off the depth of his research. It seemed to Dosh as a weak attempt at magnanimity. "You seem to have bought the stock well. You run a good business. Your cost basis must be in the tens."

"Ten dollars and thirty-three cents," Dosh admitted.

"My firm has already purchased shares in a private transaction." Tandy dropped another bomb.

Dosh reached his hand up to his hair and grabbed ahold. How had he not seen this coming? How could this be a complete surprise? How was his career not at its end?

Tandy continued to talk. "We would like to secure your stake. With your shares, my firm would be close to having voting control of Fremont."

Dosh regained his business senses. *Negotiate a favorable outcome*, he thought. *If he made millions for his company, how bad would his situation be?* "Control comes at a premium price," he mustered.

Tandy unleashed a wheezy laugh. "Of course you need to save face. You will not get the prize, but a tidy profit takes away the sting." Tandy was nothing if not blunt.

Now that he had asked Tandy to pay a control premium, he had to make one up on the fly. He continued to question himself: *How much over fifteen dollars can I go? Does any amount save my job? What would Tandy see as reasonable?* "Six bucks per share over our cost," Dosh offered.

"Done. $16.33 for the whole stock position owned by Nextdoor Auto Parts. You make a 58 percent return on your money. Not bad for a few weeks' work."

"One more thing," Dosh demanded. "Our exclusive parts deal stays."

"I am afraid that I cannot meet that demand. My people do not believe in exclusives," responded Tandy. "What if we say your firm is favored? No one gets a better deal than you?"

Dosh held silent.

"Take it, Dosh. Take it, and truck number 341 will be first off the line. It will be delivered with my compliments."

37

Sitting at his monitors in Nova's dinette, Arch saw a news alert. On his monitor, the usual yellow text on a black background was replaced by a thin rectangle of yellow that stretched across the screen. The words were in black text. The alert scrolled slowly downward. It moved line-by-line toward the bottom of his screen, seeming to flash with every declination.

An Edward Tandy company has acquired Fremont Motors for cash consideration of four hundred million dollars. Nextdoor Auto Parts has agreed to tender their shares.

Like being baptized, the fragile belief that Arch had been forcing was dispatched for the real thing. He felt his fecklessness leave. It was like something that he had been practicing for weeks finally integrated into his muscle memory.

In life, you took risks. Sometimes they had negative consequences. You took your lumps. When the next one comes along, make up for it. You bet bigger.

His phone would ring in a matter of minutes. He knew what his boss would say. Arch had listened intently when his father offered employees what he called "corrective action." These overheard conversations were some of a few memories from Arch's childhood. His father often offered employees corrective actions over weekends. Often those interventions happened during court stipulated father and son time.

Arch knew the pattern. He would be admonished. Disappointment would be expressed. Conditional support would be offered. The sequence was right out of the corporate human resources manual. His father had taken it seriously, but to Arch, it was all part of a Saturday game.

Sensing the need to play his part of contrite subordinate, Arch felt a sudden desire to dress for the occasion. He got up from the chair and skated on his socks to the bedroom. Newly facile with his splint, he replaced his T-shirt with a collared company polo shirt. Stopping at the bathroom on his way to the dinette, he combed his hair and made a quick pass with a beard trimmer until he perfected designer stubble.

The phone was vibrating by the time he returned to the front of the house. When Arch accepted the Facetime call, Skyler's face filled the screen. This interlocutor he had not expected. Skyler being the caller could mean a variety of things. Either management was not alarmed, or they needed a layer of distance between themselves and their star. Testing his premise, Arch explored his newly rediscovered aggressiveness. "How can you keep that phone so close to your face?"

"It's kind of my thing," replied Skyler. "OMG, dude, we are so screwed. Did you see the deal value? I don't want to say I told you so, but yo."

Admonishment delivered. Arch almost found himself rooting for Skyler. It was not exactly textbook. Skyler was too informal. However, he mostly did what he had likely been coached to do. Knowing the procedure, Arch also understood that he could not accept the accusation unchallenged. "You never said that you expected a takeover offer."

Skyler looked down. Arch could see him checking notes. "I specifically told you that I did not like the volume," he said. He seemed to scan down a transcript. "I said that someone was accumulating shares."

"So the firm is disappointed," he emphasized, "that I did not translate those inputs into the appropriate action items to protect our exposures." Arch's father had fully versed him in corporate speech.

Skyler looked like a high school kid asked to read aloud from his unfinished Spanish assignment. Translation was slow. Skyler made jokes, selected gambling lines, and provided advice. This role was not one for which he had volunteered.

Arch made decisions. He intended to stand by them, even if a negative assessment would be placed into his permanent record.

Skyler reverted to his area of comfort. "I'm seeing a small arbitrage on the deal. Fremont Motors is trading a few pennies short of the deal price. The Street apparently thinks that this one is going to close. I do not see a reason to suspect antitrust scrutiny. This situation looks like a done deal to me."

Arch became wary. Skyler had not completed the steps. He knew the corporate reprimand was not over, but he accepted the direction of his friend. "Get out of the position," said Arch. "Buy to cover."

Skyler's face blurred on the screen. Arch could see him further in the background. Another face entered the frame. The face was one that he did not recognize. Arch heard muffled voices, not just Skyler and the other face. Some of the other voices were ones he could identify. Management, senior leadership, apparently, was involved in the call.

Skyler would need more training. He had not demonstrated the skillset required to justify an expanded role. Arch actually felt sorry for him. Separately, he felt nothing but contempt for management, who was hiding behind Skyler's inexperience. *Conditional support*, Arch silently coached.

"No go, on the buy to cover," Skyler resumed. He read from a new notepad. "By authorization of Mr. Kimball, your trading authorization has been suspended until further notice." He kept reading. "Quote. So you don't do anything stupid."

38

A few weeks later, the stock market started bottoming. President Johnson had been waiting patiently. The plan was to let the economy sort itself out. With evidence of stability, he assembled a group of his economic advisors.

The Situation Room was dark. Most of the lighting seemed to come from the video screens on the walls. One of those screens broadcast the presidential seal. Last to arrive, the president took his position near the head of a trapezoidal conference table. The gold stripe that bisected the table ended at the president.

The Chief Executive was dressed in a light grey suit. The attire almost looked casual, like he was a guest at a spring wedding.

The Tennessean was not known as a formalist. He sat, and he rolled forward until the buttons on his suitcoat tapped the table surface. He must have liked the sound of metal on wood. He repeated the contact. "It is time to go to work," he began.

"Easier said than done," said Philip Anaclet. "Workers are afraid to return to their duties. Our numbers suggest that only about 30 percent of displaced workers have returned to their jobs. These figures are below my original projections."

"People need a reminder of what life was like before the lockdown." the president replied. "After two months at home, people have forgotten what it was like to work in an office."

"The press continues to scare the citizens," said Chief of Staff Marco Guiterrez. Five years retired from the Air Force, he maintained his military demeanor. "Frankly, some former members of the Pandemic Working Group are not helping."

"What did you expect?" said the president. "They were looking forward to decades of government funding. No BOOST Act means no funding."

"Kenworth," Anaclet interjected. "We have let the economy and the market contract. We have not countered the decline with talk show appearances and press conferences. The time has come to change that. We need to instill confidence."

"What do you advise?" asked the president.

Anaclet resumed. "Let's put a new doctor out there, one who is focused on treatment instead of prevention. How about Doctor Peter Andrew? He has some clinicals supporting his care plan."

"Counter programming. I like it. Get him out there and have the new surgeon general back him up."

"We do have to do something, Mr. President," appealed Guiterrez, "for your sake."

"My sake? Who the hell cares about my sake?"

"Your approval ratings are in the low twenties. We barely held off a primary challenge."

The president shifted his attention from the Chief of Staff to his key economic advisor. "Philip?" prompted the president.

"We are starting to see some signs of life in the economy, sir. Consumer confidence is rising from its lows. Leading indicators have bottomed out. The Economic Surprise Index is showing some positives. The recovery that we forecasted is coming. Based on our data, it could take three or four more months."

"We do not have that much time," complained Guiterrez. "Election day is ninety days away."

"Business leaders are with us, even if the people are not quite there yet," offered Anaclet. "Get back out there, Kenworth. Start talking about some wins in the stock market. Highlight some deals. I saw a few mergers last week. Give people something about which to feel good."

I agree," said the president. "It is time to start broadening our message." He turned the Chief of Staff. "Round up some business leaders. Find some executives who can walk and chew gum at the same time. Ask them to join me on a little speaking tour."

39

After what passed for a lunch rush on Tuesday afternoon, Maurice was out in front of the restaurant. He wore black jeans and a T-shirt covered by a white apron. He was carrying a wrapped charcuterie board filled with treats. He looked like a waiter carrying a tray in his palm.

Maurice left the shade of the awnings. The front edge of the blue-and-red-striped canvas fluttered in the soft breeze. Looking up at the stripes, he realized that the colors no longer resembled the Dutch flag. The sun had changed their complexion as it had changed his.

The weathered awnings drew his attention to the whole storefront. The restaurant was starting to look as if it were an outpost, the brave landmark on the Iron Belle Trail. It might have been a historic stop, but it did not have the appearance of a thriving enterprise.

The more he looked, the more he appreciated that Full Board paled in comparison to its new neighbors. New neighbors were plentiful. Most of the storefronts were filling. When they opened, the arrivals had freshness and energy.

Small businesses were roaring back from the lock-down. The suburbs were repopulated after a brief COVID flight. The returnees seemed to value community more than ever. The errors of the pandemic taught them to trust their friends and not their leaders.

While the restaurant may have needed renewal, Maurice did not. His world was as he liked it. It was a place where you could shake hands and hug, share a bottle of wine, and have a civil conversation.

Maurice walked down the sidewalk. Breathing deeply, he expanded his chest. If he had worn a sash, no doubt would remain. As it was, he appeared to be the mayor of the mall.

He strolled past a rack of dancewear on the sidewalk. As he passed the store's open door, he greeted his new friend Diane. Her store had been open for ten days. "How's business today?" he inquired.

"Not bad. We had a few customers over the lunch hour," she replied. "After-school programs are resuming." Maurice found

Diane to have a singsong voice. The melody reminded him of the springtime that he, along with everyone else, had missed this year.

The next store was one Maurice walked quickly past. The new owner sold hydroponics. In one week since opening, the store had generated steady traffic. That was good for the mall. However, Maurice distanced himself once learning that the proprietor named Johnny was lactose intolerant. Johnny had declined the welcome gift, a plate of food from the restaurant.

The next store in the line had merchandise stacked on tables and arrayed on racks. From what Maurice could tell, it was a women's boutique. Window-shopping, he could see racks of purses, earrings, and scarves. A retirement-aged woman was arranging neon letters in the inside of a plate glass window. In hot pink, the letters spelled-out "GRAND OP," which he took to be the beginning of "Grand Opening."

He entered the store and introduced himself. "Maurice Bakker," he said. "I own the bistro down on the end."

The woman climbed down from a stepladder, and she offered her hand. The woman wore an African-looking print, and she had a string of red glass beads holding glasses around her neck. "Maurice, I'm Marla," she said. "By our names, we already have much in common," she laughed. "I've eaten your food," she continued. "Several times, actually. My husband and I order online and drive up for takeaway."

"I cannot thank you enough," he replied. "Because of you and others like you, our little family business made it through the pandemic."

"Don't thank me," Marla said, "I think your cheeses are to die for... and the metaworst!" Marla laughed again and finally withdrew her hand.

Maurice looked at the tray in his left hand. He studied the meats and cheeses. "I think we put some metaworst on this board. If not, I will get you some." He presented the gift to Marla.

"How nice," she said. She walked the board back to an open table. "Would you like a tour?" she asked. When he accepted, she guided him around the store. "This store is a hobby for me," she admitted. "I'm so tired of being cooped-up at home. I hope it makes money, but if not, I'll be fine as long as I do not lose too much."

"A hobby," he repeated, "I envy you. My daughter claimed inheritance of the restaurant during the pandemic. She does not understand being in business for a purpose other than maximizing profit. She likes numbers and ratios. I prefer to be inventive with food. She will broaden her perspective in time."

"I've tasted some of your inventions. Don't let her spoil your fun."

Hearing the phrase, Maurice realized something. Working in the kitchen and chatting with the customers, he was having fun. Yes, Nova had been complaining and undermining, but she had not separated him from his passion. Moreover, working with his daughter had given him some chances to say a few things he otherwise would not have had occasion to say. "Best of luck, Marla. Come down to the restaurant anytime. We are open for lunch and dinner, and we cater."

"I intend to take full advantage," Marla laughed again.

When Maurice exited the boutique, he turned back toward his restaurant. A ride-sharing sedan had stopped in front of the building. He could tell by the "Hitchhike" sign glowing in the window. A young man stepped out of the car. The man took an unusually longtime observing his surroundings. It was like the man knew what he was seeing, but he had never seen it before.

40

Arch exited the ride-share, and he surveyed the scene. As Nova had advertised, the auto parts store had taken over part of the parking lot. A team of four red shirts stood framing a table filled with auto supplies. After dropping off Arch, the Hitchhike driver drove over to the pit crew. She rolled down her window and waved a red coupon.

As the driver received auto service, Arch focused on the restaurant. He drew a large breath, hoping to catch a scent of something. Having never been to a charcuterie restaurant, he was not certain what smell to expect. He imagined a scent of meat juices and sharp dairy. Although he tried to savor the aroma, the air he inhaled held neither odor.

Satisfied that he had absorbed what there was to experience, Arch breeched the curb and headed for the front door. As he neared, he saw a middle-aged man hurrying down the sidewalk toward him. The man grabbed for him, and Arch stepped back to protect his arm. The man had stunning blue eyes.

"I'm sorry to stop you, sir," said Maurice. "Guests are not allowed inside yet." He held a flat hand to his mouth as if hiding a secret. "We think the restrictions will get removed next week."

Arch struggled for language. He felt something profound about looking the enemy in the face. The enemy was a normal-looking guy, a guy wearing an apron. It was hard to tell from a few words, but he did not seem to be the oafish character that his daughter described. *What do you say to a man whose overthrow you have had a part in plotting?* "I'm here to see Nova," was the best Arch could muster.

The enemy seemed to make a quick assessment of the situation. "You must be Arch," Maurice said. Maurice moved close.

Arch was slightly wrong footed by the suddenness of the encounter and the realization that he was not unknown to Maurice. So much the better, he decided. He was here to push his luck. Arch offered his good hand. "It is nice to meet you, Mr. Bakker."

Maurice grabbed Arch's good hand and held it much longer than a friendly greeting would permit. The hold reminded Arch of the grip once given to him by a clergyman. That handshake was not released until corrective instruction had been delivered. While he concentrated on the hand, the shade of the blue eyes altered. They now beamed icicles. "What you are doing is no way to live," Maurice said.

Nova must have seen the encounter on her video monitor. In seconds, she appeared in the doorway. Like her father, she was wearing an apron over black clothes. The similar outfits helped highlight the lack of family resemblance.

Nova reached her hand to touch Arch's. "Maurice, let go," she demanded.

Maurice did as he was instructed.

Arch felt restrained from responding to her father. Having imagined for years a faceoff with his own father, he felt ready to take on a bad parent. He was anticipatory, but Nova had prevented the confrontation. She led Arch into the restaurant.

Arch felt as if he had entered into an abandoned home. Tables were pushed into corners, and some of them were draped. Some chairs were upside down atop tables, and some were stacked four high. In contrast, the counter was lighted and organized. "So this is where you work," he said, "the family business."

Something about how Arch stretched the word "family," must have irked Nova. Arch could see the muscles in her arm tighten. "I know why you're here," she said. "It isn't to see the family business."

Stripped of his trading authority, Arch had little to occupy his time. He required an adrenaline rush. Showing up at Nova's workplace was the riskiest thing he could think of doing. The fact that she understood his need was positive sign to Arch, the first one in a while. She cared enough to know what made him tick.

Someone burst through the kitchen door carrying a bagged board filled with cheeses, crackers, and meats. Nova pushed Arch out of the way. "Watch out," she scolded him gently. "You have to keep this aisle clear."

The worker with the board disappeared out the front door. Maurice grabbed the open door and entered the restaurant behind the runner. He walked toward the kitchen. "Nova," he seemed to summon her. "Weren't you going to show me some numbers on the effectiveness of free samples?"

"Not now," she snapped.

"No, go ahead," Arch said loudly enough for Maurice to hear. "Restaurants fail all of the time by giving food away for free. Free samples. Free meals. Nova, you should show him the data."

Nova moved to the counter and picked up her laptop. She disappeared into the kitchen. Arch wrestled a chair over to an uncovered table. He sat ready to enjoy the firestorm he hoped he was creating.

41

Nova moved Arch behind the counter that had become her command center. She opened her laptop, and she gave him an electronic tour of the business. Before she was finished, Nova heard her name called. She dashed into the kitchen.

Nova was gone for what seemed to Arch as a long time. He toggled through her spreadsheets on his own. By the rising tenor of activity around him, he guessed that dinner service was starting.

The fight that he tried to arrange had never materialized. He heard no accusations. No voices were raised. He thought he had done enough to prompt a father and daughter supposedly at odds. He was disappointed, and he was growing bored.

Nova rushed past. She must have been talking into her headset. "Will there be anything else?" she asked. "We have amazing desserts." The answer must have been a negative. "Okay," she agreed, "we should have that ready for you in about twenty-five minutes. We'll deliver it to your car window when you pull up."

With Nova seemingly occupied and with little else to do, Arch was thinking about confronting Maurice directly. The man clearly did not like him. Arch did not think he would have to work too hard to get Maurice to finish his reprimand. "What exactly is no way to live?" he would ask.

Nova passed Arch again at a full sprint. She shouted to stop a runner who had passed carrying charcuterie. "Bethany, don't move another inch! What do you think you are doing?" Nova grabbed Bethany's arm and tugged her back to the counter. Nova selected a cutting of ribbon and tied a red bow around the glossy protective bag. "We seal the bags. Customers get these boards home, and they disinfect them. We cannot let the disinfectant come in contact with the food. You know that."

Having been abandoned for the third time, Arch reached the determination he was on his own. He knew from his upbringing that running the business took precedence over everything else. He respected enterprise enough to withdraw from his self-appointed role of agitator.

While it may not be the time for family drama at Full Board, Nova's empty home offered even less stimulus. He decided that he would stay. Eventually, his lingering presence would become incendiary.

Arch turned on the television, and he flipped channels. To his surprise, he found a live baseball game. Baseball was the only sport that had resumed its season. The afternoon game at Wrigley Field had a token crowd. The game was in the bottom of the seventh inning. The Chicago Cubs were up a run on the St. Louis Cardinals.

Wrigley, like all stadiums, played simulated crowd noises. The sounds magnified cheers far beyond the crowd's capability. The amplified noises also seemed to have a slight time delay. Cardinals' shortstop made a good defensive play to take away hit. A few seconds after the out at first, the mechanical crowd reacted with "oohs" and "boos."

Real fans would change the betting odds, Arch knew. To his view, some players needed attention from crowds to perform. He knew the ones. He had been betting against their teams for weeks. With a touch, the sports wagering app opened on his smartphone.

Baseball prop bets were endless. As the Cubs took the field for the top of the eighth, Arch placed a bet, predicting that Paul Goldschmidt would get his second hit of the game. By so doing, the bet for multiple hits would cash. Arch wagered $500. The Cardinal first baseman was due up second.

The leadoff man fouled out with a short fly down the first base line. The next batter, Goldschmidt, lined the first pitch into right field. Arch pumped his fist and cashed his bet.

Nova made another high-speed pass. Carrying a tray of satchels, she breezed toward the storefront. Perfectly balanced, her pace was phrenetic. It was not hard to imagine her as a waitress. She had performed those duties since she'd been a teenager. He would have to talk to her about her pace. Hero managers never succeeded for long. Somehow, his father had been one of the few to defy the odds.

A few minutes later, the ninth inning began. Arch returned to his smartphone. He took the "over" on fifteen as the number of pitches to be thrown in the top half of the inning. The Cubs starter, Kyle Hendricks, remained in the game. He had thrown ninety pitches and eight shut-out innings, but he looked to be tiring. Arch was counting on enough ineffectiveness to bring in a reliever.

Hendricks walked the first batter on six pitches. On a 2-2 count, the second batter, catcher Yadier Molina, put the ball in play on the right side. The batter was out at first. It was strike one on the next batter. Arch needed five more pitches.

"What do you think of the business?" asked Nova on a fly by.

"Where's Maurice?" he responded, feigning aggression. She pointed toward the kitchen, and she walked into it through the swinging door.

Arch looked up to see the batter swinging on a 2-0 count. He bounced a ground-rule double over the center field ivy. Arch needed only two more pitches to win his second bet. The Cubs' manager emerged from the dugout, calling for a reliever. It was the first genuine excitement that Arch had experienced all day. He tensed as if he himself were the next batter.

A few seconds later, Nova emerged from the kitchen. She wiped her hands with a shop towel. She walked over, picked up the remote, and turned off the television. "If you're going to sit here," she said. "I need you to do some work, finance guy. We have a lot of inventory. Sausages take five days to cure. Edam cheese, our best seller, needs to age three months. Save me some money on working capital."

Arch demanded the remote. "I have something riding on these next few pitches," he said. He heard desperation in his own voice. He knew his reaction was out of proportion, but psychologically, he was growing desperate for a win.

"C'mon," she said.

He pivoted to his phone. He tried to check his phone for the play by play, but the game cast was not updating fast enough. "Okay," he replied, haughty and hostile. "If you want my finance guy view, I'll tell you. I've encountered some of the best business managers in the country. I grew up with one of them. Those people make necessary investments. They provide strategy and direction. They task their people. I'm not seeing any of those things here. You have far bigger problems than inventory."

As if on cue, Maurice walked in from the kitchen.

"Just a minute, Maurice," Nova asserted.

Arch continued, "It's not him, it's you." His tenor rose another level. "What sort of a business leader refills printer tapes, takes orders, ties ribbons, and makes snacks?"

"Someone who leads by example," she fumed. "Someone who cares about the details." Nova punched his sling and turned away.

Arch rose and grabbed her arm.

"That's enough!" bellowed Maurice. "Young man, take your hand off of her!" He walked quickly to Arch. "No more shouting. No more grabbing. You two, this is not okay, especially not here." Maurice and Arch came eye to eye. "It's time for you to go," Maurice demanded.

42

The next morning, Nova rose from her bed. She fitted herself into exercise gear. At her bedside, she began ballistic stretching. Bouncing on the balls of her feet, she would kick above her waist, hyperextending her quads and glutes. Following another series of moves that looked like she was flinging her arms from a pogo stick, she began isometrics. She pushed and pulled against progressively harder surfaces in her room. Her poses moved her from the mattress, to the dresser, to the walls.

The extreme stretching did not ease the bindings in her muscles. The muscles felt like a guitar string fighting a pluck. The pulsing was more like being over-caffeinated than injured. Her lack of fitness bothered her. It was unusual for Nova to suffer physical consequences from a fight. She chastised herself. This was emotional, not physical.

The fight at work had resumed at home. In her view, it had been a great give-and-take. Oh, how she liked to trade mostly figurative and some actual punches. They fought for hours. Arch proved that he had his spirit back. Ten rounds. No knock-downs.

She wondered why he needed constant stimulation.

He asked why she could not have a normal conversation. Why everything was a fight?

She insisted that he did not value her accomplishments at work.

He retorted that she did not value his advice.

The fight was great. Epic. Full of truths that only an intimate could voice. However, unlike the ones in previous days and weeks, this one ended badly. They may have pushed each other too far. Perhaps it was the overextension that she was feeling in her muscles. She stretched some more.

The battle ended with Arch packing. He moved out of the bedroom and slept on the sofa. Prior to the packing, she had not been sure he was really leaving. The big job and the big city did not seem to be the draw that they once must have been. His imminent exit seemed more about leaving than about where he was going.

While time was short, she was not ready to engage. Instead, Nova proceeded immediately to her workout room. Through twenty minutes of intensive elliptical, she could not settle her feelings. Had the last two months been exciting? Somewhat. Was he someone who could match up with her? Most of the time. Was confrontation any basis for a relationship? She struggled to answer. Physical strain was easier than mental strain. She moved on to weights.

When Nova emerged from the workout room, she was beyond a glistening sweat. She was outright drenched. Performing the circuit had required more effort than usual. A grey bath towel hung around her shoulders, and she kept raising its corners to her reddened face. Needing space to walk off the strain and cool down, she approached unsettled ground at the front of the house.

Near the front door, Arch's duffel bag and both suitcases were filled and zipped. He had dumped one of his computer monitors into a reusable grocery bag. He must have continued the packing job while she was in the gym. She had not seen the full array of bags since the day he had arrived. As it did then, it looked unsuited to him now. He had arrived with a startling amount of baggage. He was leaving with more.

Arch met her in the hallway. "I think I packed everything," he said. He motioned toward the suitcases. "I made my travel arrangements. I'll be out of here in about an hour."

She hesitated to respond. *What was she feeling?*, she asked herself. Many things. She had no more use for him at work. However, to her surprise, she did not want him to go. Yet how strong of a man was he if he was leaving? She may have required too much of the man. But the whole gender owed her a debt.

Arch filled the void. "I bought a car," he explained. "I used one of those online dealers that delivers to your driveway. The vehicle will be delivered here. Deliveries start at 10 o'clock, and I should be the first one." He swept his good hand toward the front of the house. "I'll keep an eye on the driveway."

"You bought a car?" Her mind kept racing. How could he buy a car on impulse? If he could, why had she been driving him around for months? Had he taken advantage of her? It was supposed to be the other way around.

"I bought a Lincoln MKZ with 75,000 miles on it," he said as if reading the Internet posting. "I like luxury nameplates, and this one has lots of power. People have not resumed buying cars, I guess. The dealer was nearly giving this one away."

"Are you driving to New York? That'll take you two days. Can your arm handle two days in a car?" This was starting to sound like concern, she realized. "With all of your travel perks, and frequent flyer miles, and gold statuses, why do this?"

He stopped and met her eyes. "I'm not going to New York," he said.

She did not see the longing she had seen before. He did not even look at her chest. "Where are you going then?"

"I like cars. I always have. I saw my dad on weekends as a teenager. Every time I visited him, it seemed that he had a new one, sometimes two or three. He would let me sit in the driver's seats. When I was old enough, he let me drive around the neighborhood." Arch seemed lost in a moment of recollection. "I haven't had a good drive in a few years. In New York, cars are a nuisance."

Nova knew nothing about cars, and she cared for them even less.

"From here, I think I'll drive up the coast. I might visit some lighthouses." Arch changed the subject. "The car will be here soon. I want to show you something on the computer before I go." He headed for his seat in the dinette. "Do you remember how to log into your FIRE account?"

She was so confused. He was leaving. He was driving. He was impassionate. He was evasive. Now was she getting one final finance lesson?

He entered the log in. "I want you to see what's in here." He turned the monitor to show her what was on screen. The account value showed $2,432. "I invested both months' rent. You have some gains from your stock calls. Do not spend this money. You are on your way to an early retirement."

She finished looking and said nothing.

Arch stowed the rest of his electronic gear and moved his bags to the porch.

Nova felt some breaths get short. A sick feeling started in her stomach. Only once before in her life had she felt this vulnerable. She rushed back to the heavy bag in the gym. She felt like punching something.

43

President Johnson stood between White House pillars above the south lawn. A breeze was gently fluffing the American flags posted behind him. A group of men were seated in white folding chairs, three on each side of the podium. A passing cloud exposed the sun, making many on the portico fumble for sunglasses.

The south lawn descended from the great building, and seating had been arranged in two tiers. In the front tier, dignitaries sat below the president to his left. The press occupied the first tier to his right. The public sat in the second tier. Several hundred Washington, D.C., tourists had been cleared to attend the national address.

Music played at eardrum splitting volume. Tom Petty's "I Won't Back Down" could probably be heard as far away as the Washington Monument. The turf, the banners, and the music gave the setting elements of a state fair.

"My fellow Americans," began the southern gentleman. "The country is rapidly recovering from the pandemic. Every day 'we the people' are getting better and stronger. Today, we have assembled a tremendous panel. They will tell you that business is improving. Moreover, they are seeing a comeback by the American consumer. Now, I am someone interested in a comeback." He paused for laughter, and he got some. "These gentlemen are going to tell us how to do it."

"The crisis is over, and this economy is starting to roar back. You can see it in the stock market. We are getting merger and acquisition activity once again."

"Without further ado, let's get on with this terrific program. Let me introduce one of the smartest guys I know. He's the Chairman of the Council of Economic Advisors, Dr. Philip Anaclet."

A mix of applause and boos covered Anaclet's bounding to the podium. He wore an electric blue sport coat over a white turtleneck. "Ladies and gentlemen," he began, "I am here to highlight the ongoing recovery in the economy." The crowd seated in the first tier flipped pages in their press briefing packets. They seemed to be reading the speaker's bio and comparing the man to the glossy headshot. The crowd had a soft murmur, perhaps disfavoring the comparison and certainly discrediting the speaker.

"Many things led to last quarter's recession," he continued over the hum, "the lock-down, masking, and social distancing, to name a few. However, the data suggests that the recession is over, and thankfully, the slowdown was one of the shortest on record." He waited for applause. What he got was forced. "We have current information that indicates that the economy is strengthening. The Economic Surprise Index increased from negative fourteen to positive two. The change in sign, from negative to positive, means that the economy has turned the corner. Other economic measures confirm the reading." He turned to face the seated president. "Mr. President, from the perspective of the Council of Economic Advisors, the economy is advancing. The crisis is over."

The crowd was not showing evidence of being won over. Anaclet looked into the sun and out over the occupants of the chairs on the lawn. Most heads were down. They seemed to be focused on the next bio in their packets. "Now that you know that the data is positive, you probably want to hear some real-life experiences." Anaclet readied to summon the next speaker. "Next I would like to introduce a prominent member of our business community, the CEO of Nextdoor Auto Parts, Benjamin Dosh."

The applause was polite and short. A gangly man in a dark suit and a red tie ambled to the podium. If he had possessed a stovepipe hat and had grown a beard, it would have appeared that Abraham Lincoln had returned to the White House. "Good afternoon, ladies and gentlemen. I have a question for you." He waited for some anticipation to build. "Do you miss driving your car?" He got a mixed response from the audience, some crowd noise, and a few claps. "Do you miss driving your truck?" He got howls from the back rows, and he smiled.

"I have an F-150." Some in the back shouted back, listing their models. "I missed driving my truck so much that I drove all the way here from Michigan—over 545 miles." The whole crowd cheered. "Judging by the lack of traffic, not many of you drove to the capital city today. Anybody else out there from Michigan?" He solicited a few hoots.

"We have all given up so much during the lock-down. Our lives have changed, and not for the better. I have been taking an inventory of what I miss. Driving is one thing. Please join me to identify the rest. Do you miss going to stores?" He paused. "I think I hear some 'yeses.' Not sure. E-commerce is great, but touch and feel is better. Do you miss going to church?" He paused and listened. "I hear about as many pilgrims as those who miss shopping. Your religious leaders want you back. After that meek response, you may want to try out the confessionals." He heard a few laughs. "Okay, here's a big one. Do you miss going to sporting events?" The crowd erupted. He heard some team chants. Before they settled, he spoke again. "What about dinners out?" He waited. The chorus grew. "Do you miss family events and Sunday dinners?" He got a loud response. He slowed to settle the ruckus.

"You can see that I like questions." He paused again so that the assembly could agree. "You are getting pretty good with the answers. Here is the big question: Are you ready?" The crowd buzzed. "My question for all of you is what are you waiting for?" He continued. "Why would you continue to miss these things?" His good hand was open and extending from the elbow as if pleading.

"Stores are open."

"Say it with me. What are you waiting for?" The crowd responded.

"Stadiums are refilling."

Dosh prompted the gathering. "What are you waiting for?" they chanted.

"Mom and Dad's house is always open."

"What are you waiting for?" the chorus grew.

He paused for a drink of water from a bottle below the dais.

"I told you earlier that I drove here today. Something about seeing the country through your own windshield is quintessentially American." Applause erupted again, along with some "Damn right" comments from the back. "Home of the automobile. Home of the drive-ins and drive-throughs." He tamped down the voices. "My message to you today is to get in your car. Or truck. Get out on the open road. See this great nation. Fill up your gas tank. Stop at a roadside attraction. Get a car wash. Put on some new windshield wipers." The crowd seemed engaged, intent on his next words. "Be it off-road or easy ride, your country needs you. Here is my question again," he said. "What are you waiting for?"

As Dosh returned to his seat, the applause was thunderous. He acknowledged it with a wave before he reclined. As the clapping turned into a standing ovation, Philip Anaclet rushed to the podium. "What are you waiting for?" he repeated. The now raucous crowd in the back said the phrase again.

"Business leaders like Ben Dosh are what makes America great, am I right?" Another round of applause ensued. Dosh waved again. In his dark sunglasses, Philip Anaclet looked like a Wall Street subreddit meme. "We have other great business leaders with us today. We have Howard Denizen and Neal Grigio." More clapping. "Go ahead, give it up for them," he said. More applause ensued. "I am pleased to announce that many business leaders are signing on to our get back to work initiative. Over 100 businesses have signed on to our plan. You probably know this by now. Our plan is called 'Actual Beats Virtual.' If you are here with us today, you are living the message: Actual Beats Virtual."

44

President Johnson complimented Dosh, "What a speech!" The speakers had gathered for a small reception in the East Wing Lobby. "Big Ben has a talent for stump speeches. You know that, don't you, Ben? 'What are you waiting for?'" he repeated. "You had them eating out of your hand. You could run for office."

Dosh was entertaining exactly that thought. Since his business deal had been scuttled, he had been marking time until his mandatory retirement. He felt less animated each day, as if the world was chipping away at his soul. Politics had elements that he did not like, but a political career might be a lifeline.

One of the president's aides scurried through the small crowd. She brought him a Post-It-sized note. He read it and shoved it into his jacket pocket. "This is good news, Big Ben." The president patted his pocket. "The preliminary ratings indicate a nice viewing audience for our address. Twenty million unique views. 'Uniques' is what they call them," he said as if he had invented the word. "It is not *The Mandalorian*. You are no Baby Yoda, Ben. But that's pretty good."

The East Wing Lobby was a narrow space, further compressed by the heavy presence of wood paneling. Further constricting the area, a long wheelchair access ramp ran nearly the length of the room. Although it was tight, the space was big enough to fit the presenters and their guests.

Most of the other guests were circulating on something like self-guided tours. The lobby was filled with official portraits of the first ladies. A full-length Nancy Reagan in a red gown seemed to attract the most attention.

Dosh stilled and selected a cranberry juice from a tray of selections offered by a member of the kitchen staff. Even without the comments from the president, he knew that he had connected with the crowd. Ignoring the fact that he was standing next to the Chief Executive, He felt as if he were the main attraction at the after party. *Something could come of this*, he thought, *some purpose for his future.*

The Press Secretary stepped close to Dosh. Rowan Nelson had a youthful face and boyish build that made his forty years look like the man was barely drinking age. Long brown hair curled behind his ears. The fresh face was a few weeks into the job. He spoke at a near whisper and then he corrected himself. "Fox television had a focus group watching the address. It was a group of eight likely voters."

"I have seen those," remarked Dosh. "As lines of the speech are delivered, the network graphs response rates on the television screen."

The grimace on Nelson's face suggested that Dosh was welcome as a listener and not a talker. Dosh understood why the man had gained a nearly instant reputation at being good at handling the press.

"The data tracks voter impressions on a minute by minute basis," Nelson said. "The focus group was lukewarm to the president." He glanced toward the president as if asking forgiveness. "However, once Ben Dosh began speaking, that changed everything. Approval numbers spiked. The charts moved upward to the right." As the Press Secretary spoke, he grew more animated. "The response was similar from both Republicans and Independents. Even better, from the time of your speech, Ben, the viewers engaged for the remainder of the program. You saved the whole event. Congratulations."

"Big Ben got the ratings? Not exactly a face for television," teased the president. "He brought in better numbers than I did?" The president turned toward Dosh, and he seemed to raise his voice to be heard by the group. "Not good to outshine the president, Big Ben." He patted Dosh on the shoulder. "Not good." His next words seemed delivered in jest, but they also seemed to have some malice. "You better watch out."

Nelson moved to console the president. "The event was a success, sir. Satisfaction levels ended on the highs. Mr. President, we think this outcome will add about five points to your poll numbers."

Senator Sasson emerged from the crowd. He gave a nod to the president as he approached Dosh. "Well done, Dosh. With a speech like that, you should take it on the road," Sasson said. "It is not too late for a dark horse campaign. I would not want to be a Michigan incumbent."

"You are too kind, Senator," demurred Dosh. While downplaying the idea, it grew on him. Representative Dosh? Senator Dosh? He tried on both titles.

The Chief of Staff engaged in the conversation. "The Senator has a point. Your speech will travel well. I have an idea. Dosh, the president leaves tomorrow on a four-state tour to promote his agenda. You seem to have the ability to rouse a crowd. Would you like to join us?"

The president did not seem thrilled when he turned back to Dosh. "Opening act, Dosh," said the president. "Warm up act. Remember, it's the headliner that fills the stadium."

"We fly to Arizona the first thing tomorrow," continued Marco Guiterrez. "The stadium in Tempe is sold out," he said as if to affirm the president. "From there, we go to Erie, Pennsylvania, for an evening rally at the convention center. Day two is North Carolina and Florida. We're hoping to draw people to the entertainment venues. The tour concept aligns perfectly with your speech."

Dosh hesitated to respond. He sensed that a political future could be at hand, but events were moving fast. Few things were worse, in his opinion, than being presented with opportunity and not being prepared. "I would deliver my same speech?" Dosh confirmed.

"Nothing permanent," Johnson reminded him. "Just a few days."

"How would you like a ride aboard Air Force One?" said Guiterrez. "I'll get you a good seat."

45

Two days later, Dosh was back in his truck. It was no worse for wear after being babysat by White House interns. Even better, it was gassed up and detailed. Although it was after dark when he retrieved his vehicle from a parking lot near Blair House, he was not ready to call it a night. He started the engine.

In less than four hours, he could drive to the Pittsburgh area. Following his talk in Erie, he submitted to a radio interview. On that call-in show, he had obligated himself to return to the region. He saw no time like the present.

While he remained wired from the four-city tour, he'd use the energy to drive. Dosh headed away from the beltway toward

Interstate-95. He was further invigorated by the nightscape of streetlights.

His thoughts went to political careerism. He now knew that he could rally crowds. He was learning to let them take him where they wanted to go.

Erie Radio station WJET secured time with Dosh following his second tour stop. To his surprise, the administration facilitated the interview. Dosh was instructed to promote Actual Beats Virtual. However, after a brief introduction, the radio host went straight to calls.

"Mr. Dosh, you're an inspiration," began a caller. Dosh pledged to himself to remember this call forever. Businessmen were seldom deemed inspirational.

"I'm a member of Lake Erie Corvette Club. We are over 100 members strong. Combined, we own 175 vehicles, including everything from 1955 models to the latest off the line."

"Fantastic," Dosh replied. "I have been to many Corvette shows. Also, I owned a C5 once."

"At your suggestion, we're scheduling an outing for next weekend. The club plans to drive sixty miles to Geneva-On-The-Lake. Our members have not hit the road in about two months. Nothing beats seeing fifty American sportscars rumbling down the highway together. Thank you for getting us moving again."

"My pleasure," said Dosh. "I would love to see all of those cars. Send me a picture."

The host switched to the next caller. "Caller, you're on the air."

"Mr. Dosh?"

"Yes," Dosh replied. "Go ahead."

"You may not remember me. We have only met once. I am the regional manager of Nextdoor Auto Parts responsible for Pittsburgh, Cleveland, and Erie."

"I remember," said Dosh. "I think I remember. Amir Ach…"

"Amir Achyara," he reminded. "The team at Nextdoor Auto Parts loved your speech. We're proud to have our leader trying to make a difference for the country. We have sixteen stores in the area, and we'd like to ask you to visit. You were last here as recently as two years ago. However, after your national address, we think your presence would be a great draw. We believe that our customers liked your speech as much as we did."

"I am overwhelmed," Dosh had replied. "I am traveling with the president tomorrow, but I promise you, Amir, that I will be driving through here on my way home to Grand Rapids. You can count on me for as many store visits as you would like." Dosh relived the exchanges as he drove west. For some reason, the administration never arranged another interview.

Having exhausted his memories of the radio show, he thought back to the rally. The crowd during the previous evening kept building and building. By the time the president's jet landed, the seating erected on the airport tarmac was already full. Dosh saw bleachers topped with jackets and hats. People seemed to have come prepared for a long wait on a cooling night.

A large gathering remained outside of the security fence, and groups of people kept approaching the queue. From where he sat, looking out a portal on Air Force One, it looked like thousands of people were patiently waiting to pass security. While the president's party was debating how long to push back the start of the event, patrons began a spontaneous outbreak of patriotic songs. Dosh sat and strained to listen as he heard some words to "God Bless America."

Half an hour later than originally expected, Dosh took the stage. He wore a corvette jacket over a red turtleneck. American flags waved throughout the crowd. He wondered if someone copied the free flag idea he used for the protest marches. He tried to point out swag from the automakers and unions: hats, jackets, and a few flags.

A few phrases into his speech, he realized that many in the audience had heard it before. They anticipated words before he voiced them. "Get out on the open road," they said in unison.

Dosh started feeling some license. This crowd knew him, knew his speech, many knew his story. Surprising those who had rehearsed his lines, he slipped in a joke about Fremont. Sympathetic applause erupted.

When he reached the end of his talk, the assembly delivered his now famous question. In a singular voice, they screamed, "What are you waiting for?"

Dosh could feel it. He was connecting. The greatest country on earth was reawakening.

46

When the adrenaline wore off, Dosh stopped at a hotel for the night. He awoke the next morning in time to see the sunrise over the Allegheny Mountains. As he loaded his truck on the hotel parking lot, sunlight glowed yellow behind the craggy green hills. A few clouds were shaded pink and orange overhead.

The spectacular drive through mountain valleys featured streams and woodlands. He imagined exploring the ravines to find the famous coal seam. As he motored, he realized that he had taken his own advice, headed out for the open road.

Nearing Pittsburgh, Dosh steered toward the Fort Pitt tunnel. Dosh remembered the tunnel from an earlier visit. He thought it to be one of the most spectacular entries to a city anywhere in America.

As he exited the dark tunnel shaft, he got his first glimpse of the light-flooded cityscape. Seconds later, the truck started over the span of one of Pittsburgh's girder-framed bridges. The Monongahela River flowed below him. The city's castle-inspired skyscraper drew him across.

Over two days, he made stops in Franklin Park and Newcastle on his way to the lakeshore in Erie. Dosh visited stores in each city, and he proved to be a draw. Stores filled with dozens of people for meet and greet events. He signed autographs on Nextdoor Auto Parts merchandise, and in several cases, he delivered sections of his speech.

Those stops went so well, each one with a larger crowd than the last that Dosh decided to hopscotch his way home. Now with more advance advertising, he made several stops in Cleveland. The publicity must have alerted Arthur McBride, the owner of the Cleveland football team to Dosh's presence in the area. Dosh had met McBride during his ownership bid several years before. Having learned Dosh to be a political ally, McBride asked Dosh to dinner. Dosh entertained thoughts about hosted fundraisers. His campaign started to feel like it had national aspirations.

Dosh was on an emotional high when he finally reached Western Michigan. However, when he reached his home, his mood changed suddenly. A car that he did not recognize occupied his driveway. It blocked his path to the garage. The Lincoln was fleet car white with a heavy layer of mud around the running boards. A paper temporary license plate curled in the wind.

After a brief pause on the street, Dosh pulled into the driveway abreast of the car. He opened the garage door, and he noticed that a small boat that he usually kept in the third stall was missing. He had not realized until that moment that people likely knew his whereabouts for the last several days.

Until he saw the derelict car, the thought had never occurred to him that the political life had risks. Half of the populace disagreed with any stance. He had insufficient benefactors to secure him and insufficient celebrity to protect him. He was on his own.

Dosh returned to the truck and removed a pistol from a locked storage compartment under the front seat. The door connecting the garage to the house was unlocked. He opened it carefully and entered. Down a short hallway, he could see a light in the center of the house. It was a bulb that he would not have left burning. Leading with his gun, Dosh approached the kitchen.

Dosh entered the kitchen doing his best reproduction of what he had seen on cop shows. He moved gun first down the blind corner by the oven and stove. With careful steps, he closed the distance to the kitchen island. The pantry door was cracked open.

He approached, pulled it back with force, and aimed his gun past the edge of the door to the opening. No one was there.

Through the kitchen window, he thought he saw movement. Keeping himself out of the frame of the pane, he closed on the window. Looking from the side, he took in as much of the scene as he could. Down at the river's edge, he could see the missing boat tied to the dock. A man was next to it. He had something black in one of his hands.

Dosh slumped to the floor and dialed 911. "I think he has a gun," explained Dosh. After a moment of silence, he said, "So do I." The police dispatcher advised him not to use it. He was not inclined to follow that suggestion. However, he knew that a shooting incident might end his political career before it had started.

He took another peek out the window. The man was coming closer, walking up the hill at a leisurely pace. Dosh ran through the kitchen, down the hallway, and back into the garage. He entered his truck, locked the door, and started the engine. Dosh rolled down his window, reached out, and pointed the gun. He began to back up the truck.

The man rounded the house, moving faster. Dosh was focused on the surprisingly large blackness around one arm. Automatic weapon, he thought. Backed onto the street, Dosh took aim.

While Dosh targeted the black, the man moved the other arm. He waved up and down with an open hand as if he were doing a jumping jack. The movement began to look like a greeting. With perspective and a better line of sight, Dosh realized that the blackness was a medical device. Dosh brought his pistol back within the truck.

"Hello, Dad," came a greeting from the top of the driveway.

47

Back inside the house, Dosh retrieved an elixir. Normally he drank only to maintain business customs. On this occasion, he needed one to settle his nerves. A home invader and a wayward son—either could ruin his political opportunity.

Dosh took one sip and let the alcohol burn his throat. The fleeting pain convinced him of his resilience. He set his glass on the kitchen counter and moved the earlier abandoned suitcase back to his bedroom. Along the way, he kept noticing things out of place, a few days' worth of wear.

When Dosh returned from the bedroom to the living room, Arch had reclined on his father's sofa. The kid's shoes were off, and his feet were up. Arch held a glass filled with ice and two fingers of bourbon that he had poured for himself. Dosh's drink was moved to the coffee table.

"Here's to my first ever drink with my father," said Arch. Dosh felt certain that Arch was right about that. The boy was twenty-six. Dosh had not laid eyes on him in at least half a decade. Dosh had heard of such ceremonies being important for some fathers and sons, a rite of passage. He picked up his drink, toasted, and sipped.

Fatherly moments did not come naturally to Dosh. In an awkward silence following the toast, he appraised his son. The young man was unkempt, but tall and lean. He had taken his mother's maiden surname. Dosh was not certain whether to start with that question, or to start with the obvious interrogatory about the splint. He did not have to decide.

"I shorted your stock," Arch blurted. His smile showed the satisfaction of a hyena feasting on a lion's kill.

The familial moment was a short one. Perhaps the toast was perfunctory or ironic. To Dosh, Arch's statement contained malice. The son he barely knew seemed to understand his sensitivities well. Any animus that the son maintained for his absentee father was best taken out on the love of his life, the business.

That sort of scandal could ruin everything. Son betting against father would shorten his business career and end his political one. While some wounds were lifelong, he had not known about any sort of vendetta. His and Arch's had been a peaceful coexistence.

Dosh checked himself. He may have been reading this situation all wrong. After many years, context clues were lacking. He decided to err on the side of camaraderie. "What did you do that for?" he said playfully. "You know I run a good business."

"I know," Arch admitted. "Everything I know about running a business I learned from watching you." He took a sip of bourbon. "I shorted the stock to try to impress a girl. She works next to your Benton Harbor store, so she knows the brand," he explained.

"When I learned that you were behind the demonstrations, I thought you could be in a bit of trouble."

As he thought about it, Dosh was happy that Arch had collected information on him. "You thought that I was under suspicion? That hedge fund you work for must have a ton of resources." Dosh had tracked his son's business career as well.

"We scan court filings and police blotters. We know which law firms represent which executives. We have so many information feeds, you wouldn't believe it."

"What do your systems say about me now?" Dosh asked.

"You are a rock star," said Arch. "Your speeches have been trending on social media. Your name recognition is way up. You've become a national figure."

"'A national figure,'" he repeated. The statement confirmed the momentum that he felt. He had crowds in Pennsylvania and donors in Ohio. The audience had repeated his speech to him in Florida. He thought back to his star turn with fondness. He could win an election, and these days senators served well into their eighties.

"Why do you want that?"

"What do you mean?" Imagining his forward path, Dosh was startled by the question.

"My generation will be the first one whose standard of living is lower than the generation before. Besides a few billionaires run things, and you are not one of them."

Dosh realized that his motives were selfish ones. He wanted an occupation. He tried to cast his quest as altruistic. "I think killing the stimulus bill was the first step in reversing some of those negatives. I had a part in that."

"Okay, you get full points for that one. You managed to kill the bill before the billionaires secured a big payday for themselves," Arch said convincingly. "Anyway, with you being a media darling, it must be helping the firm. Maybe I should go long your stock this time," continued Arch. "Come to think of it, I probably will. Should I buy straight equity, or should I use leverage? How are your numbers looking?"

"Be professional," snapped Dosh. "You know very well that I cannot divulge information about company performance to an investor. If I told you anything, it would be bad for both of us. I would have to make a public filing. Your firm would be prohibited from trading."

"I'm playing around," softened Arch.

Dosh changed the subject. "Do you want to tell me about the girl that you were trying to impress?"

"She's tall," he deadpanned. "She's got an amazing body."

"Watch yourself," Dosh cautioned. "While I realize it has been a long time, I am still your father, and you are still my son."

"Right you are," Arch said. He toasted in Dosh's general direction. "The girl. We've dated for a year. Not joking about the body this time, she's an athlete. I figured out early on in our relationship that I could take her on adventure trips. I have tried free diving, heli-skiing, and zero gravity. Going from zero-gravity to 2Gs is where this came from." He raised his splint.

"You have learned that you cannot keep that up. You will run out of money, or run out of thrills, or run out of body parts." Dosh thought he understood. He had seen plenty of women bleed his business associates dry.

"Oh, it's not the money," Arch bragged. "I've taken some big bets, and they have paid off. My philosophy is that the country is screwed in the long-term. So I'd better get mine now. Money," he said again. "Money is not the problem. My annual take home pay is probably more than yours."

Dosh was now certain that Arch was bearing some sort of grudge. At the very least, the kid felt the need to be his better. He was not sure that he could agree that more cynical meant better. So why, he wondered, was an independently wealthy young man with an adventurous girlfriend sitting on his couch?

"The girl seems to see this splint as a weakness."

"She sees a broken bone as a weakness?"

"It took me a while, but I realized that she's an endorphin junkie. She gets off on exercise, thrills, and combat. She picks fights with people almost every day for the sport of it. With one arm to box with, I must not have been much of a match. I need to understand if there is more to the relationship than adrenaline."

"So you got away. I notice that you did not go far." Dosh understood that the boy was not here to see him. It was a trip of proximity. The boy was weakened and bloodied. He needed to regroup.

"Comparative analysis," Dosh opined. "Strengths. Weaknesses. Opportunities. Threats. You need to figure out if she is a risk you can live with or an investment you can live without," he concluded. "I'm glad you are doing that upfront instead of making the mistake that I made with your mother." Dosh rose and picked up his glass, along with some scattered dishes Arch had used before

Dosh's return. He headed for the kitchen. "Now that you have moved yourself in, feel free to stay here until you figure it out."

48

After the travel lag and the excitement from the day before, Dosh slept past the dawn. He returned to the corporate office, arriving at an unaccustomed late hour, eight o'clock in the morning. He walked past five workers crowding around a coffee pot in the break room. Communal use seemed to have restarted.

Down the hall, he could not help noticing that nearly every cubicle was occupied. Dosh could see faces, as only about one in ten wore a mask. He saw smiles. He heard conversations.

Once reaching his office, Dosh looked past his reflection in the exterior glass. The city was moving again. People walked on the sidewalks. Cars rolled through the streets. Gone were the pleasure boats in which escapists made V-shaped wakes when they powered downriver.

With growing strength in the economy, along with Dosh's new celebrity, business was booming. Most of his stores had reopened. On top of that, the pit crews had become so popular that Dosh left them in place. He had a message on his desk from the professor, who Dosh presumed wanted to discuss next steps post Fremont. It was either that or he wanted to detail the dismal start for the Indianapolis football team.

Dosh's cell phone rang. The caller ID identified the number as coming from the White House. As happy as Dosh was about the business momentum, this was the call he really wanted. His political future was on the line.

"Good morning, Ben. This Marco Guiterrez, the President's Chief of Staff. We spoke briefly on the trip."

Dosh remembered him fondly. Like himself, Guiterrez was a former business professional with a political sense. "Hello, Mr. Guiterrez."

"I'm calling with some results. The tour raised the president's approval rating by seven points. As you may remember, that is much more than we expected."

"Excellent. Where does that put him," asked Dosh, "forty-five or 46 percent favorable?"

CHAPTER 48

"Forty-six," Guiterrez replied. "That is not enough to get reelected, but the race is starting to look competitive." Guiterrez continued, "Here's a piece of data you will really like. We have some polling on Ben Dosh from Gallup. Your favorables are about ten points higher than those of the president. Also good for you, your negatives are about twenty points lower than his. For him and especially you, I'd have to say that the four-city tour was a success."

"We attracted great crowds," agreed Dosh. "The president's instincts were correct. People needed a reason to get out of their homes. They needed confidence that leaders did not see any great danger in crowds."

"These tours may be our best asset," Guiterrez agreed.

"Where are we going next?" asked Dosh. "Given their status as swing states, may I suggest Michigan and Wisconsin? I am up for another drive."

"The president thought you did a great job," responded Guiterrez. "People loved your speech. You scored us some points." Guiterrez seemed to gulp some air. "Dosh, we're planning to use football stadiums on the next leg of the tour, 50- or 60,000 people."

Dosh was imagining larger crowds and greater responses. He could see his name recognition growing. He was on his way.

"I'm sorry to have to deliver this message, but I wouldn't be doing my job if I failed to do so." Guiterrez sounded apologetic, even chastened. "The president thinks of you as quote, 'small time.'

The campaign is going bigger. If we're doing stadiums, he says, we need the whole focus to be on the headliner."

In the chief of staff's statement, Dosh heard the president's warning as he had delivered it in the East Lobby. The president must have felt as if he were upstaged. Dosh was clear on the ramifications. He was out. His fledgling political career had come to a sudden halt.

After hanging up the phone, Dosh wanted to escape. However with a houseguest, home was no respite. Dosh closed his office door and lowered his window shades. He sank heavily into his office chair. He had seventy-four short days left until mandatory retirement. As of today, that date would be his end.

49

A few days later, hired movers were transferring half of the restaurant furnishings into an outside storage pod. Inside Full Board, the workers rolled tables and carried chairs. Nova shrieked every time a piece of furniture bumped into a door or a wall.

Her disposition was sour, initially not for reasons originating at the restaurant. She thought she deserved to hear from Arch. He owed her an apology for the way he'd left, how he'd calmly drove straight away. She felt cheated out of the last rounds of a fight, along with the subsequent make up. He owed her for reclaiming him. Despite what she was due, Nova grew less certain that a call would come.

A mover rough-rolled a table as if it were a wooden wheel on a washboard road. She reprimanded, "We will need these back in a few weeks. Try not to destroy them." The interior of the restaurant could open, but diners had to be six feet apart. To meet those spacing limits, half of the tables had to go.

After a chair knocked against the handle of the back door, Nova decided to get further involved. She shed her grandmother's replica apron and folded it carefully on the counter. She engaged in the move, carrying chairs herself. Without nearing a wall or a door, she muscled them out. "This is not hard," she professed to each mover she passed.

She tried to make carrying furniture into something of a workout. Nova had skipped the morning routine she'd choreographed during the pandemic. The empty house prompted her to make her return to the exercise studio. She made arrangements with her former personal trainer.

The exercise physiologist would be waiting for Nova before work tomorrow. After an assessment, they would update her training regimen. Her body was ready for something more strenuous.

Carrying potential revenues out of the door put Nova further into a fighting mood. She thought of the speed bag. She had not punched one in months. She had some pent-up frustrations to pound out. Not that she had ever hit him in the face, but she might visualize Arch as she pounded.

Maurice was outside. However, he was not visiting cars. No cars were idling. Instead he sat under the white tent. He seemed to be trying to make sense of two new tables underneath it. The wrought iron patio sets had honeycomb grates fit to a round. He tried to drape a tablecloth over one of the surfaces.

Nova finished insulting the movers, and she walked through the restaurant and out to the front curb. She selected a chair next to Maurice's, and they both stared at the parking lot. She had appealed to the owners of the Real Estate Investment Trust that owned the strip mall. She was told that her lease did not permit the drive-up that she tried to preserve. Nextdoor Auto Parts had secured a claim regarding additional parking spaces. Many of the slots were filled with used Fords. For Full Board, the new conditions felt confining.

"You wanted the lock-down to be over," she quipped. "This is what we get—social distancing, outdoor tables, and scattered service."

"Yes, I wanted it to be over," Maurice admitted. "Perhaps I was wrong to hope for that." He cracked his knuckles. "I wanted resolution for our sake, yours and mine. This time period has been hard on both of us. You have been frustrated with me, and rightly so. I am not a business manager. However, I have so much more to show you about running a kitchen. I would like to have time for that. What I really want is to get back to some sense of normal."

"Pre-pandemic normal? No such thing anymore. People won't forget what happened."

"What did happen?" he mused. "We all had a tremendous overreaction to a health scare." Maurice considered a stand-up hand sanitizer dispenser next to him. "How long do you think we will keep disinfecting and distancing?" He did not seem to be expecting an answer. "I know, germophobia has become a comfort. I am glad most authorities pivoted once learning the original ideas were wrong. Giving up on prevention to focus on treatment was the right move. Treatments are having remarkable success: Dexamethasone, Ivermectin, Hydroxychloroquine, antivirals, monoclonal antibodies, all of them seem to be working. I hear about them every afternoon on the news."

"All I hear about is our people calling in sick. I get one or two every day." Nova put plastic clips on the edge of the tablecloth, pinching it to the table. "We will make this work," she said. As she said it, she realized that the phrase might mean many things— outdoor dining, the restaurant the relationship.

"I may be a creative," Maurice responded, "but I know that having half the tables is no way to make ends meet."

"I've thought about this, Maurice." Nova couldn't believe that he had just come to that conclusion. "People will not likely come right away. I see no need to staff up. When diners come, we should expect them to linger. No one has been out to dinner in a while. Tables will not turn."

Nova continued as if delivering a master's thesis. "My plan is to sell more alcohol. We didn't sell a lot of alcohol in the drive-thru. The law restricts open containers. We could sell only full bottles. Drinks are our highest margin business. We will have wine specials. Our waiters and waitresses will be trained to upsell."

"I hope you are right. I have a lot of hopes for you: that you have your own passions... that you find your peace."

Nova felt disarmed. "Stop it, Dad."

Maurice straightened up. "Your plan is a good one." He popped his wrist, revealing more of the carpal tunnel he'd suffered after thirty years of knife work. "I like it. I will recommend some good wine pairings to you."

"If it doesn't work, we'll have to make layoffs," she said. "I'll handle it."

"Handle it gently," he concluded, "with dignity."

50

Nearly three weeks had passed without contact with Arch when Nova's phone chirped. She had spent part of that time claiming the front of her house, where Arch mostly had resided. Prior to his arrival, she had not used the space. However, her original vision of hygge, a warm-looking and untouched memorial to her grandmother, had been soiled. Now that he had employed the sofas and chairs, their ephemeral quality had dissipated.

Nova buried herself amongst the pillows covering her chair and a half. The front of the house struck her as having a quality in common with the restaurant. In both cases, a man had taken tributes to her grandmother and altered them, made them something less than they had been before.

In that way, she felt an even greater kinship with her grandmother. While she was ruminating, her brain thought of new rules and systems to give her control back. Something like: the sofa could only be used on weekends, or the dinette must be cleared and cleaned once used. As always, the penalty would be violence.

Nova had to admit to herself that squeezing some pillows and wrestling with others kindled some childhood memories. She had done the same sort of cuddling in her grandmother's hearth room. Times were infrequent in which she allowed herself comforts. Softness was something to be contrived, not experienced.

She thought twice about answering the phone. Arch would be reentering the front end of the house in a way. Her rules were not ready. Access was uncontrolled, and accountability was not established. Nova was vulnerable, and that was unacceptable.

Her mind told her not to engage. Keep a distance. Circle the ring. However, the muscle tension that she had not felt since he left resumed. She followed the signal from her body. "Hello," she said to the video screen.

"Where are you?" Arch asked. "You look like you are under blankets or something. Are you okay?"

Nova realized how it must look. Arch knew her well enough to know that she was not the type to embrace creature comforts under nearly any circumstances. She would not be explaining herself.

She responded the only way she really knew, with hostility. "Where the hell are you?"

"I have big news," he said. Arch panned the camera down from his face to his arm. "No splint," he showed. "I got it off today." What he did not tell her was that it was against the doctor's advice. The doctor wanted him to wear it for two more weeks if nothing else for protection. Arch had not exactly taken care of the medical apparatus, which was dirty and dented. Neither did he take care of the arm beneath.

"Congratulations." She flashed back to the accident and her escape from California. She marveled at the man's change from being everything she deserved to nothing she wanted in a matter of minutes. She realized that thought process was similar to the one she was having about her living room.

"The doctor gave me some physical therapy exercises to do for a few weeks. I tried them out tonight." Arch set his phone down, balancing it on its pop socket. He demonstrated elbow curls and wrist curls. "These exercises are low intensity as you can see. I'm supposed to build up over a few phases. When I was reading about my program, it occurred to me that I could use an exercise coach. Naturally, I thought of you. What do you say? Would you like to help me relearn how to use my arm?"

"I do not usually accept clients in your physical condition," she scoffed teasingly. "I do peak performance training. This seems more like rehab."

"But I've heard you are the best," he said.

"I'm the best," she agreed. "Let me see the arm again."

He held it up to his phone camera.

"With time, I could get you back into shape."

Like the businessman that he was, Arch seemed to take "yes" for the answer. "Can I begin my training this weekend?"

"Am I flying somewhere?" She relished the thought. She and Arch were at their best together when they did something spectacular. She had not been on a trip in nearly two months. She was ready to be catered to.

"No, I'm coming to you. I'm in Grand Rapids, about an hour away. I'll drive down on Sunday morning. Sunday is still your off day, right?"

"Wait, hold on. What are you doing in Grand Rapids? You were scheduled to be back in New York weeks ago."

"I've been recuperating at my dad's house. Estranged dad. I hadn't seen him in ten years. I landed on his doorstep. Actually, I let myself in while he was away. He was nice enough to let me stay."

Nova's head was getting fuzzy processing the rush of new information. He'd never left the area. He had a father who lived nearby. He was showing up at her house again. She was just now coming to terms with his previous visit. He was coming in a few days.

When she hung up, Nova threw off the pillows. She rose from the chair and rushed the place she really lived, slept, and sweat, the back of the house.

51

A few evenings later, Maurice had reached the end of his part of the dinner service. He was not feeling inventive, so the kitchen was closed. Serving in-person diners gave him energy, but even that spirit had its limits.

The restaurant was doing well enough, which was to say not dying quickly. He had few new concerns about the business. The food was good—of that he was certain. He found himself worrying more about his daughter. He had been taking particular notice of Nova when their work intersected. He was not seeing change.

Despite his repeated advice and example, Nova remained oppositional and self-centered. The lack of a personal relationship, dare he think love interest, did not seem to change anything. She was demanding and unforgiving.

Not knowing what to do other than more of the same, Maurice was content to observe. Nova worked at her computer behind the counter. She became increasingly obvious about her desire for diners at two lingering tables to leave.

Partially in support of Nova's mission and partially to take in some news, Maurice turned on the television. The prime-time reopening rallies were the newsmakers. He made a production of taking off his chef's jacket and laying it across a chair. When none of the guests moved, he turned up the sound.

"Every day we hear good news," said the president. He commanded the stage in front of 30,000 at Phoenix's Chase Field. The dry wind was blowing hard, sometimes taking over the microphones. "A major steel maker announced that they will be building a new plant in Kentucky. The plant will employ 2,000 workers. It will be a big part of the manufacturing renaissance."

The response continued.

"There's more. There's more," said the president. He quieted the throng. "This one is even better. A major cleaning company, whose products sold out during the pandemic, is now disinfecting whole movie theatres and entire airplanes. Even the most vulnerable amongst us can go back to those venues. My friend Ben Dosh would say…"

The crowd chanted, "What are you waiting for?"

"What?" prompted the president.

"What are you waiting for?"

"Exactly. Big Ben is okay."

The crowd laughed.

The larger of the lingering tables began to break up. Three couples arose comfortably. One couple stumbled to their feet. Four uncorked wine bottles remained on their table. Maurice had curated the wine flight. Given the lack of remains, it must have been a success.

Nova emerged from the counter, and she offered to call a Hitchhike. She was assured that the impaired were not driving. The group made slow progress toward the door.

Perhaps feeling the pressure of being the last, a solo couple packed their shapes. It was not clear that the young couple had eaten anything. However, the daters' creations were extensive. The shapes fit well enough into two take-home containers.

Nova finished bussing the tables, and she shuttled glasses and napkins into the kitchen. When complete, she sat beside Maurice. She had barely reclined before she took her smartphone out of her apron pocket.

Maurice realized that the phone had become her constant companion in recent weeks. Unlike many in her generation, Nova had not previously been captive to the device. Maurice wondered if this newfound hobby was a byproduct of her recent relationship or a compensation for that relationship's end. He watched her swipe and type. As much as he disliked Nova's coupling with Arch, cyber relationships appeared worse.

Nova seemed to be enjoying herself. That reaction made him even more curious. He listened to hear Nova saying words like "*bam*" and "*pow.* "For him, it was like watching the original *Batman* television series. Hearing Nova was a strange contrast to the cheers and boos the president elicited.

When Maurice heard Nova laugh out loud, he had to ask, "What are you reading?"

"Social media," she said. "Johnson trolls. This stadium rally is itself an affront to public health. I'm getting a big response to this post, 'Johnson is an economic terrorist.'" She continued typing as she spoke, "He should be locked up."

"The president is a terrorist?" he challenged. "Why do you talk like that?"

"You only get a few characters to make your point," she said. "This is how people of my generation communicate. Clickbait."

"So you do not really mean it. You do not believe that he is a murderer?"

"On the contrary," she said without looking up, "I'll defend it to the death, especially against an anonymous post. Those people are the very definition of no courage."

"Your phone is where you fight," he observed. He now understood the sudden phone fascination. "You have not given up on sparring. You just lost your live-in opponent, and I am not much of a challenge." He thought of Nova as Don Quixote, turning windmills into imaginary enemies. Temperament stopped him from voicing that viewpoint.

Nova kept typing.

"Do Tweets and Instas mean that you can get into a fight anytime of the day or night?" Maurice was proud of himself for knowing some of the slang. He knew that he was not getting through to her otherwise. He tried to communicate on her terms.

"Don't forget TikTok," she said. "Yeah, sure. I can get into an argument anytime. People are angry about the BOOST Act veto, the lost weeks during the pandemic, and the fact that nearly everything that your Pandemic Working Group said and did was wrong. It's fun. If I can shut someone up with a few well-chosen words, and generate some likes for myself in the process, that's a winning round."

"May I give you a little fatherly advice?" Maurice turned towards her and set his hand gently on hers. *Perhaps touch would help*, he thought. He wanted her to feel humanity. He clutched her forearm and moved her phone away from her face.

Nova did not answer the original question. She seemed to know that she was getting advice whether she wanted it or not. She probably also knew that Maurice's intervention would be over quickly.

"Nova, this carries over into your relationships. People are not this oppositional in real life. This is not how you communicate with people face to face."

"You don't say in real life, Maurice. It's IRL."

52

A Sunday morning in early September, Dosh sat alone in his living room. He was looking out over the trees and down to the river. The dog days of summer had given every plant a tinge of burnt brown. He could relate to the leaves, singed and a short time away from detachment.

Dosh flipped through a stack of reports from his political action committee. One page showed the president's poll numbers. Although he was not certain he wanted to see them, he could not help himself. The polling continued to rise. Since the first tours started, the president's approval rating had increased by nine points. Two points had been added since the stadium tours began.

Was two points worth ruining his political second career? Apparently so. The beautiful rush of popularity that followed his appearances had faded. Interviewers had stopped calling. Political organizers were no longer recruiting. Dosh had not felt less welcome since his audience in the Senate Dining Room.

He was not certain what was worse, being ostracized or being plagiarized. The candidate had assumed the speech that could have launched Dosh's political career. Apparently, politicians were not above stealing attention from fellow partisans. Just as Dosh never had wanted to be saddled with the legal and procedural parts of governing, he was repulsed by the power plays. The level of narcissism that he'd experienced was sickening. As a result, Dosh would not be campaigning for the man who sacked him. He had a political action committee with no apparent political action.

A few moments of self-pity later, Dosh set aside the election reports. He had plenty of work he could do to maximize the next 397 days at Nextdoor Auto Parts. He reviewed a set of business updates. The data indicated that his billionaire status, lost during the stock market correction, might not be recoverable.

"Dad have you seen the Grid news?" Arch rushed through the door from the garage. He sounded and looked wired. The whites of his eyes seemed twice their normal size.

"What is wrong with you?" Dosh asked. He wondered what sort of problems he had brought into his house and how he might be blamed. "Where were you?"

Arch seemed to ignore the questions. "Oh my God," he said. "This is crazy. You won't believe it."

Dosh was getting uncomfortable. Arch smelled of sweet smoke.

"It's a cyberattack. Edward Tandy and the Chinese launched a cyberattack." Arch was slurring and agitating. His forehead dripped with sweat. "It's Grid."

"Why would anyone cyberattack Grid?" Dosh asked. "Why would they do it now? A month or two ago, everyone was using it. It would have had a much greater impact then."

"The attack is not *on* Grid," peppered Arch. "It is *from* Grid. The data breech is massive." Arch talked rapidly. "They initiated a reverse ransomware-type of attack. This is huge. I need my computer set up."

Still struggling to decide on which new information to focus, Dosh asked, "A reverse what?"

"Ransomware!" Arch snapped. "Instead of stealing your data and holding it hostage for money, they released the recordings of every Grid call made during the last three months. You have to pay the hackers a ransom to take your information down."

"That must be millions of calls and meetings," Dosh said. He tried to contemplate how many Grid meetings he had conducted himself. A hundred? He began to get a sense of the size of the potential problem.

"The sheer volume may be the saving grace for someone like you," said Arch. "This data doesn't appear to be catalogued. The hard part for guys like me will be finding a call of interest and spending the time to listen to it."

"What do you mean? How am I saved? What should I do?"

"I just listened to part of a Grid meeting between you and the senior staff of Nextdoor Auto Parts. I learned all about your marketing strategies. Spending fifty dollars gets you twenty off if you are a ride-sharing service. Anyone can download your information. Your competitors will. It's just a matter of time."

Dosh snapped to attention. He started to understand the implications. His board meetings, his management briefings, and even his protest sponsorship would be exposed. What Arch was saying was that anyone with dedication and some technical savvy could penetrate his private business. The disclosures could ruin his company. Worse, it could ruin his reputation. Leaving at the top might no longer be an option.

"You should get someone working on this," Arch suggested. "Protect your data. Buy back the Grid calls that could hurt you the most. After that, you need to go on offense. You might be able to capture some data from your competitors."

"I, I will," Dosh staggered. He was trying to think who to call on his tech team. "How is this legal?"

"I'm not sure that it is legal. I think the recordings are the property of whoever makes them."

"So how can Tandy do this? Tandy and the Chinese?"

"I guess we're finding out that when you have content on someone else's social media platform, you're at risk."

"I wish that I would have known that."

"So does everyone else."

Dosh was beginning to collect himself from the initial shock. "What do you think is the purpose of these data dumps?"

"My people," said Arch, intent on having Dosh recognize his superior business connections, "are saying that the intent is to halt the recovery. Without the stimulus program, the stock market was barely stable. It hasn't functioned without government intervention for more than a decade. Banks were bailed out. The healthcare sector was nationalized. We were just figuring out whether Wall Street could survive without the new money that would have flowed from the BOOST Act."

Dosh looked like he had just learned the identity of the Easter Bunny.

"You're kidding me, right?" Arch reacted. "The whole market is a giant meme. Leverage the short-term because the long-term does not exist."

"When did you become so cynical?" asked Dosh. It was bad enough that the father had little hope for his future. Now he saw that his son felt the same.

"Let me tell you why this was a brilliant move," Arch continued. "Tandy buries the country in data. His people control the short term. Highlight one call. Disappear a few others. Three thousand companies take a week to change how they communicate. Half of them probably rethink business plans because everyone with a computer will know the old strategies. Parts of the market freeze as businesses are re-evaluated. No Congress. I think they all left Washington, D.C., So no bail out. How many of your peers you think can run a business without an institutional backstop?"

Arch spoke with such authority that he began to appear sober. "As people unpack this data, we'll find out that somebody out there said something illegal. Moreover, we're bound to find some embarrassing personal disclosures as well. Celebrity executive's heads will roll. Revelations will go on for days. This market is toast."

"Is this an act of war? Are we at war?"

"So far, it seems like Grid users were completely unprepared. We trusted one of our key means of communication to a hostile actor."

"God help us," said Dosh.

"God help you. Your company is a goner if you don't react to this quickly."

53

A few minutes later, Arch was unpacking. His laptop, docking station, and monitors had been cushioned in clothing inside a soft-sided grocery bag. The bag had been untouched since his arrival. He had enjoyed the charge that he felt from ghosting his employer. It made him feel powerful.

Arch untied the arms of a sweater from around a monitor, and he wondered why he had taken such care of the technology. He must have had time to waste waiting for his car purchase to arrive at Nova's.

Cords dangling, he placed the monitor atop a poker table near the bar in Dosh's walkout basement. He repeated the process, freeing the other equipment from T-shirts, sweatshirts, and khakis.

Once liberated, he arranged them and secured the plugs. The monitors lit up and the computer booted.

Rekindling his work from home office took only a few minutes. While the machines were familiar, he took a moment to consider his surroundings. The basement walls were also well known in his memories.

The room matched the mental picture he had retained from his childhood. Sunlight angled through a glass sliding door. The illumination was enough to overpower the overhead floodlights. He glimpsed the gas grill outside the door, and he recalled his mother barbequing there. His father never seemed to be home on time for the task.

The poker table conjured a better memory of his father. Arch had learned to bluff and fold in a few late-night games. At the time, his father said that it was a business skill, like golf. Arch realized that he used that skill nearly every day.

The rest of the basement was darkly lit. The décor was 2000s vintage, and it seemed to suffer from excessive attention. The shabby chic sofa and loveseat seemed as if they had seen a cleaning crew far more often than they had been used.

Situated, Arch took his smartphone out of his pocket and dialed Skyler at home. He thought it would be fun to hold the Facetime call a little too close to his face. When his friend answered, he responded with the disgust that Arch had hoped. Arch said, "Skyler, we're back in business."

"Dude, what are you talking about?" Despite numerous call attempts over days, Skyler had not connected with Arch. At work, Skyler faced regular questions about the whereabouts and the state of mind of his teammate. Inability to answer had not been career enhancing.

"The Grid hack changes everything," Arch said. In volatility, he saw opportunity. When he saw opportunity, he couldn't wait. Arch's mind sizzled like he had filled the roof of his mouth with Pop Rocks candy. He had focus and enthusiasm. "Let's go."

"Go? Go where? It's Sunday. You are persona non grata. You have no trading authority." Skyler spoke with unease, as if he had encountered an old flame more than a few years after having been left at the altar.

"The company needs me," claimed Arch flatly.

"Don't be so sure, cowboy. You're on the shit list. Taking vacation weeks after being called back to the office was a bad move, man. You put me in a terrible position."

"Are you done with your little fit yet?"

Skyler was not spent. "You're weeks overdue. Everyone else is back in the office. Your job being at risk may not bother you, but I'm pretty sure they're getting ready to fire me. Do you even care?"

"I'm back. They won't fire you now. If they had dismissed you, I would've brought you into my next venture."

"Sure.," Skyler did not sound comforted.

"Skyler, it's simple," Arch said. "This firm has the ultimate program to exploit this Grid situation. We have massive computing power and an algorithm tailored to scan spoken language. The thing is made to detect key words and phrases. We might be able to process this new data faster than anyone. Imagine what we can learn about companies, managements, and products. No one knows how to task the algorithm better than I do."

"If that's your pitch, I can run it by the Powers That Be." Skyler must have set his phone down on his desk. Arch could see the white grooved tiles of the block ceiling along with an air vent. After a moment, he heard voices and saw shadows blocking the overhead lights.

"You screwed us on your last trades," said Skyler.

"Everybody is wrong once in a while," replied Arch. "I've made this company tons of money."

Skyler sounded as if he was being force-fed words. "The firm isn't fond of the disappearing act," he said as threateningly as he could muster.

"We don't have time for this," erupted Arch. "Millions, maybe billions, are at stake over the next few days. I'll need full access and as much server power as we can spare." As if he had almost forgotten something in his haste, he added, "Oh, and I want Skyler to have an employment contract and a guaranteed bonus."

Arch heard nothing. The only thing that he could see on the video was Skyler's ear. A new voice replied. "Give us thirty minutes," it said.

54

Ten days later, Dosh's life had taken a radical turn. No longer a pariah, he was back in public demand. The Grid Dump, as the hack was being called, had not hampered him or his company. Instead, it had saved them.

The Nextdoor Auto Parts Boardroom glowed from key light, fill light, and backlight. Video cameras focused on the CEO, whose office was professed by the portrait on the wall behind him. He settled into his executive chair. It might have been the first time that he'd sat down since the attack.

Never before had Dosh experienced such staging and production. Behind the camera and across the desk were several members of his communications and media team. The team had been inundated with media requests. One of them extended their fingers to count down from three.

In the case of Nextdoor Auto Parts, the Grid Dump had backfired. Dosh proved unable to keep the public from most of his company's recordings. To his great surprise, they loved them. Nextdoor Auto Parts experienced a swell of support.

While the reaction was great for the company, it was even better for Dosh. He was back in the public spotlight. This time, he'd vowed to himself to make it count. He had a message, and he had a call to action.

"In our feature story, Nextdoor Auto Parts may be the biggest winner of the Grid Dump," began a CNBC anchor. She was blonde and ruddy, and she maintained a seemingly perpetual smirk. "When customers became privy to private discussions at many of their favorite corporations, they did not like what they saw. However, when consumers replayed the management meetings at this auto parts retailer, they uncovered a kindred spirit. Perhaps we should have known from the political speeches of their chairman calling us to the open road. Gar guys and gals run Nextdoor Auto Parts. This company breathes exhaust and bleeds motor oil. In several of the calls, Nextdoor Auto Parts managers selected Grid backgrounds displaying their favorite vehicles. If you are a fan of Corvettes, you have friends at Nextdoor Auto Parts. If you prefer muscle cars, you now know where the enthusiasts work. It took this crisis for the gear heads to see that plain fact for themselves. Chief gearhead Ben Dosh joins us by secure video. Mr. Dosh, why did it take a national disaster for you to establish this connection with your customers?"

"Thank you for having me on, Carmen," began Dosh. He was wearing a red button-down shirt that looked something like a jersey typically worn by a NASCAR race driver. The shirt had patches and decals from dozens of auto parts brands. He had a GMAC emblem above his left pocket, and a Pennzoil patch above his right. A Champion logo crossed his left pocket flap, and a Mopar insignia was stitched on his right. "Obviously, we are bad at marketing."

"That's quite a shirt," observed the host. "Is this your marketing solution?"

He modeled, showing patches on the sleeves, chest, and back. He looked like a scarecrow wearing remnants of a quilt. "This is not my usual attire," admitted Dosh. "I am wearing this shirt to support our partners, some of whom are having a hard time with this Grid Dump situation."

Dosh knew that he already had consumers on his side. If he could improve vendor relationships, the windfall for the firm would be multifaceted. "We support our partners," he said. Off-camera, his marketing team approved.

"Most companies are having a hard time," continued the anchor. "It's difficult to imagine something more destructive to the business environment than what has happened. Business plans have been abandoned. The volume of lawsuits is overwhelming many firms. Yet with all of that going on, a few firms are breaking out. Your firm is thriving. The stock is skyrocketing."

"As the world has seen through our Grid meetings, our group believes passionately in the firm's mission. On a regular day, we spend hours discussing things like short throw shifters, grill inserts, interior LED mods, and roof wraps. In the service area, we took a racing concept, pit crews, and adapted it to the needs of our customers."

"Maintain and modify, that's your corporate culture. Someone said that on one of the calls. I have watched the recordings several times," the host admitted. "Your meeting videos could be a Harvard business case study. Have you seen a positive response in your business trends?"

"Sales are picking up," Dosh said. "As much as we like the immediate attention, it feels like the new business is sustainable. Sales are tilting toward do-it-yourself items. In other words, people are investing in their cars and in themselves."

"That sounds like one of your political speeches, Mr. Dosh." Carmen shifted poses and cameras. "Ben Dosh appeared as a speaker at several of the reopening our country rallies."

"I will not make any new stump speeches," Dosh demurred. "Given this awful moment in our country's history, I would like to direct a few words at our leaders."

"Go ahead."

"The country has taken some setbacks, both the virus and the Grid Dump. As a people, we will certainly prevail. If nothing else, you have seen that people are out here who know how to make things work."

Dosh took a calculated turn. "Some in government realized that a few months ago. Those leaders prevented passage of the BOOST Act. A government takeover of both the medical and nonprofit sectors would have made the economy slower. The government would have become so large that it would have taken over a third of the entire economy. No market-based system could survive that. We would have seen supply shortages and inflation. Everyone would have been worse off. America is a much better place today without the nasty hangover from the BOOST Act. Good decisions like that are how I know we will emerge from the Grid crisis better and stronger."

"Let's get back to the Grid situation," steered the anchor. "Now among the surviving corporations, many of them have taken a reputational hit. What do you say to those corporations whose unfavorable cultures have been exposed? How do they move ahead?"

Dosh had expected the question or one like it. He intended to use it as his springboard. His team had prepared a call to action. If he delivered it correctly, he might have the whole economy subject to his words. "Carmen, do you keep any secrets?"

"Yes, certainly," she responded uncomfortably.

"Everybody does," he affirmed. "At times in our country's history, secrets were attractive. We have celebrated covert research and development centers, and we have secret recipes. Colonel Sanders, for example, built a restaurant business on a secret recipe."

He leaned forward and stared into the camera. "Since secrets are common to our experience, and some of them are favorable, perhaps we should accept their presence. They exist although they are sometimes harmful."

"You can say that again," encouraged the host.

"My appeal today is for discretion." He raised a stick holding a hand-sized image of a stop sign. "To my fellow business owners, I ask them to stop. Stop exploiting the data from your competitors. Stop the legal actions." He dropped the sign and raised it again. "To my fellow consumers, I say the same. Stop. Stop the demonstrations. Stop the boycotts. Stop."

"To use the mythological expression, you cannot put Pandora back in the box, can you, Mr. Dosh?"

"We may not be able to unwind the last few days. However, we can stop escalating this crisis. Just stop." He tilted the sign back-and-forth.

"Ben Dosh, the car guy, communicates with traffic signs. That seems fitting."

"I am asking our political and business leaders for a pause, not just a slow-and-go," he joked. "The country needs a reset. Could we take one day, one single day, and focus on forgiving one another for these painful revelations? This will sound strange coming from a workaholic like me, but could we pause? Could we stop fighting among ourselves? Could we center on fighting the real enemy? I am asking the nation to take a day off, one day, and reset."

"You have heard it first on CNBC. Ben Dosh calls for a one-day pause, a National Day of Forgiveness. The secret is out. Good luck, Mr. Dosh."

55

Arch was one of the few citizens unhappy with the National Pause. He worked until the moment that it started. A full day reset was likely to mark the end of his run.

Arch had been a kid at play. When he found untoward facts, he would disclose some and crash a stock. If his algorithm found a positive kernel, he would withhold the finding and load up his position.

After days in his father's basement, Arch felt a film over his whole body. He had not shaved or showered. He had no time for grooming. The splint that he still wore on his arm most days smelled like rot. Every speculation he'd ever imagined had been at his fingertips.

Still wanting to maintain the buzz from his multiday market bender, Arch remembered that he hadn't contacted Nova since the Grid Dump began. After days of neglect, she'd be an even greater challenge than usual.

Although he was eager for a fight, he knew that he might be overmatched. The last time that Nova had days to scheme, she'd destroyed him completely. Working up courage took him a few minutes. The danger compelled him. He still hoped for a relationship, so the real prospect of loss added to the threat. He stewed. The delay probably did him good.

Arch dialed, and Nova picked up the phone. "Yes," she said. She sounded groggy.

"Are you asleep?" questioned Arch. "Aren't you usually up by now?" He did not intend to act as her alarm clock. He did not mind that he did. She could start the day angry.

"Nice of you to call," Nova said. A slow awakening probably kept her from sounding hostile. "I have not had a day off during the workweek since that trip to Los Angeles," she said. "I was sleeping in. What time is it?" It sounded like she knocked something over while searching for a clock. "Almost 10:00," she mumbled, then she yawned. "If I ever get a chance, I'm going to thank the guy who came up with this pause idea."

Arch was not sure how much to say. How could he tell her that the very man slept in the upper level of the house in which he was staying? At least, Arch thought Dosh slept there. He had not seen or heard from his father in a week. Arch presumed that like him, Dosh was at work. Arch's last attempt at a family disclosure had gone poorly. He decided against that particular fight.

"Hold on," she said. Arch could hear a muffled thump. He thought the noise to be blankets unfolding. He detected the squeak of a bedspring. She was likely now standing. He allowed himself to picture what she might be wearing. Hearing a few more noises, Arch could tell that Nova was doing her morning stretches. The apparent priority of her physical needs fueled his willingness to spar.

"I feel like a lot has changed since I talked to you last," he said.

"It's been more than a week. Things happen in a week," she agreed. "Like everybody is out of a job. I have more applicants than customers. Nobody seems to have money all of the sudden."

For better or worse, the target of her ire was not him. "My business is the best it has ever been," he boasted. With silence on the other end of the line, he could tell that she had not received that news favorably. His insensitivity should've been a plus.

"What are we doing?" she asked plaintively. The tone of the question gave it a double meaning.

He was not sure either.

Possibly realizing that she revealed something, Nova tried to take back any sense of sentiment. She asked, "When are you going to spend some of that money on me?"

Instead of calling the question on their dating, the semiserious path was the easier one. "Want to go glamping? RVing?" he asked. "I'm reading that people who were trying to get away from the cities and experience open spaces are giving up reservations. The whole outdoorsy trend is over. We could take over someone's adventure for pennies on the dollar."

"Yeah," she said, "when did you become really lame?" For the second time, she struggled with the words, seeming to realize that she meant two things. "I did not mean anything about your weak arm," she recovered. "At least you didn't start with asking me to Netflix and Chill."

"No way on a movie night. Bingeing video is totally over with. Too bad I upgraded your router when I stayed there." Arch heard no rebuttal. Failing to get too far on a fight, he thought to move to what should be some common ground. "I'm thinking of a revenge activity."

"Revenge activity?" she reacted. She seemed to show real interest for the first time on the call. "Revenge like you wanting a chance to take me on head-to-head?"

"Maybe."

"Revenge like me getting even for your disappearing act? I could get into that!" she exclaimed.

He was encouraged that she still thought enough of him to taunt. He launched his idea. "Want to go skydiving?"

"That's the revenge?" She seemed disappointed. "You getting even with an aircraft? Will that fix your precious ego?" She groaned while she changed stretches. "Wait, what's in this for me? Is it somewhere exotic?"

The way the words came out was less of the invitation than they were meant to be and more of a dare. When he said it, he knew that she would take it as the latter. "You'll have to trust me with your life."

56

On Monday, Arch and Nova walked into a hangar near Grand Haven, Michigan. The structure was about three stories tall, and it contained four small aircraft. The nested hangar door was open to the runway. Through the door, Arch could see a windsock flapping in the bright sun.

Having changed into grey Lycra jumpsuits, Arch and Nova could have passed for high-sheen Ghostbusters. Arch thought the attire to be overkill, but he went along with it. They were only going up to 12,000 feet. In addition to the jumpsuits, helmets were offered to them. Nova accepted, and Arch declined. He had a low tolerance for useless safety features.

Near one of the planes, a man with short red hair and a matching goatee was packing a tandem parachute. Careful fold followed careful fold, and he pulled to test several straps. He wore a T-shirt and cargo shorts. A bandana spilled out of his back pocket. The middle-aged man was chewing gum as if he were measuring every bite. Slow and meticulous, he may have been Arch's antithesis. Arch disliked him immediately.

Every few seconds, the redhead turned his head skyward as if visualizing something pleasant. As he approached, Arch got the sense that the man was visioning his time being lashed to Nova, where he could grab and when he could squeeze.

Nova must has sensed the same thing. Halfway across the glossy floor, she stopped and removed something from her travel bag. She belted her jumpsuit, snugging it around her tiny waist. In a similarly subtle motion, she lowered the zipper from her neckline to provide just a hint of what the garment held beneath.

Arch enjoyed the show. He had never seen Nova broadcast her features like that. She had never flirted with dive instructors or ski guides. She must have wanted to inspire this guide, so he would bring every bit of expertise to bear.

While Nova secured safe passage, Arch packed his own chute. He stuffed the ram-air canopy into what looked like a backpack. He fastened the flap of the backpack with a clip. The clip attached to a pull cord. He fiddled with an altimeter, which hung from the bottom of the pack. He was following his version of routine. Although he had never been to this airport before, the jump would be his tenth.

A man, who Arch presumed to be the pilot, emerged from the open door of the King Air. This man had jet-black hair and a collarless jacket. He wore mirrored sunglasses. The man talked as soon as his feet hit the hangar floor. "May I have your attention," he began.

The pilot walked to the table where the parachutes had been packed. When the pilot started pointing, Arch realized that the table had a graphic of the airfield secured to its top. "The primary landing zone is on the south side of the runway. Our tandem jumpers will be landing in the designated area for tandem groups." He looked at the redhead. "If you are off course, we strongly advise you to land in either the alternative landing zone on the west side, or in the high-performance area. The high-performance area has some water so be particularly careful if you divert to that location." He stared right at Arch. "No stunts. No radical turns. Are there any questions?"

Nova shot up her hand. The Lycra pulled taut against her chest, causing all three men to look. "How long until we jump?"

Arch was happy to see her engaged, not oppositional, and having a good time.

The pilot answered, "It will take about fifteen minutes to reach altitude. At that point, we'll line up to the jump zone, and open the doors." He started toward the stairs to the plane. "Does anyone need a drink or a bathroom?" No one did. "Load up."

Nova, Arch, and the redhead followed the pilot into the plane. After a short taxi to the end of the airstrip, the turboprops revved. To Arch, it sounded like the fan blades broke the air into chunks.

Once the plane was comfortably in the air, the redhead stepped into a harness. He double-checked straps and fasteners. Once secure, he motioned for Nova to back into him. She unbuckled her seat belt, rose unsteadily, and backed in half steps until she made contact. Once in place, she stepped through two thick black straps. The redhead fastened a belt around her waist and two more around her shoulders. He put on goggles and handed her a pair.

The redhead turned to address Arch. To be heard over the cabin noise, he did so at a full shout, "We pull the ripcord at 4,000 feet. That will give you about forty-five seconds of freefall. Keep your altimeter in your hand," he said and demonstrated.

Arch nodded. He put on his pack.

The plane leveled and slowed. He glanced over at Nova. She looked as if she were a marionette with a few inches of string back to the crossed wood of the control panel. Her sense of the situation must have been the same. She made some robotic arm and leg movements. She made the best of being lashed to an unfamiliar man.

Like the seatbelt sign on a commercial airliner, the King Air had a light panel. The indicator light on the panel turned from red to green. The redhead backed to a pushbutton on the fuselage. He pressed it and opened the door. "Are you ready?" he asked. Nova nodded. The redhead turned his body, positioning part of her outside the plane. "One, two, three," he yelled. They jumped on three.

Arch rushed to the open door, and without a pause, flung himself out. With lower mass, he would have to streamline to catch them. He dove face down. Quickly, he drew even with the tandem. Arch flattened himself to try to match their rate of fall.

Nova gave him a thumbs-up.

Both hands and both legs spread wide, maintaining a perfect banana shape, he returned the signal. When he did so, he remembered that he was supposed to be holding the altimeter. He reached his good arm down near to his waist, and he captured the instrument. The altimeter indicated 9,000 feet.

With a few seconds to spare, Arch decided to take in the view. The day was clear. One way, the pale blue sky ended in the deep blue of Lake Michigan. In the other direction, he could see the topside of both the Grand Haven and Holland lighthouses. Sand dunes rose along the coast. The shore breeze pushed him gently toward the dunes.

Arch saw the redhead point at him. Then he saw the tandem parachute deploy. The yellow and red rectangular canopy opened above, and seconds later, he was hundreds of feet below the rectangle of fabric.

Arch moved his recovering arm to the ripcord. The ripcord was wavering in the wind, and he had some trouble capturing it. Even when he did, he did not get a solid sensation in his hand. He closed his hand as tight as he could, and he felt numbness in his forearm and a pain sensation in his elbow.

Fighting the ailment, Arch pulled the ripcord. When he did so, nothing happened. He looked down to see whether his arm had followed the command from his head. He was not confident that it had, at least not with sufficient force. He willed his energy into his weakened arm, and he pulled again. Sharp pain shot from his wrist. It radiated all of the way up his arm. He had not felt pain like this since the hospital. It was as if the rod had separated from the bone.

Falling at 120 feet per second, each moment amplified. Arch broke into a cold sweat, and he started breathing heavily. He had the presence of mind to check the altimeter. 3,100 feet. 2,900 feet. He released the instrument from his stronger arm, and he swung the working appendage to his chest. He fumbled for the ripcord, missed it in the rush, found it again, grabbed, and pulled. A blue and white canopy appeared over his head. It caught wind and slowed him with a jolt.

He looked up at his chute. Past the canopy he noticed the tandem. It was more than 1,000 feet above and half a mile to the northeast. The tandem was nearing the shoreline. He was still out over the lake.

Handles dropped from the parachute chords. He reached up to grab them and felt pain in his injured arm. Something was definitely wrong, and he doubted his ability to control the chute. His mind processed the information. He knew he would be unable to reach the landing zone at the airport. Worse, if he admitted what happened, he knew that his time with Nova would be over.

Arch was below 1,000 feet and falling at twenty feet per second. He needed a landing plan, and apparently he needed one in which he could only turn left. That sort of maneuver would be technical. A left turn would thrust him into the face of the twelve-knot wind that was blowing him over the beach.

The landscape to his east looked largely forested. A mile or two inland, he saw a two-lane road. That narrow strip would be hard to hit with the control he possessed. He had water, dunes, roads, or wilderness. Twenty seconds and nowhere safe. He only had one chance to save his relationship. He decided to try something spectacular.

57

A detective asked, "What is your relationship to the deceased?" Staring fixedly through the open hangar door to the empty black tarmac, Nova had not seen the man approach. She startled at the question, but she had already accepted its information. In the two hours she had been detained, she saw search parties assemble, depart, and resignedly return.

She noticed that the man had sandy hair, a matching moustache, and droopy eyes like a Bassett hound. He wore a milk chocolate-shaded suit and a coordinated tie. Nova could not help picturing that he had come directly from a church service. While she studied him, the detective waited for Nova to answer his question.

She assessed him to be nonthreatening, So Nova decided that she was willing to answer. "Friend," she said. She realized as she spoke that her answer sounded implausible. "Girlfriend, I suppose. We had been dating for about a year." She was embarrassed to call herself a "girlfriend." That term seemed old world. However, she was feeling dispossessed. She guessed that feeling made her more than friend.

"May I have the deceased's full name, please?"

"What? Why?" she stammered. Upon the second mention, the word "deceased" hit harder. However, it was not the shock of Arch's sudden death that she felt most. Instead, she realized how little she really knew about him. It was his job to know about her, not hers to know about him. "I don't think I know his full name." Embarrassment made her feel exposed. The exposure made her hostile. She clenched and unclenched her fists.

The detective must have sensed her discomfort. He moved back to give her space. "Easy, miss. Tell us what you can."

"I know his name is Arch Crockett. I don't even know if the Arch is short for something. Archie? Archibald? I never thought about it," she said. "That's all that I know." She spelled the last name. "C-R-O-C-K-E-T-T." She had tried on his last name once or twice, like she was living in the last century. To her surprise, the composition, Nova Crockett, did not offend her. As far as the boy's name was concerned, she had stopped there.

The detective wrote on a notepad. "Arch—something —— Crockett," he repeated. He seemed disappointed. "Do you happen to know his middle name?"

"I told you that I don't. Are you deaf?" Nova had lost her sparring partner. She resolved that she'd fight all comers. A forty-five-year-old middleweight with a cautious demeanor would be no match.

"Forgive me, miss. I did not mean to upset you further. I realize that you are having a hard day. May I offer you a water or something?"

"I should hydrate," she agreed. Scant tears did not explain her thirst. Instead, she had failed her fitness regime, and it was nearly noon.

The redhead had been watching the interview with interest. He rose from a stool fronting a toolbox on the back wall. He was holding a blanket, airline caliber with a satin edge. He draped it over her shoulders. Then he fetched two water bottles from a cooler near the plane.

Nova consumed half of a bottle. Her stare became vacant again.

"Is this your signature, miss?" asked the detective. He showed Nova a stapled paper.

"Yes."

He turned several pages. The detective moved the paper closer to his eyes. "This liability release is not legible," the officer said. The detective turned to address the redhead. "I'm not sure what good these waivers do when you cannot read the customer's information. Did he sign? Didn't he sign? Who can tell?"

The detective returned to Nova. He raised an eyebrow to make sure that she caught his meaning. "Of course, any contest of the waiver would have to come from his next of kin." Reading the documents further, the officer said, "Miss Bakker, that's your name," he confirmed. "Do you know how to contact Mr. Crockett's next of kin?"

Arch was not the type to find fault with the people who supported risky habits. Nevertheless, this was an answer that she knew. "Arch told me that his father lives in Grand Rapids."

"Now we're getting somewhere," said the detective. "Do you have the father's address or phone number?"

"No." She knew that she sounded either evasive or airheaded. She spouted facts to try to redeem herself. "I've never met his family. He and his father were estranged. His mother passed away."

"That's okay, Miss." The detective tried to relieve her. "We have some information. Arch D. Crockett had a New York driver's license in his wallet," reported the detective.

"You took his wallet?" she asked. Nova ranted. "Yes, he lived in New York, okay? He had an apartment there before the pandemic. He hasn't been back in months, okay?" Nova had experienced enough of what she thought to be an interrogation. She was either leaving, or punches would be thrown.

"Calm down, Miss," coaxed the detective.

"Stop asking me all of these bullshit questions." She stood and menaced the officer. "I'm being inconvenienced."

The detective seemed to understand that continuing the interview would be futile, if not dangerous. "Miss Bakker, if you can do so, it would be a great help if you could attest to the identity of the body. All that we need you to do is look and confirm that you believe the body to be that of Arch D. Crockett. Can you do that?"

"I can," she said. Nova was not squeamish. Her currency was blood and bone.

She walked over to the ambulance and the detective followed. The back door was open, swinging slightly on its hinges. She climbed up the bumper and in. Once aboard, an EMT folded a white sheet from above Arch's head down to his shoulders. "Blunt force trauma," he said. Nova took a hard look and confirmed his identity.

Nova and the detective sat on a bench in the back of the ambulance. The detective put a hand on her shoulder in what seemed to be an effort to offer comfort. She knocked it off.

"Arch died doing what he liked," she said. "He died taking a risk." His daring is what she had liked about him. Her memory would be a fond one.

"Do you have a recent picture of Arch?" the detective asked.

"A picture?" she questioned. "On my phone, sure." She hit a few buttons on her phone screen and showed him a snapshot.

He asked her to text it to him, which she did.

"I'll have the photo published in the Grand Rapids media. We'll ask friends and relatives to contact us. If a name search does not lead us to his father, perhaps a tip will."

"Can I go home now?" Nova asked. She had just thought of something. The factoid was something that she wanted to keep to herself.

58

Two weeks later, Nova entered the funeral home parlor. She wore a little black dress. It was sleeveless and knee length. A choker neck gathered a cutout that plunged from her Adam's apple. The dress was provocative for a wake, but at least it was the customary black. Besides, she was not there to pay respects.

Every eye in the gathering of about two dozen turned her way. As the one female in the place, she could only be the girlfriend. She had likely been mentioned to friends and family. However, no one in Arch's orbit had ever met her. Adding to the intrigue, she had been the last person to see Arch alive.

Dosh had been meeting fellow mourners near the urn. He left two men who appeared to be his age. He received a handshake and a conciliatory shoulder pat. Dosh approached Nova.

"You must be the young lady for whom Arch stayed in Michigan," he said. Having the tall, spindly man come forward made Nova feel like a barren tree was falling in her direction. She raised her defenses.

He offered a heartfelt handshake, the kind that employed both hands. "My name is Ben Dosh."

"Hello, Ben Dosh." Nova did not register a connection. She looked around the room for a reference point. Unlike the few other visitations that she had attended in her lifetime, the room lacked video and photo cues. She finally asked, "What is your connection to Arch?"

"I am Arch's father." To her surprise, the man seemed to have an emptiness. She had not expected anguish. However, she did sympathize with someone who must have discovered his son's passing from an article in the newspaper.

Along with Arch, they had something else in common. Nova had learned of the funeral arrangements by seeing the online obituary. When she saw the plans, she made a plan of her own. She would say the right things to the father and whoever else. However, she was there with a different purpose.

"I'm sorry to meet you like this," she said. Someone walked up behind her. The person grasped her arm and guided it through the "V" in his bent elbow. She recoiled before she looked. When she looked, she was even more offended. "Maurice, what are you doing here?"

"I'm here to acknowledge the passing of a friend of yours," he said. He leaned in and lowered his voice. "I didn't like how you two conducted yourselves, but I know that he was an important person in your life."

"Do not even," she snapped. Nova turned away from her father, but his hold on her arm turned her back into the conversation with Dosh.

"Dosh?" Nova challenged. "Did you say Dosh? His name was Arch Crockett."

Dosh acknowledged Maurice with a slight bow.

"Hey, I know you," Maurice said. "You are Ben Dosh. You spoke at rallies for the president. 'What are you waiting for?' Isn't that your line?"

"Yes," Dosh said to Maurice. "Thank you for remembering." Dosh shifted the conversation back to Nova. To make the point, he put his hand on Nova's upper arm. If he noticed the muscle tone, he did not react. "Crockett was his mother's maiden name," Dosh indicated. "Arch adopted her surname when she passed away about five years ago."

"He changed his name?" she asked.

"Yes," Dosh confirmed. "He wished to honor his mother, with whom he lived most of his life. She made him aware that life is short. She inspired him to live fully." Dosh struggled to deliver the last words. He held silent for what seemed like a minute until he regained control of his emotions. "Arch may have told you that prior to the last few weeks of his life, I had not seen him in many years. I am not sure that I would have had that time if he were not trying to stay near to you, Nova. I thank you for that."

"In a way, the pandemic brought us all together," she said perfunctorily.

"I had a hunch that it was temporary," suffered Dosh. "This event is tragic but not unexpected. Somehow, I knew that he was eventually going to do something, forgive me, stupid, to try to get back in your good graces."

Maurice must have reacted with concern that some blame was being put upon his daughter. He squeezed her elbow protectively.

"Thank you for helping," acknowledged Dosh. "The picture in the paper must have come from you. It enabled me to give him a proper burial." Dosh motioned to the urn. "I know you are here to pay your respects."

"I'm not here to mourn him," Nova blurted. The sentiment sounded much worse than she'd expected. "He died the way he wanted to live."

Dosh remained quiet. He seemed to be biting his lip. His nostrils flared, and his eyes moistened. "I know that your relationship was important to him. You helped him live to his fullest. I am sorry for your loss." He turned away.

Free from Dosh, Nova also escaped from the grasp of Maurice. Her purpose seemed to be to look at the flower sprays, none of which were from her. After only two steps, she bumped directly into one of the men who had broken away from a small circle.

The group must have been made up of New Yorkers. Each twenty-something in the covey wore a well-tailored suit, more appropriate for a power lunch than a funeral. "Nova," a young man said. "It's me, Skyler."

From a few unassuming words, she could tell that he felt more connection to her than she did to him. To Nova, the familiarity was not necessarily welcome. Her plans relied on him knowing just a little and giving benefit of the doubt for the rest. "Hello, Skyler," she said cautiously. "I'm glad to meet you in person."

"I'm sorry to meet you under these circumstances," he seemed to correct her language. "I'm sorry for your loss."

"I wish people would stop saying that," intoned Nova.

59

One night months earlier, Nova had returned late from the restaurant. Arch was already in bed. She sat down at her Danish dinette table and fretted over the pile of technology atop it. If she had to suffer the boxes, screens, and wires, she would make use of its function. She logged on to Arch's computer using the information on the Post-It stuck to the back of the keyboard.

With a little searching, she found his password file. Each password seemed to relate to a place that they had visited together and the year they visited: BlueHole$19, Costa#19Rica, 20&BellaCoola. It was not hard to memorize a few codes. She reproduced a few of them on a paper that she filed in a seldom-used kitchen drawer. Since they were sharing everything, why not passcodes?

Remembering that night, she went straight for the kitchen drawer. The policeman who had driven her home from the skydiving hangar was barely out of the driveway when she secured the paper. The police had gone straight for his wallet. So would she.

Passcodes in hand, Nova raced to the back of the house. Sitting cross-legged on her bed, she powered up her home laptop. A few keystrokes later, she had access to Arch's personal financial accounts.

She gasped. Then she voiced, "Oh, my God!" To her great surprise, the account was sizable. At the top of the page, she read $4,036,271.03. She found nearly four million dollars in cash and securities.

Nova knew that Arch threw money around, but she thought that habit to be carelessness. He was a daredevil, after all. Her sense was that he was overspending to impress her. Never did she suspect that he had that kind of money. The perspective made her rethink. Had she been getting all that she deserved? She decided immediately she had not.

Arch's holdings were complex. Nova took several more minutes to try to understand. For that task, Arch had trained her well. He owned the FANG technology stocks. He held a few junk bonds. More than anything else, the man really loved his options. He had dozens of puts and calls with expiration dates ranging from days to months away. The man was basically running a private hedge fund.

As she pondered the sum, she considered her position. Technically, these were unclaimed assets. Neither Nova nor anyone else knew Arch's next of kin. Moreover, she had no way of knowing if his father would soon be found.

Staring at Skyler in the funeral parlor, She recalled the righteous clarity with which she made her move. Careful to strike every key with precision, Nova input a transfer request. Arch had established a regular pattern of transferring money, what now looked like paltry rent. She selected her account number from a list of those frequently used. Two million dollars in cash and securities moved electronically into her possession. She even affirmed the transfer using his Internet email account. Nova signed off and returned her machine to her bedroom closet.

With Arch's identity unproven, Nova figured she had a few days, or perhaps weeks, before anyone would even find the account. She had one big concern, however: Skyler. Skyler might have been the only person who knew Arch's finances.

The funeral was her point of vulnerability. Her story had to convince Skyler. She had to look Arch's former trader in the eye and assure him.

Skyler took no time to confirm Nova's suspicions. Leading her into a quiet corner, Skyler asked, "Did you know?" He crowded her face. "You must have known," he decided. "Your account? The money?"

Nova sized up the quirky-looking man in the light grey suit. She saw a dullness in his eyes, and a bulbous nose, large enough to distract from any attractive elements of his features. Her read on him was that he seemed curious, but harmless. "Yes, I was blown away," she said. She feigned being humbled. She decided that she could get to the crux of the matter by getting him to do the talking. "Did you know?" She returned the question.

"I mean, I knew he was getting back together with you," said Skyler. "That guy was really smitten. He nearly lost both of our jobs because he wanted to stay here in Michigan. I know that he had some grand plan. It involved a massive risk. I thought it was a marriage proposal. I figured this transfer had something to do with his scheme. Did it?"

She sensed that a single line would sell it. "He told me that I was a risky investment, and he loved risky investments."

60

Two days after the funeral, Dosh was back at work. In the time he had left, he resolved to work even harder. He would mourn as he was able. In the meanwhile, he had to focus on his business legacy. He no longer had a genetic one.

Dosh's smartphone rang, and he arranged it carefully to his ear. "Hello. Ben Dosh here."

"Please hold for the president," sounded the voice on the receiver.

Dosh tilted forward in his office chair, sat a little straighter, and buttoned the next-to top button on his red shirt. He cleared a document a quarter of a ream thick from the center of his desk.

"Dosh, pray tell how we are doing in Michigan?" began the president. "Purple state. Two weeks until election day. I hear we have some challenges. I have not seen Drive for Michigan getting the word out. That's okay. It's hard for people to understand. People don't know all of the things that didn't happen because we vetoed the BOOST Act. No shortages. No inflation. No rushed vaccine. No explosion of government debt. No generation of children traumatized. No zombie companies. No zombie people. The country would have spent $2 trillion to accomplish those things. People don't understand that the country dodged a bullet."

"I do understand, sir. You made the right choice."

"Saved the country from years of misery, a lost generation," boasted the president. "You get it. Yet my friend Dosh is not worrying too much about the national election. I hear that you are trying to get your guys into the state house. Small potatoes." The president paused, but he did not wait for a reaction. "My wife tells me that I am a nice guy. You are not doing anything for me, but I might do something for you."

"Yes, Mr. President. Thank you, Mr. President." Dosh had thought that he could redirect his political efforts without much attention. Apparently, he was wrong.

"Dosh, you made out pretty clean on the Grid Dump," said the president. "You got to be an American icon... a true believer in American cars. I have not driven a car in twenty years. This guy drives a pick-up truck to D.C. He plays the National Anthem before business meetings. We can barely get them played before sporting events."

"I had my reservations about Grid. I decided to have a bit of a protest one day." Dosh had been lucky, and he knew it, but he believed that luck was an outcome of work.

"Protests. You are fairly good at those, as I recall. You outfitted a whole state with signs and road flares." A momentary pause made Dosh wonder if he was hearing admiration or condemnation. The president continued, "Do you remember the message I sent to you during your last protest?"

"Stand down? Cease and desist? That's what the FBI said."

"No, that was not my message. My message was delivered through a back channel. It goes like this: 'In America, we do not arrest billionaires.'"

Dosh chuckled. He had a clear memory of the morning in his headquarters atrium when his lawyer recited exactly that phrase. "That came from you?"

"Listen, Dosh, I want to talk to you about this Grid situation. My administration is cracking down on data privacy. You know that I cannot get anything through Congress, so these are all executive orders," he confirmed. "I am issuing an order that each person owns his or her own data. I am also demanding that each person owns their metadata. The tech monopolies do not want me to do it. They say it will destroy their business models. So be it."

"That is a courageous move, Mr. President. I think your constituents will approve. Your poll numbers might get the final boost that they need."

"Before Grid, people did not know that they were being abused by the tech monopolies. The Grid thing impacted companies more than individuals. Maybe a few people woke up. We'll see."

"Are you wanting me to make a last-minute election push?" Dosh's political instincts kicked in. His enthusiasm did not. "I could make some appearances, I guess. We could work on a tie to the National Pause. How about this for a tag line, 'privacy after the pause'?"

"You like your slogans. More Dosh slogans. I can hear the chants already." He stopped to redirect the conversation. "That's not why I called."

"What can I do for you, sir?" A friend in the White House was still a friend in the White House. If the president won, it could be good for business.

"As I said before, we don't arrest billionaires. However, we do fine the hell out of them."

"I don't understand."

"My Department of Justice has arranged a settlement with an old friend of yours, Edward Tandy. Some bad blood between you two, as I understand it. Tandy took an acquisition away from you?"

"Yes, he did." Dosh recollected the phone call from Tandy. He had been squeezed and bullied by someone with a bigger pocketbook. Tandy had left Dosh aimless from a business perspective. "I can't stand the man. He and I have different allegiances."

"That's why I am kicking him out," the president gloated.

"Kicking him out?"

"I gave Tandy a choice. Divest your American assets or divest your Asian assets. Can't keep both. No more playing both sides. We had him deal to rights—tons of correspondence with foreign agents. He of all people should have known to stay off of the video calls. It will come as no surprise to you that he chose his overseas friends."

"No surprise at all."

"I am also fining him two billion dollars. I want him to pay damages to those impacted by the Grid Dump. Two billion dollars will go a long way. You might be entitled to some of that money, Dosh. I'm going to ask you to defer on that."

"Defer?"

"Listen, Ben. Tandy will be divesting some properties, at least one of which I know you want. He also owns an auto parts manufacturing business. You can be the first in line. I promise that he will be receptive to any offer that you make. All that I ask is that when you give him a bid, take your revenge, and make it hurt."

61

At eight o'clock on election night, the polls were closed in the East and Midwest. The results were coming in, with over 70 percent of precincts already reported. The tally was not burdened by issues with mail-in ballots or unexplained counting halts. Dosh felt hopeful.

He selected a red sport coat from his closet. Checking his look in the mirror, he decided that he looked like an inductee into a sports team's Hall of Fame. For good measure, he buffed his protruding forehead.

Dosh hurried to his truck, and he sped in the direction of District 78. The trip would take about one hour, and he wanted to get there in time for the first races to be called. The Northwest coast of the Upper Peninsula was normally fertile ground for conservatives. The margins in Districts 78, 79, 80, and 81 would provide a guide for the evening. Vote percentages above sixty would be a good sign.

The Billionaire Next Door arrived at the Elks' Hall to a quiet exterior. The gravel part of the parking lot was full, and trucks were arrayed on the grass. Despite the vehicles, no people were milling around. He took a long look at the one-story hall with white siding and red shutters. A lighted Elks sign glowed over the door.

Dosh walked past a shuttered window and was able to hear what he believed to be a television network calling the presidential race in a state. Illinois went for the Democrat. Although Illinois was a deep blue state, Dosh got a sudden sense of dread about the president.

When the auto parts executive and lobbyist opened the entry door, the semidarkness behind stage lighting did nothing to hide the large crowd inside. "There's Ben Dosh," someone yelled. The hall erupted.

Representative Myia Evinrude ran from the front of the room with her hands held high and layers of red, white, and blue necklaces pulsing. The political novice had owned several haircut franchise licenses before Dosh had channeled her into public service. Revelers parted to make a path. Evinrude dove into Dosh's arms and smacked his cheek with a kiss. Dosh looked up from the hug to see local election results on a video screen. Evinrude had been declared the winner. She had garnered 78 percent of the vote, effectively a landslide.

By the time Dosh had shaken hands and made it to the front of the room, the fifty-eight seats of the Republican state house majority swelled to sixty-six seats. The Republican benefactor spent the rest of the night driving from victory party to victory party, stopping at as many as he could. By 11 o'clock, five more of his candidates had emerged victorious. With a few races undecided, Dosh was one seat away from a supermajority.

Heavily caffeinated to put off the weariness, Dosh pulled back into his driveway at just before six o'clock in the morning. Dosh parked his truck and entered the house noisily, even more gangly than usual. He fumbled with a container of ground coffee beans and a pitcher of water. He probably did not need more stimulation, but he started a pot anyway. While the coffee brewed, he turned on the television.

Dosh was not the only one active at the early hour. In Washington, D.C., Kenworth Johnson was beginning his last few months in office with a flurry of executive orders. President Johnson granted pardons to some of the members of his cabinet and staff. In an even more provocative action, the president pardoned data privacy advocates Edward Snowden and Julian Assange. Dosh saw it as a parting gift to the data privacy lobby.

A spitty exhale of hot air stopped the coffee brewer. Dosh poured coffee into a ceramic mug, and he sipped it slowly as the steam rose. The whole kitchen smelled of hazelnut. He carried the mug into his living room and collapsed onto the sofa.

He opened his phone to dozens of emails. His local connections were congratulatory. The local effort was a stunning success. Email and texts from his national relationships cast blame and threatened an end to his party status.

Television reports of executive actions kept coming. The president was not leaving quietly. With the uproar, the media might take days to notice Dosh's wins. Had Dosh been awake to see more of the blitz, he would have thought it one of the best twenty-four-hour periods in his behind-the-scenes political life.

62

A week after the election, Maurice unlocked the front door of the restaurant. As he grabbed at his pants pockets for a key, he realized that it had been a long time since he had opened. Nova had been the first one in the building for the last six months.

He opened the door and flipped on the lights. As was his custom upon entering the store, he proceeded to the kitchen. He was happy to see that it was both empty and spotless. He turned a few aging cheese wheels. He was content, even feeling like he might get creative. However, it was too quiet. Maurice was on his way to turn on the television when Nova walked in.

"I'm here," she said. "Don't turn that on."

Maurice shrugged. Any noise was good noise. In his eyes, her voice would be plenty. He leaned forward over the counter. "Here I am," he said. "Why did you want me to come in early?" Before he finished the question, he noticed her hair. The color had changed from blonde to her natural black. "When did you change your hair?" he asked.

Nova retrieved her laptop. She placed it on the table nearest to the counter. "I have changed more than that," she said. She removed a fabric belt, which held together a long jacket resembling a robe. Underneath, she was dressed head-to-toe in form-fitting black. She wore a short-sleeved crop top and boy shorts.

"Have you abandoned modesty?" Maurice asked. "You were doing so well." He corrected himself. "With the exception of the funeral, I guess." He remembered questioning her wardrobe choice. "Is this about the boy? You are a beautiful girl. You will have other relationships. Better ones."

If she had a reaction to another dose of unsolicited parental guidance, she did not show it. "Come sit down," she said. She deposited herself into one of the chairs.

Maurice walked to the opposite chair, and he sat as requested. "What's on your mind?" he asked.

Nova seemed to look Maurice over. He felt like she was looking for an opening through which to land a decisive punch.

"This meeting is about the viability of the business, Maurice." Nova opened her laptop, and she turned the lighted screen toward him.

Maurice took a momentary look at a large and detailed spreadsheet. At the bottom, he saw some now familiar metrics: Free Cash Flow, EBITDA, ROE. The numbers were highlighted in red. Numbers were still not his thing, but he did his best to understand.

"You wished for an end to the pandemic." She sounded like she was casting blame.

"I got my wish," he agreed.

"Takeaway is down to near nothing. The restaurant has failed to return to full capacity."

"Perhaps a new menu item," he offered. "Suikerbrood was a hit for a while. Let me take a look at my recipe box."

"I think it's too late for another one of your creations," she said. "We're losing money, and you've been working without a salary."

"I want to hand the business over to you some day. It is a good business. We bring people nourishment and joy. As long as we do that, we are okay. We have survived tough times before."

"Not like this," she indicated. "The store is losing money coming off of the best few months we've ever seen, or ever may see again."

"You have worked so hard… all of those new systems. You told me that you shored up the finances."

"I did, Maurice." Nova seemed matter-of-fact. "The restaurant is debt free. Our obligations have been met. We were able to give our people some extra benefits. After all of that, we put a little money away for ourselves."

"You did great things, Nova. You really improved the front of the house. I am proud of you."

Nova must have felt pressure to return the compliment. "Maurice, I'm proud of your contributions to the food world. The James Beard Award can never be taken away." She swallowed hard. "However, if we continue to operate the restaurant, the good we've accomplished will go away. Every day now, we subtract from our previous investments. I've analyzed the numbers and considered options. I think that we need to close the restaurant."

Maurice's stunning blue eyes welled. Without the restaurant, he could not think of a purpose. He had spent his whole adult life making food. Outside of parenting, the bistro had been his highest calling.

"I've recently come into some money," she said.

"Money?" This he was not expecting. The idea was so surprising that he felt a daze. "You came into money? How?"

"Arch," was her one-word answer.

"Arch," he repeated. He thought about it for a second. "His father is a wealthy guy. He runs that chain of auto parts stores." Further consideration confirmed the thought. "That guy, Ben Dosh, appeared with the president." Dosh must have given Nova some stipend to comfort her loss, a nice gesture.

Nova nodded.

"So you have a bit of money. If you have money, why do we need to close?"

"I'm not interested in funding losses," she said. "One of the things Arch taught me was not to put good money after bad."

"I see," he understood. She must have thought of his years of financial and personal investment as bad money.

"For the sake of grandma's memory, I'll give you $1,000,000 if you close the store and walk away."

"A million dollars?" It was hard for Maurice to keep his thoughts on track. The money. A million? The takeover. The family. As he fought to organize his mind, the fatherly thought took over. He struggled to understand what that number must have meant about her relationship with that boy. He realized that whatever he had done in terms of moral teaching had not been enough.

"A condition of my offer is that I get your recipes. You must teach me how to do the poffertjes preparation and tell me the special ingredient that you put into Dorotha."

"Those are your heritage. They are yours no matter what." In all of his imaginings, Maurice had not foreseen an exit. He would have died happily if he had perished over the stove. "I might need some time on this," he stalled.

"Say yes, Maurice."

As he contemplated her actions, he could not help countering with what he could offer in return, more fatherly advice. "You know, Nova, closing the store is not going to solve anything. You may get rid of some financial headaches, and my foibles may trouble you less, but your problem will remain. Nothing will make you happy until you get comfortable in your own skin."

"I'm getting comfortable," she said. She flexed her arms.

Maurice breathed a big sigh. He wished to give his daughter what she wanted. For the first time in his memory, she was making it easy. How could he say no?

63

Two weeks later, Maurice stood alone in the restaurant. It was four o'clock in the afternoon. The blinds were drawn, giving the bistro a grey shadow. As it had been during the pandemic, only the counter and a corridor to the front door had lights ablaze.

His chef's attire was folded and stacked on the counter. The clothes were atop the folded Metaworst flag, which he could identify by the fringe. Pictures of patrons' food creations topped the flag. He'd removed them carefully from walls. A few remaining menus completed his stack of memories.

Since he was alone, the television blared. The sound waves were more like a tidal surge. Maurice could not hear himself think.

That was the point of the noise. He did not want to remember his achievements as a chef. He certainly did not want to relive his failings as a proprietor. His heart ached every time he remembered a detail.

"The president stands accused of treason, which according to our constitutional system, is an impeachable offense." Senator Sasson's voice came from the speaker. "Two of the men that he deigned to pardoned have demonstrably and admittedly revealed state secrets. Surveillance sources and methods were exposed to our enemies. Publication of these secrets spanned home and abroad." The senator pounded on the podium, seeming to indicate intensity. "By pardoning these men, he has emboldened our enemies and done irreparable harm to the country. I call on the impeachment managers to proceed."

The political theater continued. To Maurice's mind, it was just that. The president had fulfilled his promises. The farce of masks, and six-foot spaces, and drive-away food service was over. Restaurant workers were no longer special. Every worker was essential again.

While attuned to his community, Maurice's attention span for Washington waned. Given the lies told by the Pandemic Working Group, he had lost his tolerance for untruths. After all, corporate surveillance secrets had been released, and the outcome had been good more than bad. Companies seemed to be going forward on an honest basis. Maurice was ready for some of that outcome for his government.

"I want to talk about a man who is needy and desperate," maligned the one-time ally of the president, Senator Sasson. "As a member of the Senate Intelligence Committee, I can say that my perspective on the man has changed. The United States now sells out allies under his leadership." He continued to rebuke. "I have stood up for this president. I will do so no more. I cannot condone the actions that he has taken. My vote will be to impeach."

Maurice watched only long enough to see the Senate vote to impeach Kenworth Johnson. The president was removed from office ten days before his successor was to be sworn in. Maurice turned the television off. He did not wait to see President Warren Fairbanks follow the path of Gerald Ford and pardon the man he succeeded.

The chef felt numb and profoundly tired. Maurice walked into the kitchen like a man twenty years older than his age. Each step was deliberate, and his shoulders sagged. He made one last sweep.

The stainless-steel prep tables were gone. The kitchen supply reseller to whom he sold had picked them up the previous week. Empty spaces, dangling cables, and pipes took the place of specialty equipment. Stoves, grinders, mixers, and aging racks were no more, although he did move a few things to his garage at home.

As he walked back through the swinging door into the front of the house, he remembered a phrase from his early restaurant days. He said it aloud, "The front of the house is for show; the back of the house is where you live." Those words from long ago rang true to him. He would miss his kitchen.

Maurice shut his characteristic blue eyes to take in the moment. He pictured tables full of happy diners. For years, he had treated foodies and friends to perfectly crafted food. He had tried to rear his family in the same place. He hoped he had done some good.

After a few seconds, he gathered up his collection from the counter. He moved to the front door of the former bistro. After a last look, Maurice turned out the lights and locked the door. Tears streamed down his cheeks.

His car was parked below the red curb. He opened the trunk remotely, then closed it over his belongings. He drove home to cook dinner for his wife and son.

64

Early on a December Monday, Dosh tried to clear what seemed like miles of Chicago traffic. He appreciated his friends. They had made an effort to distract him from his son's passing, Sunday was over, and daylight was burning. He should be at work.

"Can't we go any faster?" The professor pressed his phantom accelerator in the passenger seat. He arched his back, forcing his shoulders up near the headrest. He turned his head to get a good look at the asphalt apron. He seem to be assessing whether to advise creating an improvised traffic lane.

Dosh tried to commiserate. They had hours to go. "That's one thing I miss about COVID... empty roads," said Dosh.

"Empty roads! Empty roads," repeated the professor. "You're the one that told the country to get out of their houses and onto the highways. This traffic nonsense is all your fault."

Knowing that charge was likely true, Dosh also appreciated that traffic would have been worse had they tried to make this same trip after the game. They both would have been more irritable managing the clothing layers and shaking off the chill during his three- to four-hour commute home.

It was much better to have a hot shower and be treated by his friends, the Murdykes, to dinner. The owners of the Chicago team often had an entertaining angle on the game. The insider viewpoint tended to involve the potential dismissal of an offensive line coach or questioning the blocking schemes employed by the special teams coordinator.

Last night, the owners had been in a particularly salty mood. The opposing quarterback had shredded Chicago for 402 yards passing. The home team allowed passes to seven different receivers. The outcome was not close.

Thirty minutes later, stop-and-go traffic was beginning to break up, and so was the professor. Dosh's F-150 finally cranked up to the speed limit. Before long, he rounded the southern edge of Lake Michigan. The exits for Gary, Indiana, were in his sights.

Dosh's cell phone rang. The device in his pocket was connected to the vehicle's communications system. The call lit up his center console. Dosh saw that it originated from a New York number. "Do you mind if I take this?" he asked his testy companion.

The professor nodded and made a circular gesture with his hands that seemed to communicate acquiescence as long as the speed of the truck increased.

A shaky voice curled from his car speakers. "Hel... hello, Mr. Dosh?" The caller sounded like a repentant child forced by his parents to place a call to make amends.

"This is Ben Dosh. Go ahead. If we have a bit of an echo, it is because I am mobile in my truck."

"Oh, I hope I'm not bothering you." The caller paused. Without an answer, the young-sounding man continued. "Mr. Dosh, this is Skyler. I am a friend of Arch's." After another moment of silence, he said, "We met at the wake."

"I remember you, Skyler." In truth, his memory was fuzzier than usual. Dosh could not place Skyler among four or five members of the New York contingent. Their conduct seemed fraternal. This voice was different. He could not tell if the caller was timid or mournful. He guessed mournful. "Thank you for being there for Arch."

"Sorry for your loss," Skyler said. "May I bother you for a minute?"

Dosh had an immediate thought. The call must regard further arrangements. He guessed that Arch had belongings in New York. Dosh was learning a lot about his son by settling his affairs. "Go ahead."

When Skyler struggled to continue, Dosh tried to draw him out. "What can I do for you on a Monday morning? I am just about to turn north and get the sun out of my eyes." Aiming some words at the professor, he said, "That should help us pick up the pace."

Skyler was silent again.

Dosh decided that it was the driving that may be confusing him. Dosh understood that the idea of motoring to be somewhat foreign to a New Yorker. He wondered if Skyler even had a driver's license. "It's okay, son, I am perfectly fine. It is a wide highway, and I will be back in my home state in the next few minutes. What did you want to say?"

Skyler blurted, "Mr. Dosh, I'm calling about Arch's brokerage account."

"Brokerage account?" That topic was something truly unexpected. "I didn't know he had a brokerage account. I guess that makes sense he would have something like that."

"He does. He was a very active trader, both personally and at work. Very active. Quite a lot has been going on with the account." He hesitated again. "Let me explain. Arch had some sizable gains in the last month, basically increased his assets by a third." Skyler took an audible breath. "Then there was this transfer on the day of his death."

"Oh?" Dosh had no idea what Skyler was talking about.

"Two million dollars."

"That is some account," he acknowledged. He kept his focus on the road ahead, trying to determine what losses he would be asked to cover.

Skyler paused so long that it nearly demanded further response. "Then the firm wanted to settle the margin loan. Which it did. He also had dozens of options contracts. Many of them were short-term options, exercising in a few hours or a few days. We tried to do the best that we could on Arch's behalf, but these were some crazy positions, straddles, butterfly spreads. It was hard to unwind."

"What are you trying to tell me, Skyler? Do I owe you money or something?"

"No, no," he replied. "Not at all. Many of those trades were favorable. After reconciliation, Arch was left with about $1,500,000 in his account. He put you down as his beneficiary."

Dosh needed all three lanes to take in the message. He squeezed the steering wheel with both hands and veered into the right-hand lane. The truck decelerated back to the speed limit. As it did so, the professor winced.

"My son left me with over $1,000,000? You're kidding. Is this a joke?"

"No, Mr. Dosh, for real. For realzzz," Skyler repeated, seeming to suddenly think himself funny. "All that I need you to do is to send me a copy of the death certificate. I think there are some inheritance taxes, but otherwise, the money will be yours."

"I'll be damned," exclaimed Dosh. He pounded both palms on the leather-wrapped steering wheel. "I put the kid through graduate school, or at least my wife forwarded the money I gave her for that purpose. Otherwise, I never gave him a dime. He must have made that money on his own."

"Arch was what our company calls a 'highly compensated individual,'" reported Skyler. "He had a knack for making money in the financial markets."

"I always thought he was too reckless to put him anywhere near a business," Dosh admitted.

"He seemed to have found a profession that fit his personality, Mr. Dosh. I worked with him nearly every day. I know. He took great risks. When he believed he was right, he had constancy then. He wouldn't sell until he achieved his price."

"So you are telling me that if I send you a form, you are releasing more than $1,000,0000 to me?" Dosh started to think of the situation as unreal. The son whom he hardly knew was a successful businessman. In something of an ironic twist, the boy left his billionaire father a million bucks. "Do I have any instructions? Is there something I should do with this money?"

"There are no strings attached," Skyler resumed. "From what I know, Arch had no other family. He wasn't religious. He didn't align with any charitable endeavors. He wasn't politically active. Pretty much all he did was gamble and try to impress his girlfriend."

Dosh thought about the possibilities. A mile rumbled under his tires. As he passed an exit, an idea occurred to him. "Skyler, I am thinking about what a fitting use of Arch's money would be. You have been kind to help me with this situation. Could I keep the money there at your firm?"

"We would've to open a new account in your name, and then transfer the assets," said Skyler. "Procedural stuff, but we could do that."

It was a quick decision, but it felt like the right one. "I think that the best thing that I could do to honor Arch's legacy is to use this money for an investment purpose. I've a financial speculation in mind, and it's risky as hell."

"Sounds perfect," agreed Skyler.

65

A week later, Skyler sat in front of his computer console in New York. Traders resided in an open series of three-quarter cubicles. Despite the presence of female traders, the area retained its traditional name, the bullpen. Each workspace had four to eight monitors stacked two high. The number of computer screens indicated seniority. Skyler had six. Every screen was alit with digital figures.

"Are you ready, Mr. Dosh?" Even over FaceTime, Skyler's eagerness seemed palpable. Arch had involved Skyler in many speculations, but he had never assigned him responsibility for assembling a beneficial interest in a public company. The fact that the shares were trading for $1.44 each made buying over five percent of the firm a distinct possibility. The low price also made every penny matter. The job was a perfect challenge for an experienced Wall Street trader. He would have to use the full suite of his tricks: block trades and dark pools. "The time is 9:21 Eastern. The market opens in nine minutes," Skyler announced.

Eight hundred miles away, Dosh saw Skyler's nose and left eye fill his screen. Despite the strange apparition, Dosh barely glanced at his phone. He stood at the wall of windows in the back of his office, mostly looking at his own reflection in the glass. He focused on his usual red shirt. The indirect light at his back diffused the image of the shirt and it was made more prominent by the overcast beyond the architectural glass. The gloomy sky of fall, winter, and spring had returned. More so today than any other day, the redness of his shirt made an impression on Dosh. He could see his life's work in it.

When he finally spoke, Dosh sounded contemplative. "Mourning a son that I barely knew raises challenges," he said. Dosh looked back on the decisions of his life, not only the business ones. He had driven away his wife. Until recently, his son was someone he had seen a few Sundays a year ten years ago. Why was he so driven by work? What kind of a man puts his family last? Whatever kind of man that was, Dosh knew it described him. He would have no family at his own funeral. Red shirts would be there. It would be politically expedient to attend. "Red shirts," he repeated aloud. The words bounced back off the plate glass.

Will I leave anything of lasting value?, he asked himself. He thought not. Markets change quickly. How many of the S&P 500 companies were the same ones as twenty years ago? Less than half? Damn few. Nextdoor Auto Parts had a shelf life.

"What did you say?" asked Skyler. "Red shirts? I do not understand that instruction." After a few more moments of silence on the line, Skyler spoke again. "This trade honors Arch," he said. "In fact, it may be better than anything he would have come up with himself."

"Is honor what is merited?" Dosh asked. "What sort of a legacy is risk-taking?"

"Most people don't have the courage," replied Skyler.

Courage could just as easily be described as recklessness, Dosh thought. He suffered in knowing that he had failed to teach his own child the value of a life. Dosh paused for a long time. He cleared his throat to purge the glob of regret that he had swallowed. "I sincerely apologize to you, Skyler. I have reconsidered."

"Nooo," Skyler responded. "Not now. I'm ready to execute. I need to start positioning. What you have proposed is a terrific speculation. The plan is a good one. Now is the time. We must trade now."

Dosh checked his watch. It displayed two minutes until the opening bell on the New York Stock Exchange. Time pressure was not going to get the better of him. He had already decided. The original plan did not matter any longer. He did not need to improve his business fortunes, using his dead son's money. "No, Skyler. Trading is not approved. I repeat. Not approved."

"You are kidding me, man? Owning enough of a company to pressure management for a board seat is a good legacy," Skyler said.

"Arch would probably have wished that I'd attended fewer board meetings," Dosh replied. Maybe it would have helped to have a dad around to tell him not to drive fast, live hard, or play dangerous games. Dosh never put that voice in Arch's ear. He never put any limits on his son at all. That would have taken too much time.

"I'm sure you were a good father," said Skyler. "You gave him a lot of resources."

Dosh ignored the statement. He knew that many people confused money with quality of life. "Arch died with nothing of value. He spent money on experiences. Everything else he had in the world ended up at a thrift store."

"Except his computers, right?" Skyler asked, "you sent those back to us?"

"Yes, of course." While handling the perfunctory detail, Dosh strengthened his resolve. Arch's trader did not seem to understand what Dosh was really thinking about his own life choices.

Dosh decided to be explicit. "Skyler, the extreme risk taking that we were ready to celebrate…I now see it for what it was…that activity killed Arch." Dosh let that statement hang in the air. "As some point, most people realize their mortality. They skin a knee or break an arm. They feel pain. The next time they ride a bike or run down a set of stairs, they exercise caution. Arch had not developed that filter."

"He could not wait for that splint to come off so he could go jump out of a plane," Skyler agreed. "Pain was not a demotivator for him. That's for sure. I've heard some stories…"

"Exactly. Acting on the extreme, he tried to make a virtue out of physical challenges, sports gambling, and stock speculating. In truth, he was an adrenaline junkie. As a parent, I surrounded him with permissions and stimulants. I used to leave him unsupervised on the river behind our house."

"Arch. That guy was a wild man," said Skyler unenthusiastically. "So what now?"

66

Before January was over, Nova had become disgruntled. Taking control of the family legacy had not proven satisfying. The remaining money would last for a while, but not forever. She spent most of her time in the gym, pushing her body harder and harder.

Amid the weight machines one morning, Nova overheard some of the semi regulars confess to training for a winter trip. Skiing, she guessed by the leg exercises. She remembered her heli-skiing adventure with Arch. Without hesitation, Nova determined that exotic travel was what was missing from her life.

Six days later and halfway around the world, Nova was nearing the midpoint of a clifftop walk. She would have preferred the outing to be a run, but the trail was snow covered. Gendarmstein to Viemose was an icy, flat trail with the occasional peak at lime green grass. Only an infrequent tree blocked spectacular views along the coast. The Sonderborg Baht looked grey blue. Waves broke into chunks of ice on the shoreline.

As she reached the turn at the eight-kilometer mark, Nova tired. The exercise was harder than it should have been. She blamed both the cold wind and the jet lag. Nova zipped her insulated windbreaker to her collar, fighting back against the gale. The Dybbol Molle windmill slightly inland from the path turned fast.

Her lethargy might more properly be the result of the food, but she was not ready to admit that to herself. Nova had already discovered Sonderborg's cuisine. Restaurants were replete with Danish pastries and Scandinavian dishes with which she had some familiarity. Her first meal in town was Kafferbord, coffee, and seven different cakes. Her only other time eating such a gluttonous flight was in her Oma's American kitchen.

She picked up speed on the path back toward town. Soon, the Sonderborg skyline started to fill her field of view. The hotel Steigenberger Alsik, the only tall building on the waterfront, jutted skyward. Towering over the rise in the path despite being across the sound, the black modern building looked out of place in its environment.

As she pushed further up the trail, the more fitting cathedral spire and the Sonderborg Castle gradually rose into view. The 800-year-old castle was square, with a light brown roof and dark brown walls. It occupied a spectacular peninsula, where it guarded the waterway.

Sonderborg, Denmark, was the city of Oma's youth. However, Nova did not remember hearing stories about the castle. She did remember talk about the jetty. The jetty extended from the castle to the King Christian X's Bridge, the full length of the downtown. In grandma's tales, sailboats and steamers tied up along its length. Nova imagined what it must have been like to be a child on the jetty. You could play across the planking, view the bounty of the sea, and hear at least three languages spoken.

In Nova's time, the jetty was populated with statues and empty carts for summer street vendors. A passenger ferry was at the dock, and a tour boat was tied next to the ferry. A heavy layer of frost on the tour boat revealed that it had been idle for some time. The seafaring heritage she'd wished to claim did not seem evident in the winter.

Although the jetty had not met the picture in her mind's eye, the town was living up to expectations. The pastel buildings were quaint, especially with snowcapped roofs. The surrounding fjords looked other earthly.

Oma had to have family here, Nova believed. Not everyone fled the Nazi occupation, as Oma had. If nothing else, she would find ancestry archives. Sonderborg was one of those cities that revered its dead. Blomskobbel, Skelde, on the outskirts of the city, had burial mounds going back thousands of years.

If family connections proved impossible, she intended to find places. The jetty would require more exploration. Mostly, however, she wanted to locate Oma's house. From stories, she knew what the kitchen must look like. However, that would not be much help in finding its location. She promised herself to try to rent or buy the house once she found it.

Nova's outing ended back at the bridge. She paused to take another look at the city before crossing. Amidst the surroundings of her grandmother's youth, Nova's connection never felt stronger. This, she determined, was the pure, uncommercialized, unadulterated culture, full of ancestors and artifacts, to which she was entitled. When she returned to her apartment, she found it ransacked.

67

Dosh stood on risers in front of the Cardinal State University graduating class of May 2021. He wore a black cap and a gown paneled in red and black. He looked like a black cherry candy stick from a roadside tourist stop. The garments signified his honorary degree, Doctorate in Business Administration.

The invitation and the honorary degree were both the product of a large donation. Dosh had granted $3,000,000 to the school's research institute for mental health. New signage identified a legacy, the Dosh wing of the institute. The money supplemented an even larger donation from the owner of the Indianapolis football team. The whole institute was named for the largest donor, and the new building was nearly complete.

On stage, Dosh felt recognized, and he felt contented. He believed that he had done right by Arch. Extreme risk- taking was not something to perpetuate. Instead Dosh had learned that speculation was already so common among people of Arch's generation that it had become a scourge. The behavior was a product of a widely held fatalistic outlook, something Dosh only recently experienced when his job was threatened. With the benefit of experience, he could show these kids. He could help them. He hoped he had the right words.

Dosh stood from a row of seated academics, all in regalia. When summoned, he sauntered to a podium and began the commencement address. "Congratulations on your graduation day." The students seated on the floor of the field house all applauded. "I hope it is a thrill. I must admit that it has been about forty years since I last attended a graduation. Since I was not planning to attend my son's ceremonies, he did not walk the stage to receive his diplomas. Most of my life, I have had trouble with the work-life balance. Actually, no balance existed. Work prevailed. Students, if your parents are here today, listen to their advice. They figured out something about parenting that I never did."

"As the Dean said, my name is Ben Dosh. Some of you may know me from speeches that I made on behalf of the former president. If you do remember my talks about American cars and the open road, you will easily complete this phrase, 'What are?'"

"You waiting for," answered about half of the assembly.

"Thank you," he said. Although this response was less enthusiastic than the ones he'd encountered on the tour, he nevertheless relived the earlier experience. Realizing that he was this event's headliner, he had a feeling of inhibition.

"We are here today because you graduates heeded that call. You did not wait to complete your education. Half of your colleagues took skip years, or they quit for financial or COVID-related reasons. The 2,000 of you that are here today, the smallest graduating class in fifty years, are the ones who did not wait to get back to work. You did not wait to complete your studies. I think I speak for the whole business community in saying that we have been waiting for people like you."

The assembly applauded.

"As I mentioned earlier, today is a thrill. Before you move on to outings with your family and friends, I want to talk to you about thrills. Milestones can be thrills. My question for the graduates today is this: Can a single thrill be enough for you?"

Chatter emerged from the crowd as attendees mumbled answers. One of the graduates shouted above the din. "One is never enough! Wooo!"

A massive cheer ensued.

"I would like to talk to that young man after the assembly," said Dosh. He squinted into the crowd of caps and gowns to try to see the culprit. He pointed to an open wing of the field house floor seeming to identify a meeting place.

A white noise rose from the crowd. It seemed to indicate that they approved of his humor.

"With one exception," he looked again for the thrill seeker, "I think I'm talking to a group of realists." Dosh continued, "I hope this will become the greatest group of realists in the history of our nation. You know that our experts lied to you. You have seen the madness of crowds. Yet none of those things have blocked your path. None of those things drove you to despair. Fatalism dies here today."

This time the applause came from the upper decks.

"I am here today because my son Arch succumbed to a fatalistic view of things. He lacked confidence in the future. He decided to live for the now. As a result, Arch took excessive, some would say extreme, risks. He did this both professionally and personally."

"Many of you will be moving on to careers. Arch was able to direct what I will call 'his disorder,' into a highly successful career. Wall Street has a place for excessive risk takers. If stocks are not enough, try shorting. If shorting does not satisfy, try futures and options. If traditional derivatives are not risky enough, zero-day options may be to your taste. Graduates, if you picked your employer because the risks and potential rewards were limitless, listen well."

"What is risky behavior on the personal level? That manifests in lifestyle choices. Investing legend Charlie Munger used to call it liquor, ladies, and leverage. From my son's experience, I would add drugs, gambling, and extreme situations. Consider. What if these are all symptoms of something greater?"

"What if there is an addiction to high sensation experiences? Can you be addicted to base jumping? Half pipe? Extreme kayaking? Cliffside selfies? We think that it is possible. The purpose of the Dosh grant is for the university to study high sensation addictions."

"The young man who earlier wanted more than one thrill... this crowd cheered for you. That is a common response. People want to see the crazy risks and the daring feats. In just a few hours, you may be daring a friend to take that fifth celebratory vodka shot or to tattoo her degree on her arm." Dosh spoke solemnly. "Craving high sensation experiences can do lasting harm. I can tell you, it is not always so pleasant to watch the crash."

"As you prepare to go out into the world, I join your faculty and administration in wishing you long, happy, and successful lives. In wishing you well, I urge you to be careful of adrenaline. Enjoy your thrill today. One thrill is enough."

68

The commissioner's suite held most of the league ownership. The elite group looked out on a raucous, sold-out crowd ready to enjoy Super Bowl LVI. As a special guest of the Indianapolis team owner, Ben Dosh watched the spectacle.

The owner, Dale Rosen, had been in the crowd for Dosh's commencement speech. Following the ceremony, the two met and discussed the impetus behind their parallel donations. Rosen said that his interest was personal. "I have a drive to do crazy stuff that I just don't understand," he said. He was a twenty-eight-year-old mountain climber, who had summited three of the seven highest peaks in the world. The football team he had just inherited should have been enough to satisfy his competitive need, but it was not.

During that conversation, Dosh had mentioned that football had become a salve for his son lost to unchecked risk. He recounted the recent Chicago game, and he mentioned that his friend, the professor, held season tickets for the Indianapolis team. With an immediate kinship, Rosen offered Dosh the ultimate in football therapy, Super Bowl tickets.

Down on the field, Joe Burrow and the Cincinnati Bengals had taken their sideline. Matthew Stafford was about to be announced with the offense of the Los Angeles Rams. The crowd was ecstatic for their hometown team. Seventy thousand fans were screaming. Dosh took a moment to realize that the stadium would have been half empty if not for the veto of the BOOST Act. He realized that the experience was all of the thanks he would ever receive.

The glass separating most of the owners from the field was vibrating from the sound. While deafening outside, inside the suite, it was a low din of conversation. "Who do you like?" asked Rosen.

"Los Angeles is strong on both sides of the ball," replied Dosh. He felt comfortable talking football with anyone. Sports conversation seemed like a social equalizer. Sports ownership was likely the opposite. "Home field advantage in the Super Bowl. That will be too hard for the Bengals to overcome. Do you have a rooting interest, Dale?"

"I always root for the AFC."

The men turned their attention to the field for the National Anthem. Dosh faced the flag and placed his hand over his heart. The pose must have reminded Rosen of the Reopen the Country rallies. When the song ended, he told Dosh that he looked like a politician. Dosh accepted that maybe he did. This football game was the first at which he had ever worn a suit. The only salvation to having a coat was that it was a temperate sixty-three degrees at gametime.

"Who let Dosh in here?" asked Arthur McBride. He walked forward, patted Dosh on the back, and shook his hand. "It's nice to see you again. I promised you a seat in an owner's box one day. Frankly, I was thinking of a home game against a non-divisional opponent," he chided. "Rosen brings you to the Super Bowl?"

"Do you two know each other?" Dale Rosen inquired.

"Yes, we do," said Dosh. "We spent some time together on one of my road trips. He gave me a behind-the-scenes tour of the stadium."

After "America the Beautiful," McBride started back. "You give Rosen a few million, and he gives you a Super Bowl ticket." McBride really seemed to be enjoying himself. "I tell you what,

Dosh, you give one of my charities a million, and I'll get you a sideline pass."

Marion Tucker, the new majority owner of the Detroit team, walked nearby. She had her head down, seemingly intent on getting to her seat for the kickoff. Arthur McBride stopped her. "Marion, you should know Ben Dosh," he said. "Ben is in the auto aftermarket business."

Dosh offered his hand. "I grew up watching Detroit," he said.

"Me too," replied Marion. She motioned toward the field, and she walked away.

While Dosh was recovering from what he felt to be a rebuff, Dale Rosen interjected, "We should have you meet some other people." After several minutes of conversation, all three men reacted to a *thump*. They looked toward the turf. The ball was nearing the top of its arc, and Cincinnati scored its first three points.

Rosen continued, "What about Jay Warner? Do you know Jay?"

Dosh indicated that he did. Warner was another billionaire who Dosh knew from press clippings and charity events. "My firm carries a few of his products."

Rosen walked past the glass and down a few steps into the rows of seating on the field side of the box. He returned with a man on the dark side of seventy. Apparently fighting his age, he sported a ponytail and a thick, dappled beard that was also gathered with a band. The man had a western-style shirt and a bolo tie. The tie clasp was a dull metal with a cast of the league logo. "Jay Warner, I'd like you to meet Ben Dosh. Ben runs Nextdoor Auto Parts. He says they sell some of your stuff."

"It's a pleasure to meet you, Ben."

"Nice to meet you as well," said Dosh.

"I'm here to try to learn the formula for success in this league. I haven't found it yet. As you may know, my team has the top pick of the incoming college prospects."

"A franchise quarterback will help," replied Dosh. "From what I can tell, it looks like you will have your choice of three in the top slot." His energy returned when he was able to talk football again. "Three quarterbacks, including the Heisman trophy winner, are projected to be among the top five selections."

"You know your athletes, Mr. Dosh."

"Ben wants to become an owner someday," offered Rosen.

"I bought my team at auction," said Warner. "I used a New York dealmaker. I'll introduce you to her if you want that. I'm not sure you want that. I probably overpaid. Auctions of attractive properties seldom favor the buyer." Warner smiled, showing a somewhat crooked bottom row of teeth. "However," he continued, "it has been a ride, and here we are."

"You have made some great moves," Dosh commented. "I like your new head coach. His play calling is imaginative. After what you did in free agency, your offensive line will be one of the best in the league."

Warner seemed to be enjoying Dosh's fandom. He nodded and sipped from a highball glass. "I am having a post-game party," said Warner. "Why don't you come? We can talk about your ownership aspirations. I will tell you what it's like to compete with these guys," Warner motioned to Rosen and McBride.

Dosh glanced at his friends, seeking their approval. It was given.

"It's hard to break into this league, auction or not." Warner turned to the men surrounding him. "Between the three of us, we should be able to figure out something for Mr. Dosh."

69

Two years later, Ben Dosh sat in the owner's box in the stadium outside of Washington, D.C. He wore a mustard-colored shirt and a maroon tie. From a distance, he resembled a foot-long hot dog in a bun. His statue-worthy hairline had receded a bit further, and the top of his head was shining in the sun.

Being on display contented him. It seemed like a passive form of celebrity. Being contented with passivity is a new skill that he was learning. It required less than his former six days a week and sixteen hours per day.

Following Dosh's national pause, momentum continued at Nextdoor Auto Parts. Business was going so well that Dosh's term as CEO was extended. As a condition of his continued employment, he surprised everyone by insisting on taking both Saturdays and Sundays off. He even reserved a weeklong vacation, his first. Dosh took a driving tour of the remnants of Route 66.

Some of that business momentum came with the help of the Michigan Congress. The legislature, that Dosh had worked to strengthen, blocked loads of wasteful government spending, notably incentives for electric vehicles. Without those incentives, EVs became uneconomic, too expensive for most consumers.

With EVs relegated to being more of a pricy hobby, Detroit recommitted to internal combustion engines, transmissions, and drive train parts. With the home of the auto industry removing favored political status from the electrics, most of the rest of the country followed. Dosh gladly pivoted the assets he had acquired from Tandy.

Secure that the future included road trips, carburetors, and radiators, Dosh wanted one last look at his empire and his people. The farewell tour began in Benton Harbor. Over three months, it covered every store and city. Upon return to Grand Rapids, he transferred the leadership mantle to his handpicked successor.

While Dosh's business thrived and his wealth peaked, his leisure pursuit became more affordable. The Indiana research institute produced its first studies on sensation addiction. The assembled input from base jumpers, free divers, and heli-skiers uncovered that sports gambling was the extreme recreation equivalent of a gateway drug.

Faced with that data, the major sports leagues disengaged from the sports gambling business. Following the precedent of the tobacco industry decades before, all advertising was blocked. The retreat came at a large cost to the value of sports franchises.

The Washington football team was one of the worst hit. The fall in revenue from sports gambling ties cemented the franchise's decline. The owner wanted to sell.

Dosh had a growing group of football friends. He turned to sports after his son's passing. It earned him something of a sympathy vote. Dosh assembled a coalition, bid for the team, and won.

Following the management changeover, Dosh moved decisively. He hired the best general manager he could find. Next, he guided the GM on hiring a head coach. A welcome surprise to most of the fan base, Dosh then disappeared.

Football began a new era for Dosh. He selected his leadership team, delegated to them, and distanced to an arm's length away. The results were immediate, and they were spectacular.

Dosh watched from the owner's box as his management team's improvements manifest. Increasingly, he was in the company of a female former racecar driver. Although separated in age by twenty-five years and height by more than a foot, both were starting their second acts. Cameras often caught them breaking off conversation to celebrate touchdowns.

After a home playoff win, a member of the press asked Dosh about the relationship. Dosh said, "it is about competitions, cars, and clean slates." Harkening back to his once famous line, he added, "This is what I have been waiting for."

www.ingramcontent.com/pod-product-compliance
Lightning Source LLC
Chambersburg PA
CBHW030801260626
47169CB00001B/144